John Galsworthy was born on 14 A
in Surrey, the son of John and Blanc
of four children. John Galsworthy senior, whose family came
Devon, was a successful solicitor in London and a man of 'new money', determined to provide privilege and security for his family. They idolised him. By contrast, their mother Blanche was a more difficult woman, strict and distant. Galsworthy commented that, 'My father really predominated in me from the start . . . I was so truly and deeply fond of him that I seemed not to have a fair share of love left to give my mother'.

Young Johnny enjoyed the happy, secure childhood of a Victorian, upper-middle-class family. Educated at Harrow, he was popular at school and a good sportsman. Holidays were spent with family and friends, moving between their country houses. After finishing school, John went up to New College, Oxford to read law. There he enjoyed the carefree life of a privileged student, not working particularly hard, gambling and becoming known as 'the best dressed man in College'. But he could also be quiet and serious, a contemporary describing how 'He moved among us somewhat withdrawn . . . a sensitive, amused, somewhat cynical spectator of the human scene'.

The period after university was one of indecision for Galsworthy. Although his father wanted him to become a barrister, the law held little appeal. So he decided to get away from it all and travel. It was on a voyage in the South Seas in 1893 that he met Joseph Conrad, and the two became close friends. It was a crucial friendship in Galsworthy's life. Conrad encouraged his love of writing, but Galsworthy attributes his final inspiration to the woman he was falling in love with: Ada.

Ada Nemesis Pearson Cooper married Major Arthur Galsworthy, John's cousin, in 1891. But the marriage was a tragic mistake. Embraced by the entire family, Ada became close friends with John's beloved sisters, Lilian and Mabel, and through them John heard of her increasing misery, fixing in his imagination the pain of an unhappy marriage. Thrown together more and more, John and Ada eventually became lovers in September 1895. They were unafraid of declaring their relationship and facing the consequences, but the only person they couldn't bear to hurt was John's adored father, with his traditional values. And so they endured ten years of secrecy until Galsworthy's father died in December 1904. By September 1905 Ada's divorce had come through and they were finally able to marry.

It was around this time, in 1906, that Galsworthy's writing career flourished. During the previous decade he had been a man 'in chains', emotionally and professionally, having finally abandoned law in 1894. He struggled to establish himself as an author. But after many false starts and battling a lifelong insecurity about his writing, Galsworthy turned an affectionately satirical eye on the world he knew best and created the indomitable Forsytes, a mirror image of his own relations – old Jolyon: his father; Irene: his beloved Ada, to name but a few. On reading the manuscript, his sister Lilian was alarmed that he could so expose their private lives, but John dismissed her fears saying only herself, Mabel and their mother, 'who perhaps had better not read the book', knew enough to draw comparisons. *The Man of Property*, the first book in *The Forsyte Saga*, was published to instant acclaim; Galsworthy's fame as an author was now sealed.

By the time the first Forsyte trilogy had been completed, with *In Chancery* (1920) and *To Let* (1921), sales of *The Forsyte Saga* had reached one million on both sides of the Atlantic. With the public clamouring for more, Galsworthy followed these with six more Forsyte novels, the last of which, *Over The River*, was completed just before his death in 1933. And their appeal endures, immortalised on screen in much-loved adaptations such as the film *That Forsyte Woman* (1949), starring Errol Flynn. The celebrated BBC drama in 1967 with Kenneth More and Eric Porter was a phenomenal success, emptying the pubs and churches of Britain on a Sunday evening, and reaching an estimated worldwide audience of 160 million. The recent popular 2002 production starred Damien Lewis, Rupert Graves and Ioan Gruffudd and won a Bafta TV award.

Undoubtedly *The Forsyte Saga* is Galsworthy's most distinguished work, but he was well known, if not more successful in his time, as a dramatist. His inherent compassion meant Galsworthy was always involved in one cause or another, from women's suffrage to a ban on ponies in mines, and his plays very much focus on the social injustices of his day. *The Silver Box* (1906) was his first major success, but *Justice* (1910), a stark depiction of prison life, had an even bigger impact. Winston Churchill was so impressed by it that he immediately arranged for prison reform, reducing the hours of solitary confinement. *The Skin Game* (1920) was another big hit and later adapted into a film, under the same title, by Alfred Hitchcock.

Despite Galsworthy's literary success, his personal life was still troubled. Although he and Ada were deeply in love, the years of uncertainty had taken their toll. They never had children and their marriage reached a crisis in 1910 when Galsworthy formed a close friendship with a young dancer called Margaret Morris while working on one of his plays with her. But John, confused and tortured by the thought of betraying Ada, broke off all contact with Margaret in 1912 and went abroad with his wife. The rest of their lives were spent constantly on the move; travelling in America, Europe, or at home in London, Dartmoor and later Sussex. Numerous trips were made in connection with PEN, the international writers' club, after Galsworthy was elected its first president in 1921. Many people have seen the constant travelling as unsettling for Galsworthy and destructive to his writing, but being with Ada was all that mattered to him: 'This is what comes of giving yourself to a woman body and soul. A. paralyses and has always paralysed me. I have never been able to face the idea of being cut off from her.'

By the end of his life, Galsworthy, the man who had railed against poverty and injustice, had become an established, reputable figure in privileged society. Having earlier refused a knighthood, he was presented with an Order of Merit in 1929. And in 1932 he was awarded the Nobel Prize for literature. Although it was fashionable for younger writers to mock the traditional Edwardian authors, Virginia Woolf dismissing Galsworthy as a 'stuffed shirt', J.M. Barrie perceived his contradictory nature: 'A queer fish, like the rest of us. So sincerely weighed down by the out-of-jointness of things socially . . . but outwardly a man-about-town, so neat, so correct – he would go to the stake for his opinions but he would go courteously raising his hat.'

John Galsworthy died on 31 January 1933, at the age of sixty-five, at Grove Lodge in Hampstead, with Ada by his side. At his request, his ashes were scattered over Bury Hill in Sussex. *The Times* hailed him as the 'mouthpiece' of his age, 'the interpreter in drama, and in fiction of a definite phase in English social history'.

Other Forsyte novels by John Galsworthy and available from Headline Review

The Man Of Property
In Chancery
To Let
The White Monkey
The Silver Spoon
Swan Song
Maid In Waiting
Over The River

The Forsyte Saga
Flowering Wilderness

John Galsworthy

First published in Great Britain in 1932

This paperback edition published in 2007 by HEADLINE REVIEW
An imprint of HEADLINE PUBLISHING GROUP

1

ISBN 978 0 7553 4092 7

Typeset in Sabon by Palimpsest Book Production Limited,
Grangemouth, Stirlingshire

Printed and bound in Great Britain by
Clays Ltd, St Ives plc

Headline's policy is to use papers that are natural, renewable and recyclable products and made from wood grown in sustainable forests. The logging and manufacturing processes are expected to conform to the environmental regulations of the country of origin.

HEADLINE PUBLISHING GROUP
An Hachette Livre UK Company
338 Euston Road
London NW1 3BH

www.reviewbooks.co.uk
www.headline.co.uk

To
Herman Ould

Chapter One

In 1930, shortly after the appearance of the Budget, the eighth wonder of the world might have been observed in the neighbourhood of Victoria Station – three English people, of wholly different type, engaged in contemplating simultaneously a London statue. They had come separately, and stood a little apart from each other in the south-west corner of the open space clear of the trees, where the drifting late afternoon light of spring was not in their eyes. One of these three was a young woman of about twenty-six, one a youngish man of perhaps thirty-four, and one a man of between fifty and sixty. The young woman, slender and far from stupid-looking, had her head tilted slightly upward to one side, and a faint smile on her parted lips. The younger man, who wore a blue overcoat with a belt girt tightly round his thin middle, as if he felt the spring wind chilly, was sallow from fading sunburn; and the rather disdainful look of his mouth was being curiously contradicted by eyes fixed on the statue with real intensity of feeling. The elder man, very tall, in a brown suit and brown buckskin shoes, lounged, with his hands in his trouser pockets, and his long, weathered, good-looking face masked in a sort of shrewd scepticism.

In the meantime the statue, which was that of Marshal Foch

on his horse, stood high up among those trees, stiller than any of them.

The youngish man spoke suddenly.

'He delivered us.'

The effect of this breach of form on the others was diverse; the elder man's eyebrows went slightly up, and he moved forward as if to examine the horse's legs. The young woman turned and looked frankly at the speaker, and instantly her face became surprised.

'Aren't you Wilfrid Desert?'

The youngish man bowed.

'Then,' said the young woman, 'we've met. At Fleur Mont's wedding. You were best man, if you remember, the first I'd seen. I was only sixteen. You wouldn't remember me – Dinny Cherrell, baptised Elizabeth. They ran me in for bridesmaid at the last minute.'

The youngish man's mouth lost its disdain.

'I remember your hair perfectly.'

'Nobody ever remembers me by anything else.'

'Wrong! I remember thinking you'd sat to Botticelli. You're still sitting, I see.'

Dinny was thinking: 'His eyes were the first to flutter me. And they really are beautiful.'

The said eyes had been turned again upon the statue.

'He *did* deliver us,' said Desert.

'You were there, of course.'

'Flying, and fed up to the teeth.'

'Do you like the statue?'

'The horse.'

'Yes,' murmured Dinny, 'it *is* a horse, not just a prancing barrel, with teeth, nostrils and an arch.'

'The whole thing's workmanlike, like Foch himself.'

Dinny wrinkled her brow.

'I like the way it stands up quietly among those trees.'

'How is Michael? You're a cousin of his, if I remember.'

'Michael's all right. Still in the House; he has a seat he simply can't lose.'

'And Fleur?'

'Flourishing. Did you know she had a daughter last year?'

'Fleur? H'm! That makes two, doesn't it?'

'Yes; they call this one Catherine.'

'I haven't been home since 1927. Gosh! It's a long time since that wedding.'

'You look,' said Dinny, contemplating the sallow darkness of his face, 'as if you had been in the sun.'

'When I'm not in the sun I'm not alive.'

'Michael once told me you lived in the East.'

'Well, I wander about there.' His face seemed to darken still more, and he gave a little shiver. 'Beastly cold, the English spring!'

'And do you still write poetry?'

'Oh! you know of that weakness?'

'I've read them all. I like the last volume best.'

He grinned. 'Thank you for stroking me the right way; poets, you know, like it. Who's that tall man? I seem to know his face.'

The tall man, who had moved to the other side of the statue, was coming back.

'Somehow,' murmured Dinny, 'I connect him with that wedding, too.'

The tall man came up to them.

'The hocks aren't all that,' he said.

Dinny smiled.

'I always feel so thankful I haven't got hocks. We were just trying to decide whether we knew you. Weren't you at Michael Mont's wedding some years ago?'

'I was. And who are you, young lady?'

'We all met there. I'm his first cousin on his mother's side, Dinny Cherrell. Mr Desert was his best man.'

The tall man nodded.

'Oh! Ah! My name's Jack Muskham, I'm a first cousin of his father's.' He turned to Desert. 'You admired Foch, it seems.'

'I did.'

Dinny was surprised at the morose look that had come on his face.

'Well,' said Muskham, 'he was a soldier all right; and there weren't too many about. But I came here to see the horse.'

'It is, of course, the important part,' murmured Dinny.

The tall man gave her his sceptical smile.

'One thing we have to thank Foch for, he never left us in the lurch.'

Desert suddenly faced round:

'Any particular reason for that remark?'

Muskham shrugged his shoulders, raised his hat to Dinny, and lounged away.

When he had gone there was a silence as over deep waters.

'Which way were you going?' said Dinny at last.

'Any way that you are.'

'I thank you kindly, sir. Would an aunt in Mount Street serve as a direction?'

'Admirably.'

'You must remember her, Michael's mother; she's a darling, the world's perfect mistress of the ellipse – talks in stepping stones, so that you have to jump to follow her.'

They crossed the road and set out up Grosvenor Place on the Buckingham Palace side.

'I suppose you find England changed every time you come home, if you'll forgive me for making conversation?'

'Changed enough.'

'Don't you "love your native land", as the saying is?'

'She inspires me with a sort of horror.'

'Are you by any chance one of those people who wish to be thought worse than they are?'

'Not possible. Ask Michael.'

'Michael is incapable of slander.'

'Michael and all angels are outside the count of reality.'

'No,' said Dinny, 'Michael is very real, and very English.'

'That is his contradictory trouble.'

'Why do you run England down? It's been done before.'

'I never run her down except to English people.'

'That's something. But why to me?'

Desert laughed.

'Because you seem to be what I should like to feel that England is.'

'Flattered and fair, but neither fat nor forty.'

'What I object to is England's belief that she is still "the goods".'

'And isn't she, really?'

'Yes,' said Desert, surprisingly, 'but she has no reason to think so.'

Dinny thought:

'You're perverse, brother Wilfrid, the young woman said,
And your tongue is exceedingly wry;
You do not look well when you stand on your head –
Why will you continually try?'

She remarked, more simply:

'If England is still "the goods", has no reason to think so and yet does, she would seem to have intuition, anyway. Was it by intuition that you disliked Mr Muskham?' Then, looking at his face, she thought: 'I'm dropping a brick.'

'Why should I dislike him? He's just the usual insensitive type of hunting, racing man who bores me stiff.'

'That wasn't the reason,' thought Dinny, still regarding him. A strange face! Unhappy from deep inward disharmony, as though a good angel and a bad were for ever seeking to fire each other out; but his eyes sent the same thrill through her as when, at sixteen, with her hair still long, she had stood near him at Fleur's wedding.

'And do you really like wandering about in the East?'

'The curse of Esau is on me.'

'Some day,' she thought, 'I'll make him tell me why. Only probably I shall never see him again.' And a little chill ran down her back.

'I wonder if you know my Uncle Adrian. He was in the East during the war. He presides over bones at a museum. You probably know Diana Ferse, anyway. He married her last year.'

'I know nobody to speak of.'

'Our point of contact, then, is only Michael.'

'I don't believe in contacts through other people. Where do you live, Miss Cherrell?'

Dinny smiled.

'A short biographical note seems to be indicated. Since the umpteenth century, my family has been "seated" at Condaford Grange in Oxfordshire. My father is a retired General; I am one of two daughters; and my only brother is a married soldier just coming back from the Soudan on leave.'

'Oh!' said Desert, and again his face had that morose look.

'I am twenty-six, unmarried but with no children as yet. My hobby seems to be attending to other people's business. I don't know why I have it. When in Town I stay at Lady Mont's in Mount Street. With a simple upbringing I have expensive instincts and no means of gratifying them. I believe I can see a joke. Now you?'

Desert smiled and shook his head.

'Shall I?' said Dinny. 'You are the second son of Lord Mullyon, you had too much war; you write poetry; you have nomadic instincts and are your own enemy; the last item has the only news value. Here we are in Mount Street; do come in and see Aunt Em.'

'Thank you – no. But will you lunch with me tomorrow and go to a matinée?'

'I will. Where?'

'Dumourieux's, one-thirty.'

They exchanged hand-grips and parted, but as Dinny went into her aunt's house she was tingling all over, and she stood still outside the drawing room to smile at the sensation.

Chapter Two

The smile faded off her lips under the fire of noises coming through the closed door.

'My goodness!' she thought: 'Aunt Em's birthday "pawty", and I'd forgotten.'

Someone playing the piano stopped, there was a rush, a scuffle, the scraping of chairs on the floor, two or three squeals, silence, and the piano-playing began again.

'Musical chairs!' she thought, and opened the door quietly. She who had been Diana Ferse was sitting at the piano. To eight assorted chairs, facing alternatively east and west, were clinging one large and eight small beings in bright paper hats, of whom seven were just rising to their feet and two still sitting on one chair. Dinny saw from left to right: Ronald Ferse; a small Chinese boy; Aunt Alison's youngest, little Anne; Uncle Hilary's youngest, Tony; Celia and Dingo (children of Michael's married sister Celia Moriston); Sheila Ferse; and on the single chair Uncle Adrian and Kit Mont. She was further conscious of Aunt Em panting slightly against the fireplace in a large headpiece of purple paper, and of Fleur pulling a chair from Ronald's end of the row.

'Kit, get up! You were out.'

Kit sat firm and Adrian rose.

'All right, old man, you're up against your equals now. Fire away!'

'Keep your hands off the backs,' cried Fleur. 'Wu Fing, you mustn't sit till the music stops. Dingo, don't stick at the end chair like that.'

The music stopped. Scurry, hustle, squeals, and the smallest figure, little Anne, was left standing.

'All right, darling,' said Dinny, 'come here and beat this drum. Stop when the music stops, that's right. Now again. Watch Auntie Di!'

Again, and again, and again, till Sheila and Dingo and Kit only were left.

'I back Kit,' thought Dinny.

Sheila out! Off with a chair! Dingo, so Scotch-looking, and Kit, so bright-haired, having lost his paper cap, were left padding round and round the last chair. Both were down; both up and on again, Diana carefully averting her eyes, Fleur standing back now with a little smile; Aunt Em's face very pink. The music stopped, Dingo was down again; and Kit left standing, his face flushed and frowning.

'Kit,' said Fleur's voice, 'play the game!'

Kit's head was thrown up and he rammed his hands into his pockets.

'Good for Fleur!' thought Dinny.

A voice behind her said:

'Your aunt's purple passion for the young, Dinny, leads us into strange riots. What about a spot of quiet in my study?'

Dinny looked round at Sir Lawrence Mont's thin, dry, twisting face, whose little moustache had gone quite white, while his hair was still only sprinkled.

'I haven't done my bit, Uncle Lawrence.'

'Time you learned not to. Let the heathen rage. Come down and have a quiet Christian talk.'

Subduing her instinct for service with the thought: 'I *should* like to talk about Wilfrid Desert!' Dinny went.

'What are you working on now, Uncle?'

'Resting for the minute and reading the Memoirs of Harriette Wilson – a remarkable young woman, Dinny. In the days of the Regency there were no reputations in high life to destroy; but she did her best. If you don't know about her, I may tell you that she believed in love and had a great many lovers, only one of whom she loved.'

'And yet she believed in love?'

'Well, she was a kind-hearted baggage, and the others loved her. All the difference in the world between her and Ninon de l'Enclos, who loved them all; both vivid creatures. A duologue between those two on "virtue"? It's to be thought of. Sit down!'

'While I was looking at Foch's statue this afternoon, Uncle Lawrence, I met a cousin of yours, Mr Muskham.'

'Jack?'

'Yes.'

'Last of the dandies. All the difference in the world, Dinny, between the "buck", the "dandy", the "swell", the "masher", the "blood", the "knut", and what's the last variety called? – I never know. There's been a steady decrescendo. By his age Jack belongs to the "masher" period, but his cut was always pure dandy – a dyed-in-the-wool Whyte Melville type. How did he strike you?'

'Horses, piquet and imperturbability.'

'Take your hat off, my dear. I like to see your hair.'

Dinny removed her hat.

'I met someone else there, too; Michael's best man.'

'What! Young Desert? He back again?' And Sir Lawrence's loose-eyebrow mounted.

A slight colour had stained Dinny's cheeks.

'Yes,' she said.

'Queer bird, Dinny.'

Within her rose a feeling rather different from any she had ever experienced. She could not have described it, but it reminded her of a piece of porcelain she had given to her father on his birthday, two weeks ago; a little china group, beautifully modelled, of a vixen and four fox cubs tucked in under her. The look on the vixen's face, soft yet watchful, so completely expressed her own feeling at this moment.

'Why queer?'

'Tales out of school, Dinny. Still, to *you* – There's no doubt in my mind that that young man made up to Fleur a year or two after her marriage. That's what started him as a rolling stone.'

Was that, then, what he had meant when he mentioned Esau? No! By the look of his face when he spoke of Fleur, she did not think so.

'But that was ages ago,' she said.

'Oh, yes! Ancient story; but one's heard other things. Clubs are the mother of all uncharitableness.'

The softness of Dinny's feeling diminished, the watchfulness increased.

'What other things?'

Sir Lawrence shook his head.

'I rather like the young man; and not even to you, Dinny, do I repeat what I really know nothing of. Let a man live an unusual life, and there's no limit to what people invent about him.' He looked at her rather suddenly; but Dinny's eyes were limpid.

'Who's the little Chinese boy upstairs?'

'Son of a former Mandarin, who left his family here because of the ructions out there – quaint little image. A likeable people, the Chinese. When does Hubert arrive?'

'Next week. They're flying from Italy. Jean flies a lot, you know.'

'What's become of her brother?' And again he looked at Dinny.

'Alan? He's out on the China station.'

'Your aunt never ceases to bemoan your not clicking there.'

'Dear Uncle, almost anything to oblige Aunt Em; but, feeling like a sister to him, the prayer-book was against me.'

'*I* don't want you to marry,' said Sir Lawrence, 'and go out to some Barbary or other.'

Through Dinny flashed the thought: 'Uncle Lawrence is uncanny,' and her eyes became more limpid than ever.

'This confounded officialism,' he continued, 'seems to absorb all our kith and kin. My two daughters, Celia in China, Flora in India; your brother Hubert in the Soudan; your sister Clare off as soon as she's spliced – Jerry Corven's been given a post in Ceylon. I hear Charlie Muskham's got attached to Government House, Cape Town; Hilary's eldest boy's going into the Indian Civil, and his youngest into the Navy. Dash it all, Dinny, you and Jack Muskham seem to be the only pelicans in my wilderness. Of course there's Michael.'

'Do you see much of Mr Muskham, then, Uncle?'

'Quite a lot at "Burton's", and he comes to me at "The Coffee House"; we play piquet – we're the only two left. That's in the illegitimate season – from now on I shall hardly see him till after the Cambridgeshire.'

'Is he a terribly good judge of a horse?'

'Yes. Of anything else, Dinny – no. They seldom are. The horse is an animal that seems to close the pores of the spirit. He makes you too watchful. You don't only have to watch him, but everybody connected with him. How was young Desert looking?'

'Oh!' said Dinny, almost taken aback: 'a sort of dark yellow.'

'That's the glare of the sand. He's a kind of Bedouin, you know. His father's a recluse, so it's a bit in his blood. The best thing I know about him is that Michael likes him, in spite of that business.'

'His poetry?' said Dinny.

'Disharmonic stuff, he destroys with one hand what he gives with the other.'

'Perhaps he's never found his home. His eyes are rather beautiful, don't you think?'

'It's his mouth I remember best, sensitive and bitter.'

'One's eyes are what one is, one's mouth what one becomes.'

'That and the stomach.'

'He hasn't any,' said Dinny. 'I noticed.'

'The handful of dates and cup of coffee habit. Not that the Arabs drink coffee – green tea is their weakness, with mint in it. My God! Here's your aunt. When I said "My God!" I was referring to the tea with mint.'

Lady Mont had removed her paper headdress and recovered her breath.

'Darling,' said Dinny, 'I *did* forget your birthday, and I haven't got anything for you.'

'Then give me a kiss, Dinny. I always say your kisses are the best. Where have you sprung from?'

'I came up to shop for Clare at the Stores.'

'Have you got your night things with you?'

'No.'

'That doesn't matter. You can have one of mine. Do you still wear nightdresses?'

'Yes,' said Dinny.

'Good girl! I don't like pyjamas for women – your uncle doesn't either. It's below the waist, you know. You can't get over it – you try to, but you can't. Michael and Fleur will be stayin' on to dinner.'

'Thank you, Aunt Em; I do want to stay up. I couldn't get half the things Clare needs today.'

'I don't like Clare marryin' before you, Dinny.'

'But she naturally would, Auntie.'

'Fiddle! Clare's brilliant – they don't as a rule. I married at twenty-one.'

'You see, dear!'

'You're laughin' at me. I was only brilliant once. You

remember, Lawrence – about that elephant – I wanted it to sit, and it would kneel. All their legs bend one way, Dinny. And I said it *would* follow its bent.'

'Aunt Em! Except for that one occasion you're easily the most brilliant woman I know. Women are so much too consecutive.'

'Your nose is a comfort, Dinny, I get so tired of beaks, your Aunt Wilmet's, and Hen Bentworth's, and my own.'

'Yours is only faintly aquiline, darling.'

'I was terrified of its gettin' worse, as a child. I used to stand with the tip pressed up against a wardrobe.'

'I've tried that too, Auntie, only the other way.'

'Once while I was doin' it your father was lyin' concealed on the top, like a leopard, you know, and he hopped over me and bit through his lip. He bled all down my neck.'

'How nasty!'

'Yes. Lawrence, what are you thinking about?'

'I was thinking that Dinny has probably had no lunch. Have you, Dinny?'

'I was going to have it tomorrow, Uncle.'

'There you are!' said Lady Mont. 'Ring for Blore. You'll never have enough body until you're married.'

'Let's get Clare over first, Aunt Em.'

'St. George's. I suppose Hilary's doin' them?'

'Of course!'

'I shall cry.'

'Why, exactly, do you cry at weddings, Auntie?'

'She'll look like an angel; and the man'll be in black tails and a toothbrush moustache, and not feelin' what she thinks he is. Saddenin'!'

'But perhaps he's feeling more. I'm sure Michael was about Fleur, or Uncle Adrian when he married Diana.'

'Adrian's fifty-three and he's got a beard. Besides, he's Adrian.'

'I admit that makes a difference. But I think we ought rather to cry over the man. The woman's having the hour of her life and the man's waistcoat is almost certain to be too tight.'

'Lawrence's wasn't. He was always a thread-paper, and I was as slim as you, Dinny.'

'You must have looked lovely in a veil, Aunt Em. Didn't she, Uncle?' The whimsically wistful look on both those mature faces stopped her, and she added: 'Where did you first meet?'

'Out huntin', Dinny. I was in a ditch, and your uncle didn't like it, he came and pulled me out.'

'I think that's ideal.'

'Too much mud. We didn't speak to each other all the rest of the day.'

'Then what brought you together?'

'One thing and another. I was stayin' with Hen's people, the Corderoys, and your uncle called to see some puppies. What are you catechisin' me for?'

'I only just wanted to know how it was done in those days.'

'Go and find out for yourself how it's done in these days.'

'Uncle Lawrence doesn't want to get rid of me.'

'All men are selfish, except Michael and Adrian.'

'Besides, I should hate to make you cry.'

'Blore, a cocktail and a sandwich for Miss Dinny, she's had no lunch. And, Blore, Mr and Mrs Adrian and Mr and Mrs Michael to dinner. And, Blore, tell Laura to put one of my nightdresses and the other things in the blue spare room. Miss Dinny'll stay the night. Those children!' And, swaying slightly, Lady Mont preceded her butler through the doorway.

'What a darling, Uncle!'

'I've never denied it, Dinny.'

'I always feel better after her. Was she ever out of temper?'

'She can begin to be, but she always goes on to something else before she's finished.'

'What saving grace . . . !'

At dinner that evening, Dinny listened for any allusion by her uncle to Wilfrid Desert's return. There was none.

After dinner, she seated herself by Fleur in her habitual, slightly mystified admiration of this cousin by marriage, whose pretty poise was so assured, whose face and figure so beautifully turned out, whose clear eyes were so seeing, whose knowledge of self was so disillusioned, and whose attitude to Michael seemed at once that of one looking up and looking down.

'If I ever married,' thought Dinny, 'I could never be like that to him. I would have to look him straight in the face as one sinner to another.'

'Do you remember your wedding, Fleur?' she said.

'I do, my dear. A distressing ceremony!'

'I saw your best man today.'

The clear white round Fleur's eyes widened.

'Wilfrid? How did you remember him?'

'I was only sixteen, and he fluttered my young nerves.'

'That is, of course, the function of a best man. Well, and how was he?'

'Very dark and dissolvent.'

Fleur laughed. 'He always was.'

Looking at her, Dinny decided to press on.

'Yes. Uncle Lawrence told me he tried to carry dissolution rather far.'

Fleur looked surprised. 'I didn't know Bart ever noticed that.'

'Uncle Lawrence,' said Dinny, 'is a bit uncanny.'

'Wilfrid,' murmured Fleur, with a little reminiscent smile, 'really behaved quite well. He went East like a lamb.'

'But surely that hasn't kept him East ever since?'

'No more than measles keep you permanently to your room. Oh! no, he likes it. He's probably got a harem.'

'No,' said Dinny, 'he's fastidious, or I should be surprised.'

'Quite right, my dear; and one for my cheap cynicism. Wilfrid's the queerest sort of person, and rather a dear. Michael loved him. But,' she said, suddenly looking at Dinny, 'he's impossible to be in love with – disharmony personified. I studied him pretty closely at one time – had to, you know. He's elusive. Passionate, and a bundle of nerves. Soft-hearted and bitter. And search me for anything he believes in.'

'Except,' queried Dinny, 'beauty, perhaps; and truth if he could find it?'

Fleur made the unexpected answer, 'Well, my dear, we all believe in those, when they're about. The trouble is they aren't, unless – unless they lie in oneself, perhaps. And if you happen to be disharmonic, what chance have you? Where did you see him?'

'Staring at Foch.'

'Ah! I seem to remember he rather idolised Foch. Poor Wilfrid, he hasn't much chance. Shell-shock, poetry, and his breeding – a father who's turned his back on life; a mother who was half an Italian, and ran off with another. Not restful. His eyes were his best point, they made you sorry for him; and they're beautiful – rather a fatal combination. Did the young nerves flutter again?' She looked rather more broadly into Dinny's face.

'No, but I wondered if yours would still if I mentioned him.'

'Mine? My child, I'm nearly thirty. I have two children, and' – her face darkened – 'I have been inoculated. If I ever told anyone about *that*, Dinny, I might tell you, but there are things one doesn't tell.'

Up in her room, somewhat incommoded by the amplitude of Aunt Em's nightgown, Dinny stared into a fire lighted against protest. She felt that what she was feeling was absurd – a queer eagerness, at once shy and bold, the sensations, as it were, of direct action impending. And why? She had seen again a man who ten years before had made her feel silly;

from all accounts a most unsatisfactory man. Taking a looking-glass, she scrutinised her face above the embroidery on the too ample gown. She saw what might have satisfied but did not.

'One gets tired of it,' she thought – 'always the same Botticellian artifact,

> 'The nose that's snub,
> The eyes of blue!
> 'Ware self, you red-haired nymph,
> And shun the image that is you!'

He was so accustomed to the East, to dark eyes through veils, languishing; to curves enticingly disguised; to sex, mystery, teeth like pearls – *vide* houri! Dinny showed her own teeth to the glass. There she was on safe ground – the best teeth in her family. Nor was her hair really red – more what Miss Braddon used to call auburn. Nice word! Pity it had gone out. With all that embroidery it was no good examining herself below the Victorian washing line. Remember that tomorrow before her bath! For what she was about to examine might the Lord make her truly thankful! Putting down the glass with a little sigh, she got into bed.

Chapter Three

Wilfrid Desert still maintained his chambers in Cork Street. They were, in fact, paid for by Lord Mullyon, who used them on the rare occasions when he emerged from rural retreat. It was not saying much that the secluded peer had more in common with his second than with his eldest son, who was in Parliament. It gave him, however, no particular pain to encounter Wilfrid; but as a rule the chambers were occupied only by Stack, who had been Wilfrid's batman in the war, and had for him one of those sphinx-like habits which wear better than expressed devotions. When Wilfrid returned, at a moment or two's notice, his rooms were ever exactly as he left them, neither more nor less dusty and unaired; the same clothes hung on the same clothes-stretchers; and the same nicely cooked steak and mushrooms appeased his first appetite. The ancestral 'junk', fringed and dotted by Eastern whims brought home, gave to the large sitting room the same castled air of immutable possession. And the divan before the log fire received Wilfrid as if he had never left it. He lay there the morning after his encounter with Dinny, wondering why he could only get really good coffee when Stack made it. The East was the home of coffee, but Turkish coffee was a rite, a toy; and, like all rites and toys, served but to titillate the soul. This was his third day in London after three years; and in the last two years he had been through a good deal more than he would ever care to speak of, or even wish to remember; including one experience which still divided him against himself, however much he affected to discredit its importance. In other words, he had come back with a skeleton in his cupboard. He had brought back, too, enough poems for a fourth slender volume. He lay there, debating whether its slender bulk could not be increased by inclusion of the longest poem he had ever written, the outcome of that experience; in his view, too, the best poem he had ever written – a pity it should not be published, but—! And the 'but' was so considerable that he had many times been on the point of tearing the thing up, obliterating all trace of it, as he would have wished to blot remembrance from his mind. Again, but—! The poem expressed his defence for allowing what he hoped no one knew had happened to him. To tear it up would be parting with his defence. For he could never again adequately render his sensations in that past dilemma. He would be parting with his best protection from his own conscience, too; and perhaps with the only means of laying a ghost. For he sometimes thought that, unless he proclaimed to the world what had happened to him, he would never again feel quite in possession of his soul.

Reading it through, he thought: 'It's a damned sight better and deeper than Lyall's confounded poem.' And without any obvious connection he began to think of the girl he had met the day before. Curious that he had remembered her from Michael's wedding, a transparent slip of a young thing like a Botticelli Venus, Angel, or Madonna – so little difference between them. A charming young thing, then! Yes, and a charming young woman now, of real quality, with a sense of humour and an understanding mind. Dinny Cherrell! Charwell they spelled it, he remembered. He wouldn't mind showing her his poems; he would trust her reactions.

Partly because he was thinking of her, and partly because

he took a taxi, he was late for lunch, and met Dinny on the doorstep of Dumourieux's just as she was about to go away.

There is perhaps no better test of woman's character than to keep her waiting for lunch in a public place. Dinny greeted him with a smile.

'I thought you'd probably forgotten.'

'It was the traffic. How can philosophers talk of time being space or space time? It's disproved whenever two people lunch together. I allowed ten minutes for under a mile from Cork Street, and here I am ten minutes late. Terribly sorry!'

'My father says you must add ten per cent to all timing since taxis took the place of hansoms. Do you remember the hansom?'

'Rather!'

'I never was in London till they were over.'

'If you know this place, lead on! I was told of it, but I've not yet been here.'

'It's under ground. The cooking's French.'

Divested of their coats, they proceeded to an end table.

'Very little for me, please,' said Dinny. 'Say cold chicken, a salad, and some coffee.'

'Anything the matter?'

'Only a spare habit.'

'I see. We both have it. No wine?'

'No, thanks. Is eating little a good sign, do you think?'

'Not if done on principle.'

'You don't like things done on principle?'

'I distrust the people who do them – self-righteous.'

'I think that's too sweeping. You are rather sweeping, aren't you?'

'I was thinking of the sort of people who don't eat because it's sensual. That's not your reason, is it?'

'Oh! no,' said Dinny, 'I only dislike feeling full. And very little makes me feel that. I don't know very much about them so far, but I think the senses are good things.'

'The only things, probably.'

'Is that why you write poetry?'

Desert grinned.

'I should think *you* might write verse, too.'

'Only rhymes.'

'The place for poetry is a desert. Ever seen one?'

'No. I should like to.' And, having said that, she sat in slight surprise, remembering her negative reaction to the American professor and his great open spaces. But no greater contrast was possible than between Hallorsen and this dark, disharmonic young man, who sat staring at her with those eyes of his till she had again that thrill down her spine. Crumbling her roll, she said: 'I saw Michael and Fleur last night at dinner.'

'Oh!' His lips curled. 'I made a fool of myself over Fleur once. Perfect, isn't she – in her way?'

'Yes,' and her eyes added: 'Don't run her down!'

'Marvellous equipment and control.'

'I don't think you know her,' said Dinny, 'and I'm sure I don't.'

He leaned forward. 'You seem to me a loyal sort of person. Where did you pick that up?'

'Our family motto is the word "Leal". That ought to have cured me, oughtn't it?'

'I don't know,' he said, abruptly, 'whether I understand what loyalty is. Loyalty to what? To whom? Nothing's fixed in this world; everything's relative. Loyalty's the mark of the static mind, or else just a superstition, and anyway the negation of curiosity.'

'There *are* things worth being loyal to, surely. Coffee, for instance, or one's religion.'

He looked at her so strangely that Dinny was almost scared.

'Religion? Have you one?'

'Well, roughly, I suppose.'

'What? Can you swallow the dogmas of any religious creed? Do you believe one legend more true than another? Can you suppose one set of beliefs about the Unknowable has more value than the rest? Religion! You've got a sense of humour. Does it leave you at the word?'

'No; only religion, I suppose, may be just a sense of an all-pervading spirit, and the ethical creed that seems best to serve it.'

'H'm! A pretty far cry from what's generally meant, and even then how do you know what best serves an all-pervading spirit?'

'I take that on trust.'

'There's where we differ. Look!' he said, and it seemed to her that excitement had crept into his voice: 'What's the use of our reasoning powers, our mental faculties? I take each problem as it comes, I do the sum, I return the answer, and so I act. I act according to a reasoned estimate of what is best.'

'For whom?'

'For myself and the world at large.'

'Which first?'

'It's the same thing.'

'Always? I wonder. And, anyway, that means doing so long a sum every time that I can't think how you ever get to acting. And surely ethical rules are just the result of countless decisions on those same problems made by people in the past, so why not take them for granted?'

'None of those decisions were made by people of my temperament or in my circumstances.'

'No, I see that. You follow what they call case law, then. But how English!'

'Sorry!' said Desert, abruptly: 'I'm boring you. Have a sweet?'

Dinny put her elbows on the table and, leaning her chin on her hands, looked at him earnestly.

'You weren't boring me. On the contrary, you're interesting me frightfully. Only I suppose that women act much more instinctively; I suppose that really means they accept themselves as more like each other than men do, and are more ready to trust their instinctive sense of general experience.'

'That *has* been women's way; whether it will be much longer, I don't know.'

'I think it will,' said Dinny. 'I don't believe we shall ever much care for sums. I *will* have a sweet, please. Stewed prunes, I think.'

Desert stared at her, and began to laugh.

'You're wonderful. We'll both have them. Is your family a very formal one?'

'Not exactly formal, but they do believe in tradition and the past.'

'And do you?'

'I don't know. I definitely like old things, and old places, and old people. I like anything that's stamped like a coin. I like to feel one has roots. I was always fond of history. All the same one can't help laughing. There's something very comic about the way we're all tied – like a hen by a chalk mark to its beak.'

Desert stretched out his hand and she put hers into it.

'Shake hands on that saving grace.'

'Some day,' said Dinny, 'you're going to tell me something. But at the moment what play are we going to?'

'Is there anything by a man called Shakespeare?'

With some difficulty they discovered that a work by the world's greatest dramatist was being given in a theatre beyond the pale of the river. They went to it, and, when the show was over, Desert said, hesitating: 'I wonder if you would come and have tea at my rooms?'

Dinny smiled and nodded, and from that moment was conscious of a difference in his manner. It was at once more intimate yet more respectful, as if he had said to himself: 'This is my equal.'

That hour of tea, brought by Stack, a man with strange, understanding eyes and something monk-like in his look, seemed to her quite perfect. It was like no other hour she had ever spent, and at the end of it she knew she was in love. The tiny seed planted ten years before had flowered. This was such a marvel, so peculiar to one who at twenty-six had begun to think she would never be in love, that every now and then she drew in her breath and looked wonderingly at his face. Why on earth did she feel like this? It was absurd! And it was going to be painful, because he wasn't going to love her. Why should he? And if he wasn't, she mustn't show, and how was she to help showing?

'When am I going to see you again?' he said, when she stood up to go.

'Do you want to?'

'Extraordinarily.'

'But why?'

'Why not? You're the first lady I've spoken to for ten years. I'm not at all sure you're not the first lady I've ever spoken to.'

'If we are going to see each other again, you mustn't laugh at me.'

'Laugh at you! One couldn't. So when?'

'Well! At present I'm sleeping in a foreign nightgown at Mount Street. By rights I ought to be at Condaford. But my sister's going to be married in town next week, and my brother's coming back from Egypt on Monday, so perhaps I'll send for things and stay up. Where would you like to see me?'

'Will you come for a drive tomorrow? I haven't been to Richmond or Hampton Court for years.'

'I've never been.'

'All right! I'll pick you up in front of Foch at two o'clock, wet or fine.'

'I will be pleased to come, young sir.'

'Splendid!' And, suddenly bending, he raised her hand and put his lips to it.

'Highly courteous,' said Dinny. 'Good-bye!'

Chapter Four

Preoccupied with this stupendous secret, Dinny's first instinct was for solitude, but she was booked for dinner with the Adrian Cherrells. On her uncle's marriage with Diana Ferse the house of painful memories in Oakley Street had been given up, and they were economically installed in one of those spacious Bloomsbury squares now successfully regaining the gentility lost in the eighteen-thirties and forties. The locality had been chosen for its proximity to Adrian's 'bones', for at his age he regarded as important every minute saved for the society of his wife. The robust virility which Dinny had predicted would accrue to her uncle from a year spent in the presence of Professor Hallorsen and New Mexico was represented by a somewhat deeper shade of brown in his creased cheeks, and a more frequent smile on his long face. It was a lasting pleasure to Dinny to think that she had given him the right advice, and that he had taken it. Diana, too, was fast regaining the sparkle which, before her marriage with poor Ferse, had made her a member of 'Society'. But the hopeless nature of Adrian's occupation and the extra time he needed from her had precluded her from any return to that sacred ring. She inclined more and more, in fact, to be a wife and mother. And this seemed natural to one with Dinny's partiality for her uncle. On her way there she debated whether or not to say what she had been doing. Having little liking for shifts and subterfuge, she decided to be frank. 'Besides,' she thought, 'a maiden in love always likes to talk about the object of her affections.' Again, if not to have a confidant became too wearing, Uncle Adrian was the obvious choice; partly because he knew at first hand something of the East, but chiefly because he was Uncle Adrian.

The first topics at dinner, however, were naturally Clare's marriage and Hubert's return. Dinny was somewhat exercised over her sister's choice. Sir Gerald (Jerry) Corven was forty, active and middle-sized, with a daring face. She recognised that he had great charm, and her fear was, rather, that he had too much. He was high in the Colonial service, one of those men who – people instinctively said – would go far. She wondered also whether Clare was not too like him, daring and brilliant, a bit of a gambler, and, of course, seventeen years younger. Diana, who had known him well, said:

'The seventeen years' difference is the best thing about it. Jerry wants steadying. If he can be a father to her as well, it may work. He's had infinite experiences. I'm glad it's Ceylon.'

'Why?'

'He won't meet his past.'

'Has he an awful lot of past?'

'My dear, he's very much in love at the moment; but with men like Jerry you never know; all that charm, and so much essential liking for thin ice.'

'Marriage doth make cowards of us all,' murmured Adrian.

'It won't have that effect on Jerry Corven; he takes to risk as a goldfish takes to mosquito larvae. Is Clare very smitten, Dinny?'

'Yes, but Clare loves thin ice, too.'

'And yet,' said Adrian, 'I shouldn't call either of them really modern. They've both got brains and like using them.'

'That's quite true, uncle. Clare gets all she can out of life, but she believes in life terribly. She might become another Hester Stanhope.'

'Good for you, Dinny! But to be that she'd have to get rid of Gerald Corven first. And if I read Clare, I think she might have scruples.'

Dinny regarded her uncle with wide eyes.

'Do you say that because you know Clare, or because you're a Cherrell, Uncle?'

'I think because *she's* a Cherrell, my dear.'

'Scruples,' murmured Dinny. 'I don't believe Aunt Em has them. Yet she's as much of a Cherrell as any of us.'

'Em,' said Adrian, 'reminds me of nothing so much as a find of bones that won't join up. You can't say of what she's the skeleton. Scruples are emphatically co-ordinate.'

'No! Adrian,' murmured Diana, 'not bones at dinner. When does Hubert arrive? I'm really anxious to see him and young Jean. After eighteen months of bliss in the Soudan which will be top dog?'

'Jean, surely,' said Adrian.

Dinny shook her head. 'I don't think so, Uncle.'

'That's your sisterly pride.'

'No. Hubert's got more continuity. Jean rushes at things and must handle them at once, but Hubert steers the course, I'm pretty sure. Uncle, where is a place called Darfur? And how do you spell it?'

'With an "r" or without. It's west of the Soudan; much of it is desert and pretty inaccessible, I believe. Why?'

'I was lunching today with Mr Desert, Michael's best man, you remember, and he mentioned it.'

'Has he been there?'

'I think he's been everywhere in the Near East.'

'I know his brother,' said Diana, 'Charles Desert, one of the most provocative of the younger politicians. He'll almost certainly be Minister of Education in the next Tory Government.

That'll put the finishing touch to Lord Mullyon's retirement. I've never met Wilfrid. Is he nice?'

'Well,' said Dinny, with what she believed to be detachment, 'I only met him yesterday. He seems rather like a mince pie, you take a spoonful and hope. If you can eat the whole, you have a happy year.'

'I should like to meet the young man,' said Adrian. 'He did good things in the war, and I know his verse.'

'Really, Uncle? I could arrange it; so far we are in daily communication.'

'Oh!' said Adrian, and looked at her. 'I'd like to discuss the Hittite type with him. I suppose you know that what we are accustomed to regard as the most definitely Jewish characteristics are pure Hittite according to ancient Hittite drawings?'

'But weren't they all the same stock, really?'

'By no means, Dinny. The Israelites were Arabs. What the Hittites were we have yet to discover. The modern Jew in this country and in Germany is probably more Hittite than Semite.'

'Do you know Mr Jack Muskham, Uncle?'

'Only by repute. He's a cousin of Lawrence's and an authority on bloodstock. I believe he advocates a reintroduction of Arab blood into our racehorses. There's something in it if you could get the very best strain. Has young Desert been to Nejd? You can still only get it there, I believe.'

'I don't know. Where is Nejd?'

'Centre of Arabia. But Muskham will never get his idea adopted, there's no tighter mind than the pukka racing man's. He's a pretty pure specimen himself, I believe, except for this bee in his bonnet.'

'Jack Muskham,' said Diana, 'was once romantically in love with one of my sisters; it's made him a misogynist.'

'H'm! That's a bit cryptic!'

'He's rather fine-looking, I think,' said Dinny.

'Wears clothes wonderfully and has a reputation for hating everything modern. I haven't met him for years, but I used to know him rather well. Why, Dinny?'

'I just happened to see him the other day, and wondered.'

'Talking of Hittites,' said Diana, 'I've often thought those very old Cornish families, like the Deserts, have a streak of Phoenician in them. Look at Lord Mullyon. There's a queer type!'

'Fanciful, my love. You'd be more likely to find that streak in the simple folk. The Deserts must have married into non-Cornish stock for hundreds of years. The higher you go in the social scale, the less chance of preserving a primitive strain.'

'*Are* they a very old family?' said Dinny.

'Hoary and pretty queer. But you know my views about old families, Dinny, so I won't enlarge.'

Dinny nodded. She remembered very well that nerve-racked walk along Chelsea Embankment just after Ferse returned. And she looked affectionately into his face. It *was* nice to think that he had come into his own at last . . .

When she got back to Mount Street that night her uncle and aunt had gone up, but the butler was seated in the hall. He rose as she entered.

'I didn't know you had a key, Miss.'

'I'm terribly sorry, Blore, you were having such a nice snooze.'

'I was, Miss Dinny. After a certain age, as you'll find out, one gets a liking for dropping off at improper moments. Now Sir Lawrence, he's not a good sleeper, but, give you my word, if I go into his study almost any time when he's at work, I'll find him opening his eyes. And my Lady, she can do her eight hours, but I've known her to drop off when someone's talking to her, especially the old Rector at Lippinghall, Mr Tasburgh – a courtly old gentleman, but he has that effect. Even Mr

Michael – but then he's in Parliament, and they get the 'abit. Still, I do think, Miss, whether it was the war, or people not having any hope of anything, and running about so, that there's a tendency, as the saying is, towards sleep. Well, it does you good. Give you my word, Miss; I was dead to the world before I had that forty winks, and now I could talk to you for hours.'

'That would be lovely, Blore. Only I find, so far, that I'm sleepiest at bedtime.'

'Wait till you're married, Miss. Only I do hope you won't be doing that yet awhile. I said to Mrs Blore last night: "If Miss Dinny gets taken off, it'll be the life and soul of the party gone!" I've never seen much of Miss Clare, so that leaves me cold; but I heard my Lady yesterday telling you to go and find out for yourself how it was done, and, as I said to Mrs Blore, "Miss Dinny's like a daughter of the house, and" – well – you know my sentiments, Miss.'

'Dear Blore! I'm afraid I must go up now, I've had rather a tiring day.'

'Quite, Miss. Pleasant dreams!'

'Good-night!'

Pleasant dreams! Perhaps the dreams might be, but would reality? What uncharted country was she not entering with just a star to guide! And was it a fixed star, or some flaring comet? At least five men had wanted to marry her, all of whom she had felt she could sum up, so that a marriage would have been no great risk. And now she only wanted to marry one, but there he was, an absolutely uncertain quantity except that he could rouse in her a feeling she had never had before. Life was perverse. You dipped your finger in a lucky bag, and brought out – what? Tomorrow she would walk with him. They would see trees and grass together; scenery and gardens, pictures, perhaps; the river, and fruit blossom. She would know at least how his spirit and her own agreed about many things she cared for. And yet, if she found they didn't agree, would it make any difference to her feeling? It would not.

'I understand now,' she thought, 'why we call lovers dotty. All I care about is that he should feel what I feel, and be dotty too. And of course he won't – why should he?'

Chapter Five

The drive to Richmond Park, over Ham Common and Kingston Bridge to Hampton Court, and back through Twickenham and Kew, was remarkable for alternation between silence and volubility. Dinny was, as it were, the observer, and left to Wilfrid all the piloting. Her feelings made her shy, and it was apparent that he was only able to expand if left to his free will – the last person in the world to be drawn out. They duly lost themselves in the maze at Hampton Court, where, as Dinny said,

'Only spiders who can spin threads out of themselves, or ghosts who can tails unfold, would have a chance.'

On the way back they got out at Kensington Gardens, dismissed the hired car, and walked to the tea kiosk. Over the pale beverage he asked her suddenly whether she would mind reading his new poems in manuscript.

'Mind? I should love it.'

'I want a candid opinion.'

'You will get it,' said Dinny. 'When can I have them?'

'I'll bring them round to Mount Street and drop them in your letter-box after dinner.'

'Won't you come in this time?'

He shook his head.

When he left her at Stanhope Gate, he said abruptly:

'It's been a simply lovely afternoon. Thank you!'

'It is for me to thank you.'

'You! You've got more friends than quills upon the fretful porpentine. It's I who am the pelican.'

'Adieu, pelican!'

'Adieu, flowering wilderness!'

The words seemed musical all the way down Mount Street.

A fat unstamped envelope was brought in about half-past nine with the last post. Dinny took it from Blore, and slipping it under *The Bridge of San Luis Rey*, went on listening to her aunt.

'When I was a girl I squeezed my own waist, Dinny. We suffered for a principle. They say it's comin' in again. I shan't do it, so hot and worryin'; but you'll have to.'

'Not I.'

'When the waist has settled down there'll be a lot of squeezin'.'

'The really tight waist will never come in again, Auntie.'

'And hats. In 1900 we were like eggstands with explodin' eggs in them. Cauliflowers and hydrangeas, and birds of a feather, enormous. They stuck out. The Parks were comparatively pure. Sea-green suits you, Dinny; you ought to be married in it.'

'I think I'll go up, Aunt Em. I'm rather tired.'

'That's eatin' so little.'

'I eat enormously. Good-night, dear.'

Without undressing she sat down to the poems, nervously anxious to like them, for she knew that he would see through any falsity. To her relief they had the tone she remembered in his other volumes, but were less bitter and more concerned with beauty. When she had finished the main sheaf, she came on a much longer poem entitled 'The Leopard', wrapped round in a blank sheet of paper. Was it so wrapped to keep her from reading it; why, then, had he enclosed it? She decided that he had been doubtful, and wanted her verdict. Below the title was written the line:

'Can the leopard change its spots?'

It was the story of a young monk, secretly without faith, sent on a proselytising expedition. Seized by infidels, and confronted with the choice between death or recantation, he recants and accepts the religion of his captors. The poem was seared with passages of such deep feeling that they hurt her. It had a depth and fervour which took her breath away; it was a paean in praise of contempt for convention faced with the stark reality of the joy in living, yet with a haunting moan of betrayal running through it. It swayed her this way and that; and she put it down with a feeling almost of reverence for one who could so express such a deep and tangled spiritual conflict. With that reverence were mingled a compassion for the stress he must have endured before he could have written this and a feeling, akin to that which mothers feel, of yearning to protect him from his disharmonies and violence.

They had arranged to meet the following day at the National Gallery, and she went there before time, taking the poems with her. He came on her in front of Gentile Bellini's 'Mathematician'. They stood for some time looking at it without a word.

'Truth, quality, and decorative effect. Have you read my stuff?'

'Yes. Come and sit down, I've got them here.'

They sat down, and she gave him the envelope.

'Well?' he said; and she saw his lips quivering.

'Terribly good, I think.'

'Really?'

'Even truly. One, of course, is much the finest.'

'Which?'

Dinny's smile said: 'You ask that?'

'"The Leopard?"'

'Yes. It hurt me, here.'

'Shall I throw it out?'

By intuition she realised that on her answer he would act, and said feebly: 'You wouldn't pay attention to what I said, would you?'

'What you say shall go.'

'Then of course you can't throw it out. It's the finest thing you've done.'

'Inshallah!'

'What made you doubt?'

'It's a naked thing.'

'Yes,' said Dinny, 'naked – but beautiful. When a thing's naked it must be beautiful.'

'Hardly the fashionable belief.'

'Surely a civilised being naturally covers deformities and sores. There's nothing fine in being a savage that I can see, even in art.'

'You run the risk of excommunication. Ugliness is a sacred cult now.'

'Reaction from the chocolate box,' murmured Dinny.

'Ah! Whoever invented those lids sinned against the holy ghost – he offended the little ones.'

'Artists are children, you mean?'

'Well, aren't they? or would they carry on as they do?'

'Yes, they do seem to love toys. What gave you the idea for that poem?' His face had again that look of deep waters stirred, as when Muskham had spoken to them under the Foch statue.

'Tell you some day, perhaps. Shall we go on round?'

When they parted, he said: 'Tomorrow's Sunday. I shall be seeing you?'

'If you will.'

'What about the Zoo?'

'No, not the Zoo. I hate cages.'

'Quite right. The Dutch garden near Kensington Palace?'

'Yes.'

And that made the fifth consecutive day of meeting.

For Dinny it was like a spell of good weather, when every night you go to sleep hoping it will last, and every morning wake up and rub your eyes seeing that it has.

Each day she responded to his: 'Shall I see you tomorrow?' with an 'If you will'; each day she concealed from everybody with care whom she was seeing, and how, and when; and it all seemed to her so unlike herself that she would think: 'Who is this young woman who goes out stealthily like this, and meets a young man, and comes back feeling as if she had been treading on air? Is it some kind of a long dream I'm having?' Only, in dreams one didn't eat cold chicken and drink tea.

The moment most illuminative of her state of mind was when Hubert and Jean walked into the hall at Mount Street, where they were to stay till after Clare's wedding. This first sight for eighteen months of her beloved brother should surely have caused her to feel tremulous. But she greeted him steady as a rock, even to the power of cool appraisement. He seemed extremely well, brown, and less thin, but more commonplace. She tried to think that was because he was now safe and married and restored to soldiering, but she knew that comparison with Wilfrid had to do with it. She seemed to know suddenly that in Hubert there had never been capacity for any deep spiritual conflict; he was of the type she knew so well, seeing the trodden path and without real question following. Besides, Jean made all the difference! One could never again be to him, or he to her, as before his marriage. Jean was brilliantly alive and glowing. They had come the whole way from Khartoum to Croydon by air with four stops. Dinny was troubled by the inattention which underlay her seeming absorption in their account of life out there, till a mention of Darfur made her prick her ears. Darfur was where something had happened to Wilfrid. There were still followers of the Mahdi there, she gathered. The personality of Jerry Corven was discussed. Hubert was enthusiastic about 'a job of work' he had done. Jean filled out the gap. The wife of a Deputy Commissioner had gone off her head about him. It was said that Jerry Corven had behaved badly.

'Well, well!' said Sir Lawrence, 'Jerry's a privateer, and women ought not to go off their heads about him.'

'Yes,' said Jean. 'It's silly to blame men nowadays.'

'In old days,' murmured Lady Mont, 'men did the advancing and women were blamed; now women do it and the men are blamed.'

The extraordinary consecutiveness of the speech struck with a silencing effect on every tongue, until she added: 'I once saw two camels, d'you remember, Lawrence, so pretty.'

Jean looked rather horrified, and Dinny smiled.

Hubert came back to the line. 'I don't know,' he said; 'he's marrying our sister.'

'Clare'll give and take,' said Lady Mont. 'It's only when their noses are curved. The Rector,' she added to Jean, 'says there's a Tasburgh nose. You haven't got it. It crinkles. Your brother Alan had it a little.' And she looked at Dinny. 'In China, too,' she added. 'I said he'd marry a purser's daughter.'

'Good God, Aunt Em, he hasn't!' cried Jean.

'No. Very nice girls, I'm sure. Not like clergymen's.'

'Thank you!'

'I mean the sort you find in the Park. They call themselves that when they want company. I thought everybody knew.'

'Jean was rectory-bred, Aunt Em,' said Hubert.

'But she's been married to you two years. Who was it said: "And they shall multiply exceedin'ly"?'

'Moses?' said Dinny.

'And why not?'

Her eyes rested on Jean, who flushed. Sir Lawrence remarked quickly: 'I hope Hilary will be as short with Clare as he was with you and Jean, Hubert. That was a record.'

'Hilary preaches beautifully,' said Lady Mont. 'At Edward's death he preached on "Solomon in all his glory". Touchin'! And when we hung Casement, you remember – so stupid of us! – on the beam and the mote. We had it in our eye.'

'If I could love a sermon,' said Dinny, 'it would be Uncle Hilary's.'

'Yes,' said Lady Mont, 'he could borrow more barley-sugar than any little boy I ever knew and look like an angel. Your Aunt Wilmet and I used to hold him upside down – like puppies, you know – hopin', but we never got it back.'

'You must have been a lovely family, Aunt Em.'

'Tryin'. Our father that was not in Heaven took care not to see us much. Our mother couldn't help it – poor dear! We had no sense of duty.'

'And now you all have so much; isn't it queer?'

'Have I a sense of duty, Lawrence?'

'Emphatically not, Em.'

'I thought so.'

'But wouldn't you say as a whole, Uncle Lawrence, that the Cherrells have too much sense of duty?'

'How can they have *too* much?' said Jean.

Sir Lawrence fixed his monocle.

'I scent heresy, Dinny.'

'Surely duty's narrowing, Uncle? Father and Uncle Lionel and Uncle Hilary, and even Uncle Adrian, always think first of what they ought to do. They despise their own wants. Very fine, of course, but rather dull.'

Sir Lawrence dropped his eyeglass.

'Your family, Dinny,' he said, 'perfectly illustrate the mandarin. They hold the Empire together. Public schools, Osborne, Sandhurst; oh! ah! and much more. From generation to generation it begins in the home. Mother's milk with them. Service to Church and State – very interesting, very rare now, very admirable.'

'Especially when they've kept on top by means of it,' murmured Dinny.

'Shucks!' said Hubert: 'As if anyone thought of that in the Services!'

'You don't think of it because you don't have to; but you would fast enough if you did have to.'

'Somewhat cryptic, Dinny,' put in Sir Lawrence; 'you mean if anything threatened them, they'd think: "We simply mustn't be removed, we're It."'

'But are they It, Uncle?'

'With whom have you been associating, my dear?'

'Oh! no one. One must think sometimes.'

'Too depressin',' said Lady Mont. 'The Russian revolution, and all that.'

Dinny was conscious that Hubert was regarding her as if thinking: 'What's come to Dinny?'

'If one wants to take out a linch-pin,' he said, 'one always can, but the wheel comes off.'

'Well put, Hubert,' said Sir Lawrence; 'it's a mistake to think one can replace type or create it quickly. The sahib's born, not made – that is, if you take the atmosphere of homes as part of birth. And, if you ask me, he's dying out fast. A pity not to preserve him somehow; we might have National Parks for them, as they have for bisons.'

'No,' said Lady Mont, 'I won't.'

'What, Aunt Em?'

'Drink champagne on Wednesday, nasty bubbly stuff!'

'Must we have it at all, dear?'

'I'm afraid of Blore. He's so used. I might tell him not, but it'd be there.'

'Have you heard of Hallorsen lately, Dinny?' asked Hubert suddenly.

'Not since Uncle Adrian came back. I believe he's in Central America.'

'He *was* large,' said Lady Mont. 'Hilary's two girls, Sheila, Celia, and little Anne, five – I'm glad you're not to be, Dinny. It's superstition, of course.'

Dinny leaned back and the light fell on her throat.

'To be a bridesmaid once is quite enough, Aunt Em . . .'

When next morning she met Wilfrid at the Wallace Collection, she said:

'Would you by any chance like to be at Clare's wedding tomorrow?'

'No hat and no black tails; I gave them to Stack.'

'I remember how you looked, perfectly. You had a grey cravat and a gardenia.'

'And you had on sea-green.'

'Eau-de-nil. I'd like you to have seen my family, though, they'll all be there; and we could have discussed them afterwards.'

'I'll turn up among the "also ran" and keep out of sight.'

'Not from me,' thought Dinny. So she would not have to go a whole day without seeing him!

With every meeting he seemed less, as it were, divided against himself; and sometimes would look at her so intently that her heart would beat. When she looked at him, which was seldom, except when he wasn't aware, she was very careful to keep her gaze limpid. How fortunate that one always had that pull over men, knew when they were looking at one, and was able to look at them without their knowing!

When they parted this time, he said: 'Come down to Richmond again on Thursday. I'll pick you up at Foch – two o'clock as before.'

And she said: 'Yes.'

Chapter Six

Clare Cherrell's wedding, in Hanover Square, was 'fashionable' and would occupy with a list of names a quarter of a column in the traditional prints. As Dinny said:

'So delightful for them!'

With her father and mother Clare came to Mount Street from Condaford overnight. Busy with her younger sister to the last, and feeling an emotion humorously disguised, Dinny arrived with Lady Cherrell at the Church not long before the bride. She lingered to speak to an old retainer at the bottom of the aisle, and caught sight of Wilfrid. He was on the bride's side, far back, gazing at her. She gave him a swift smile, then passed up the aisle to join her mother in the left front pew. Michael whispered as she went by:

'People *have* rolled up, haven't they?'

They had. Clare was well known and popular, Jerry Corven even better known, if not so popular. Dinny looked round at the 'audience' – one could never credit a wedding with the word congregation. Irregular and with a good deal of character, their faces refused generalisation. They looked like people with convictions and views of their own. The men conformed to no particular type, having none of that depressing sameness which used to characterise the German officer caste. With herself and her mother in the front pew were Hubert and Jean,

Uncle Lawrence and Aunt Em; in the pew behind sat Adrian with Diana, Mrs Hilary, and Lady Alison. Dinny caught sight of Jack Muskham at the end of two or three rows back, tall, well-dressed, rather bored-looking. He nodded to her, and she thought: Odd, his remembering me!

On the Corven side of the aisle were people of quite as much diversity of face and figure. Except Jack Muskham, the bridegroom, and his best man, hardly a man gave the impression of being well-dressed or of having thought about his clothes. But from their faces Dinny received the impression that they were all safe in the acceptance of a certain creed. Not one gave her the same feeling that Wilfrid's face brought of spiritual struggle and disharmony, of dreaming, suffering, and discovery. 'I'm fanciful,' she thought. And her eyes came to rest on Adrian, who was just behind her. He was smiling quietly above that goatee beard of his, which lengthened his thin brown visage. 'He has a dear face,' she thought, 'not conceited, like the men who wear those pointed beards as a rule. He always will be the nicest man in the world.' And she whispered: 'Fine collection of bones here, Uncle.'

'I should like your skeleton, Dinny.'

'I mean to be burned and scattered. H'ssh!'

The choir was coming in, followed by the officiating priests. Jerry Corven turned. Those lips smiling like a cat's beneath that thin-cut moustache, those hardwood features and daring, searching eyes! Dinny thought with sudden dismay: 'How could Clare! But after all I'd think the same of any face but one, just now. I'm going potty.' Then Clare came swaying up the aisle on her father's arm! 'Looking a treat! Bless her!' A gush of emotion caught Dinny by the throat, and she slipped her hand into her mother's. Poor mother! She was awfully pale! Really the whole thing was stupid! People *would* make it long and trying and emotional. Thank goodness Dad's old black tail-coat really looked quite decent – she had taken out the stains with ammonia; and he stood as she had seen him when reviewing troops. If Uncle Hilary happened to have a button wrong, Dad would notice it. Only there wouldn't be any buttons. She longed fervently to be beside Wilfrid away at the back. He would have nice unorthodox thoughts, and they would soothe each other with private smiles.

Now the bridesmaids! Hilary's two girls, her cousins Monica and Joan, slender and keen, Little Celia Moriston, fair as a seraph (if that was female), Sheila Ferse, dark and brilliant; and toddly little Anne – a perfect dumpling!

Once on her knees, Dinny quietened down. She remembered how they used to kneel, nightgowned, against their beds, when Clare was a tiny of three and she herself a 'big girl' of six. She used to hang on to the bed-edge by the chin so as to save the knees; and how ducky Clare had looked when she held her hands up like the child in the Reynolds picture! 'That man,' thought Dinny, 'will hurt her! I know he will!' Her thoughts turned again to Michael's wedding all those ten years ago. There she had stood, not three yards from where she was kneeling now, alongside a girl she didn't know – some relative of Fleur's. And her eyes, taking in this and that with the fluttered eagerness of youth, had lighted on Wilfrid standing sideways, keeping watch on Michael. Poor Michael! He had seemed rather daft that day, from excessive triumph! She could remember quite distinctly thinking: 'Michael and his lost angel!' There had been in Wilfrid's face something which suggested that he had been cast out of happiness, a scornful and yet yearning look. That was only two years after the Armistice, and she knew now what utter disillusionment and sense of wreckage he had suffered after the war. He had been talking to her freely the last two days; had even dwelled with humorous contempt on his infatuation for Fleur eighteen months after that marriage which had sent him flying off to the East. Dinny, but ten when the war broke out, remembered it chiefly as meaning that Mother had been anxious about Father, had knitted all the time, and been a sort of sock depot; that everybody hated the Germans; that she had been forbidden sweets because they were made with saccharine, and finally the excitement and grief when Hubert went off to the war and letters from him didn't often come. From Wilfrid these last few days she had gathered more clearly and poignantly than ever yet what the war had meant to some who, like Michael and himself, had been in the thick of it for years. With his gift of expression he had made her feel the tearing away of roots, the hopeless change of values, and the gradual profound mistrust of all that age and tradition had decreed and sanctified. He had got over the war now, he said. He might think so, but there were in him still torn odds and ends of nerves not yet mended up. She never saw him without wanting to pass a cool hand over his forehead.

The ring was on now, the fateful words said, the exhortations over; they were going to the vestry. Her mother and Hubert followed. Dinny sat motionless, her eyes fixed on the East window. Marriage! What an impossible state, except – with a single being.

A voice in her ear said:

'Lend me your hanky, Dinny. Mine's soakin', and your uncle's is blue.'

Dinny passed her a scrap of lawn, and surreptitiously powdered her own nose.

'Be done at Condaford, Dinny,' continued her aunt. 'All these people – so fatiguin', rememberin' who they aren't. That was his mother, wasn't it? She isn't dead, then.'

Dinny was thinking: 'Shall I get another look at Wilfrid?'

'When I was married everybody kissed me,' whispered her aunt, 'so promiscuous. I knew a girl who married to get kissed by his best man. Aggie Tellusson. I wonder. They're comin' back!'

Yes! How well Dinny knew that bride's smile! How could Clare feel it, not married to Wilfrid! She fell in behind her father and mother, alongside Hubert, who whispered: 'Buck up, old girl, it might be a lot worse!' Divided from him by a secret that absorbed her utterly, Dinny squeezed his arm. And, even as she did so, saw Wilfrid, with his arms folded, looking at her. Again she gave him a swift smile, and then all was hurly-burly, till she was back at Mount Street and Aunt Em saying to her, just within the drawing-room door:

'Stand by me, Dinny, and pinch me in time.'

Then came the entry of the guests and her aunt's running commentary.

'It *is* his mother – kippered. Here's Hen Bentworth! . . . Hen, Wilmet's here, she's got a bone to pick . . . How d'you do? Yes, isn't it – so tirin' . . . How d'you do? The ring was so well done, don't you think? Conjurers! . . . Dinny, who's this? . . . How do you do? Lovely! No! Cherrell. Not as it's spelled, you know – so awkward! . . . The presents are over there by the man with the boots, tryin' not to. Silly, I think! But they will . . . How d'you do? You *are* Jack Muskham? Lawrence dreamed the other night you were goin' to burst . . . Dinny, get me Fleur, too, she knows everybody.'

Dinny went in search of Fleur and found her talking to the bridegroom.

As they went back to the door Fleur said: 'I saw Wilfrid Desert in the church. How did he come there?'

Really Fleur was too sharp for anything!

'Here you are!' said Lady Mont. 'Which of these three comin' is the Duchess? The scraggy one. Ah! . . . How d'you do? Yes, charmin'. Such a bore, weddin's! Fleur, take the Duchess to have some presents . . . How d'you do? No, my brother Hilary. He does it well, don't you think? Lawrence says he keeps his eye on the ball. Do have an ice, they're downstairs . . . Dinny, is this one after the presents, d'you think? –

Oh! How d'you do, Lord Beevenham? My sister-in-law ought to be doin' this. She ratted. Jerry's in there . . . Dinny, who was it said: "The drink, the drink!" Hamlet? He said such a lot. Not Hamlet? . . . Oh! How d'you do? . . . How d'you do? . . . How d'you do, or don't you? Such a crush! . . . Dinny, your hanky!'

'I've put some powder on it, Auntie.'

'There! Have I streaked? . . . How d'you do? Isn't it silly, the whole thing? As if they wanted anybody but themselves, you know . . . Oh! Here's Adrian! Your tie's on one side, dear. Dinny, put it right. How d'you do? Yes, they are. I don't like flowers at funerals – poor things, lyin' there, and dyin' . . . How's your dear dog? You haven't one? Quite! . . . Dinny, you ought to have pinched me . . . How d'you do? How d'you do? I was tellin' my niece she ought to pinch me. Do you get faces right? No. How nice! How d'you do? How d'you do? How d'you do? . . . That's three! Dinny, who's the throwback just comin'? Oh! . . . How d'you do? So you got here? I thought you were in China . . . Dinny, remind me to ask your uncle if it was China. He gave me such a dirty look. Could I give the rest a miss? Who is it's always sayin' that? Tell Blore "the drink", Dinny. Here's a covey! . . . How d'you do? . . . How de do? . . . How do? . . . Do! . . . Do! . . . How? . . . So sweet! . . . Dinny, I want to say: Blast!'

On her errand to Blore, Dinny passed Jean talking to Michael, and wondered how anyone so vivid and brown had patience to stand about in this crowd. Having found Blore, she came back. Michael's queer face, which she thought grew pleasanter every year, as if from the deepening impress of good feeling, looked strained and unhappy.

'I don't believe it, Jean,' she heard him say.

'Well,' said Jean, 'the bazaars do buzz with rumour. Still, without fire of some sort there's never smoke.'

'Oh! yes, there is – plenty. He's back in England, anyway. Fleur saw him in the church today. I shall ask him.'

'I wouldn't,' said Jean: 'if it's true he'll probably tell you, and if it isn't, it'll only worry him for nothing.'

So! They were talking of Wilfrid. How to find out why without appearing to take interest? And suddenly she thought: 'Even if I could, I wouldn't. Anything that matters he must tell me himself. I won't hear it from anyone else.' But she felt disturbed, for instinct was always warning her of something heavy and strange on his mind.

When that long holocaust of sincerity was over and the bride had gone, she subsided into a chair in her uncle's study, the only room which showed no signs of trouble. Her father and mother had started back to Condaford, surprised that she wasn't coming too. It was not like her to cling to London when the tulips were out at home, the lilacs coming on, the apple blossom thickening every day. But the thought of not seeing Wilfrid daily had become a positive pain.

'I *have* got it badly,' she thought, 'worse than I ever believed was possible. Whatever is going to happen to me?'

She was lying back with her eyes closed when her uncle's voice said:

'Ah! Dinny, how pleasant after those hosts of Midian! The mandarin in full feather! Did you know a quarter of them? Why do people go to weddings? A registrar's, or under the stars, there's no other way of preserving decency. Your poor aunt has gone to bed. There's a lot to be said for Mohammedanism, except that it's the fashion now to limit it to one wife, and she not in Purdah. By the way, there's a story going round that young Desert's become a Moslem. Did he say anything to you about it?'

Dinny raised her startled head.

'I've only twice known it happen to fellows in the East, and they were Frenchmen and wanted harems.'

'Money's the only essential for that, Uncle.'

'Dinny, you're getting cynical. Men like to have the sanction of religion. But that wouldn't be Desert's reason; a fastidious creature, if I remember.'

'Does religion matter, Uncle, so long as people don't interfere with each other?'

'Well, some Moslems' notions of woman's rights are a little primitive. He's liable to wall her up if she's unfaithful. There was a sheikh when I was in Marrakesh – gruesome.'

Dinny shuddered.

'"From time immemorial," as they say,' went on Sir Lawrence, 'religion has been guilty of the most horrifying deeds that have happened on this earth. I wonder if young Desert has taken up with it to get him access to Mecca. I shouldn't think he believes anything. But you never know – it's a queer family.'

Dinny thought: 'I can't and won't talk about him.'

'What proportion of people in these days do you think really have religion, Uncle?'

'In northern countries? Very difficult to say. In this country ten to fifteen per cent of the adults, perhaps. In France and southern countries, where there's a peasantry, more, at least on the surface.'

'What about the people who came this afternoon?'

'Most of them would be shocked if you said they weren't Christians, and most of them would be still more shocked if you asked them to give half their goods to the poor, and that would only make them well disposed Pharisees, or was it Sadducees?'

'Are you a Christian, Uncle Lawrence?'

'No, my dear; if anything a Confucian, who, as you know, was simply an ethical philosopher. Most of our caste in this country, if they only knew it, are Confucian rather than Christian. Belief in ancestors, and tradition, respect for parents, honesty, moderation of conduct, kind treatment of animals and dependents, absence of self-obtrusion, and stoicism in face of pain and death.'

'What more,' murmured Dinny, wrinkling her nose, 'does one want except the love of beauty?'

'Beauty? That's a matter of temperament.'

'But doesn't it divide people more than anything?'

'Yes, but willy nilly. You can't make yourself love a sunset.'

'"You are wise, Uncle Lawrence, the young niece said." I shall go for a walk and shake the wedding-cake down.'

'And I shall stay here, Dinny, and sleep the champagne off.'

Dinny walked and walked. It seemed an odd thing to be doing alone. But the flowers in the Park were pleasing, and the waters of the Serpentine shone and were still, and the chestnut trees were coming alight. And she let herself go on her mood, and her mood was of love.

Chapter Seven

Looking back on that second afternoon in Richmond Park, Dinny never knew whether she had betrayed herself before he said so abruptly:

'If you believe in it, Dinny, will you marry me?'

It had so taken her breath away that she sat growing paler and paler, then colour came to her face with a rush.

'I'm wondering why you ask me. You know nothing of me.'

'You're like the East. One loves it at first sight, or not at all, and one never knows it any better.'

Dinny shook her head: 'Oh! I am not mysterious.'

'I should never get to the end of you; no more than of one of those figures over the staircase in the Louvre. Please answer me, Dinny.'

She put her hand in his, nodded, and said: 'That must be a record.'

At once his lips were on hers, and when they left her lips she fainted.

This was without exception the most singular action of her life so far, and, coming to almost at once, she said so.

'It's the sweetest thing you could have done.'

If she had thought his face strange before, what was it now? The lips, generally contemptuous, were parted and quivering, the eyes, fixed on her, glowed; he put up his hand and thrust back his hair, so that she noticed for the first time a scar at the top of his forehead. Sun, moon, stars, and all the works of God stood still while they were looking each into the other's face.

At last she said:

'The whole thing is most irregular. There's been no courtship; not even a seduction.'

He laughed and put his arm around her. Dinny whispered:

'"Thus the two young people sat wrapped in their beatitude." My poor mother!'

'Is she a nice woman?'

'A darling. Luckily she's fond of Father.'

'What is your father like?'

'The nicest General I know.'

'Mine is a hermit. You won't have to realise him. My brother is an ass. My mother ran away when I was three, and I have no sisters. It's going to be hard for you, with a nomadic, unsatisfactory brute like me.'

'"Where thou goest, I go." We seem to be visible to that old gentleman over there. He'll write to the papers about the awful sights to be seen in Richmond Park.'

'Never mind!'

'I don't. There's only one first hour. And I was beginning to think I should never have it.'

'Never been in love?'

She shook her head.

'How wonderful! When shall it be, Dinny?'

'Don't you think our families ought first to know?'

'I suppose so. They won't want you to marry me.'

'Certainly you are my social superior, young sir.'

'One can't be superior to a family that goes back to the twelfth century. We only go back to the fourteenth. A wanderer and a writer of bitter verse. They'll know I shall want to cart you off to the East. Besides, I only have fifteen hundred a year, and practically no expectations.'

'Fifteen hundred a year! Father may be able to spare me two – he's doing it for Clare.'

'Well, thank God there'll be no obstacle from your fortune.'

Dinny turned to him, and there was a touching confidence in her eyes.

'Wilfrid, I heard something about your having turned Moslem. That wouldn't matter to me.'

'It would matter to them.'

His face had become drawn and dark. She clasped his hand tight in both of hers.

'Was that poem "The Leopard" about yourself?'

He tried to draw his hand away.

'Was it?'

'Yes. Out in Darfur. Fanatical Arabs. I recanted to save my skin. Now you can chuck me.' Exerting all her strength, Dinny pulled his hand to her heart.

'What you did or didn't do is nothing. You are *you*!' To her dismay and yet relief, he fell on his knees and buried his face in her lap.

'Darling!' she said. Protective tenderness almost annulled the wilder, sweeter feeling in her.

'Does anyone know of that but me?'

'It's known in the bazaars that I've turned Moslem, but it's supposed of my free will.'

'I know there are things you would die for, Wilfrid, and that's enough. Kiss me!'

The afternoon drew on while they sat there. The shadows of the oak trees splayed up to their log; the crisp edge of the sunlight receded over the young fern: some deer passed, moving slowly towards water. The sky, of a clear bright blue, with white promising clouds, began to have the evening look; a sappy scent of fern fronds and horse chestnut bloom crept in slow whiffs; and dew began to fall. The sane and heavy air, the grass so green, the blue distance, the branching, ungraceful solidity of the oak trees, made a trysting hour as English as lovers ever loved in.

'I shall break into cockney if we sit here much longer,' said Dinny, at last; 'besides, dear heart, "fast falls the dewy eve".' . . .

Late that evening in the drawing room at Mount Street her aunt said suddenly:

'Lawrence, look at Dinny! Dinny, you're in love.'

'You take me flat aback, Aunt Em. I am.'

'Who is it?'

'Wilfrid Desert.'

'I used to tell Michael that young man would get into trouble. Does he love you too?'

'He is good enough to say so.'

'Oh! dear. I *will* have some lemonade. Which of you proposed?'

'As a fact, he did.'

'His brother has no issue, they say.'

'For heaven's sake, Aunt Em!'

'Why not? Kiss me!'

But Dinny was regarding her uncle across her aunt's shoulder. He had said nothing.

Later, he stopped her as she was following out.

'Are your eyes open, Dinny?'

'Yes, this is the ninth day.'

'I won't come the heavy uncle; but you know the drawbacks?'

'His religion; Fleur; the East? What else?'

Sir Lawrence shrugged his thin shoulders.

'That business with Fleur sticks in my gizzard, as old Forsyte would have said. One who could do that to the man he has led to the altar can't have much sense of loyalty.'

Colour rose in her cheeks.

'Don't be angry, my dear, we're all too fond of you.'

'He's been quite frank about everything, Uncle.'

Sir Lawrence sighed.

'Then there's no more to be said, I suppose. But I beg you to look forward before it's irrevocable. There's a species of china which it's almost impossible to mend. And I think you're made of it.'

Dinny smiled and went up to her room, and instantly she began to look back.

The difficulty of imagining the physical intoxication of love was gone. To open one's soul to another seemed no longer impossible. Love stories she had read, love affairs she had watched, all seemed savourless compared with her own. And she had only known him nine days, except for that glimpse ten years ago! Had she had what was called a complex all this time? Or was love always sudden like this? A wild flower seeding on a wild wind?

Long she sat half dressed, her hands clasped between her knees, her head drooping, steeped in the narcotic of remembrance, and with a strange feeling that all the lovers in the world were sitting within her on that bed bought at Pullbred's in the Tottenham Court Road.

Chapter Eight

Condaford resented this business of love, and was, with a fine rain, as if sorrowing for the loss of its two daughters.

Dinny found her father and mother elaborately 'making no bones' over the loss of Clare, and only hoped they would continue the motion in her own case. Feeling, as she said, 'very towny', she prepared for the ordeal of disclosure by waterproofing herself and going for a tramp. Hubert and Jean were expected in time for dinner, and she wished to kill all her birds with one stone. The rain on her face, the sappy fragrance, the call of the cuckoos, and that state of tree when each has leaves in different stage of opening, freshened her body but brought a little ache to her heart. Entering a covert, she walked along a ride. The trees were beech and ash, with here and there an English yew, the soil being chalky. A woodpecker's constant tap was the only sound, for the rain was not yet heavy enough for leaf-dripping to have started. Since babyhood she had been abroad but three times – to Italy, to Paris, to the Pyrenees, and had always come home more in love with England and Condaford than ever. Henceforth her path would lie she knew not where; there would, no doubt, be sand, figtrees, figures by wells, flat roofs, voices calling the Muezzin, eyes looking through veils. But surely Wilfrid would feel the charm of

Condaford and not mind if they spent time there now and then. His father lived in a show place, half shut up and never shown, which gave everyone the blues. And that, apart from London and Eton, was all he seemed to know of England, for he had been four years away in the war and eight years away in the East.

'For me to discover England to him,' she thought; 'for him to discover the East to me.'

A gale of last November had brought down some beech trees. Looking at their wide flat roots exposed, Dinny remembered Fleur saying that selling timber was the only way to meet death duties. But Dad was only sixty-two! Jean's cheeks the night of their arrival, when Aunt Em quoted the 'multiply exceedingly'. A child coming! Surely a son. Jean was the sort to have sons. Another generation of Cherrells in direct line! If Wilfrid and she had a child! What then? One could not wander about with babes. A tremor of insecurity went through her. The future, how uncharted! A squirrel crossed close to her still figure and scampered up a trunk. Smiling, she watched it, lithe, red, bushy-tailed. Thank God, Wilfrid cared for animals! 'When to God's fondouk the donkeys are taken.' Condaford, its bird life, woods and streams, mullions, magnolias, fantails, pastures green, surely he would like it! But her father and mother, Hubert and Jean; would he like them? Would they like him? They would not – too unshackled, too fitful, and too bitter; all that was best in him he hid away, as if ashamed of it; and his yearning for beauty they would not understand! And his change of religion, even though they would not know what he had told her, would seem to them strange and disconcerting!

Condaford Grange had neither butler nor electric light, and Dinny chose the moment when the maids had set decanters and dessert on the polished chestnut wood, lit by candles.

'Sorry to be personal,' she said, quite suddenly; 'but I'm engaged.'

No one answered. Each of those four was accustomed to say and think – not always the same thing – that Dinny was the ideal person to marry, so none was happier for the thought that she was going to be married. Then Jean said:

'To whom, Dinny?'

'Wilfrid Desert, the second son of Lord Mullyon – he was Michael's best man.'

'Oh! but—!'

Dinny was looking hard at the other three. Her father's face was impassive, as was natural, for he did not know the young man from Adam; her mother's gentle features wore a fluttered and enquiring look; Hubert's an air as if he were biting back vexation.

Then Lady Cherrell said: 'But, Dinny, when did you meet him?'

'Only ten days ago, but I've seen him every day since. I'm afraid it's a first-sight case like yours, Hubert. We remembered each other from Michael's wedding.'

Hubert looked at his plate. 'You know he's become a Moslem, or so they say in Khartoum.'

Dinny nodded.

'What!' said the General.

'That's the story, sir.'

'Why?'

'I don't know, I've never seen him. He's been a lot about in the East.'

On the point of saying: 'One might just as well be Moslem as Christian, if one's not a believer,' Dinny stopped. It was scarcely a testimonial to character.

'I can't understand a man changing his religion,' said the General bluntly.

'There doesn't seem to be much enthusiasm,' murmured Dinny.

'My dear, how can there be when we don't know him?'

'No, of course, Mother. May I ask him down? He *can* support a wife; and Aunt Em says his brother has no issue.'

'Dinny!' said the General.

'I'm not serious, darling.'

'What is serious,' said Hubert, 'is that he seems to be a sort of Bedouin – always wandering about.'

'Two can wander about, Hubert.'

'You've always said you hate to be away from Condaford.'

'I remember when you said you couldn't see anything in marriage, Hubert. And I'm sure both you and Father said that at one time, Mother. Have any of you said it since?'

'Cat!'

With that simple word Jean closed the scene.

But at bedtime in her mother's room, Dinny said:

'May I ask Wilfrid down, then?'

'Of course, when you like. We shall be only too anxious to see him.'

'I know it's a shock, Mother, coming so soon after Clare; still, you did expect me to go some time.'

Lady Cherrell sighed: 'I suppose so.'

'I forgot to say that he's a poet, a real one.'

'A poet?' repeated her mother, as if this had put the finishing touch to her disquiet.

'There are quite a lot in Westminster Abbey. But don't worry, *he'll* never be there.'

'Difference in religion is serious, Dinny, especially when it comes to children.'

'Why, Mother? No child has any religion worth speaking of till it's grown up, and then it can choose for itself. Besides, by the time my children, if I have any, are grown up, the question will be academic.'

'Dinny!'

'It's nearly so even now, except in ultra-religious circles. Ordinary people's religion becomes more and more just ethical.'

'I don't know enough about it to say, and I don't think you do.'

'Mother, dear, stroke my head.'

'Oh! Dinny, I do hope you've chosen wisely.'

'Darling, it chose me.'

That she perceived was not the way to reassure her mother, but as she did not know one, she took her good-night kiss and went away.

In her room she sat down and wrote:

Condaford Grange: Friday.

DARLING,

This is positively and absolutely my first love-letter, so you see I don't know how to express myself. I think I will just say 'I love you' and leave it at that. I have spread the good tidings. They have, of course, left everyone guessing, and anxious to see you as soon as possible. When will you come? Once you are here the whole thing will seem to me less like a very real and very lovely dream. This is quite a simple place. Whether we should live in style if we could, I can't say. But three maids, a groom-chauffeur, and two gardeners are all our staff. I believe you will like my mother, and I don't believe you will get on very well with my father or brother, though I expect his wife Jean will tickle your poetic fancy, she's such a vivid creature. Condaford itself I'm sure you'll love. It has the real 'old' feeling. We can go riding; and I want to walk and talk with you and show you my pet nooks and corners. I hope the sun will shine, as you love it so much. For me almost any sort of day does down here; and absolutely any will do if I can be with you. The room you will have is away by itself and supernaturally quiet; you go up to it by five twisty steps, and it's called the priest's room, because Anthony Charwell, brother of the Gilbert who owned Condaford under Elizabeth, was walled up there and fed from a basket let down nightly to his window. He was a conspicuous Catholic priest, and Gilbert was a Protestant, but he put his brother first, as any decent body would. When he'd been there three months they took the wall down one night, and got him across country all the way south to the Beaulieu river and 'aboard the lugger'. The wall was put up again to save appearances and only done away with by my great-grandfather, who was the last of us to have any money to speak of. It seemed to prey on his nerves, so he got rid of it. They still speak of him in the village, probably because he drove four-in-hand. There's a bathroom at the bottom of the twisty steps. The window was enlarged, of course and the view's jolly from it, especially now, at lilac and apple-blossom time. My own room, if it interests you to know, is somewhat cloistral and narrow, but it looks straight over the lawns to the hill-rise and the woods beyond. I've had it ever since I was seven, and I wouldn't change for anything, until you're making me

'brooches and toys for my delight
Of birds' song at morning and starshine at night.'

I almost think that little 'Stevenson' is my favourite poem; so you see, in spite of my homing tendency, I must have a streak of the wanderer in me. Dad, by the way, has a great feeling for Nature, likes beasts and birds and trees. I think most soldiers do – it's rather odd. But, of course, their love is on the precise and knowledgeable rather than the aesthetic side. Any dreaminess they incline to look on as 'a bit barmy'. I have been wondering whether to put my copies of your poems under their noses. On the whole I don't think; they might take you too seriously. There is always something about a person more ingratiating than his writings. I don't expect to sleep much tonight, for this is the first day that I haven't seen you since the world began. Goodnight, my dear, be blessed and take my kiss.

Your
DINNY

P.S. – I have looked you out the photo where I approximate most to the angels, or rather where my nose turns up least – to send to-morrow. In the meantime here are two snaps. And when, sir, do I get some of you?

D.

And that was the end of this to her far from perfect day.

Chapter Nine

Sir Lawrence Mont, recently elected to Burton's Club whereon he had resigned from the Aeroplane, retaining besides only 'Snooks' (so-called), The Coffee House and the Parthen, was accustomed to remark that, allowing himself another ten years of life, it would cost him twelve shillings and sixpence every time he went into any of them.

He entered Burton's, however, on the afternoon after Dinny had told him of her engagement, took up a list of the members, and turned to D. 'Hon. Wilfrid Desert.' Quite natural, seeing the Club's pretension to the monopoly of travellers. 'Does Mr Desert ever come in here?' he said to the porter.

'Yes, Sir Lawrence, he's been in this last week; before that I don't remember him for years.'

'Usually abroad. When does he come in as a rule?'

'For dinner, mostly, Sir Lawrence.'

'I see. Is Mr Muskham in?'

The porter shook his head. 'Newmarket today, Sir Lawrence.'

'Oh! Ah! How on earth you remember everything!'

'Matter of 'abit, Sir Lawrence.'

'Wish I had it.' Hanging up his hat, he stood for a moment before the tape in the hall. Unemployment and taxation going up all the time, and more money to spend on cars and sports than ever. A pretty little problem! He then sought the Library as the room where he was least likely to see anybody; and the first body he saw was that of Jack Muskham, who was talking, in a voice hushed to the level of the locality, to a thin dark little man in a corner.

'That,' thought Sir Lawrence, cryptically, 'explains to me why I never find a lost collar-stud. My friend the porter was so certain Jack would be at Newmarket, and not under that chest of drawers, that he took him for someone else when he came in.'

Reaching down a volume of Burton's *Arabian Nights*, he rang for tea. He was attending to neither when the two in the corner rose and came up to him.

'Don't get up, Lawrence,' said Jack Muskham with some languor; 'Telfourd Yule, my cousin Sir Lawrence Mont.'

'I've read thrillers of yours, Mr Yule,' said Sir Lawrence, and thought: 'Queer-looking little cuss!'

The thin, dark, smallish man, with a face rather like a monkey's, grinned. 'Truth whips fiction out of the field,' he said.

'Yule,' said Jack Muskham, with his air of superiority to space and time, 'has been out in Arabia, going into the question of how to corkscrew a really pure-strain Arab mare or two out of them for use here. It's always baffled us, you know. Stallions, yes; mares never. It's much the same now in Nejd as when Palgrave wrote. Still, we think we've got a rise. The owner of the best strain wants an aeroplane, and if we throw in a billiard table we believe he'll part with at least one daughter of the sun.'

'Good God!' said Sir Lawrence. 'By what base means? We're all Jesuits, Jack!'

'Yule has seen some queer things out there. By the way, there's one I want to talk about. May we sit down?'

He stretched his long body out in a long chair, and the dark little man perched himself on another, with his black twinkling eyes fixed on Sir Lawrence, who had come to uneasy attention without knowing why.

'When,' said Jack Muskham, 'Yule here was in the Arabian desert, he heard a vague yarn among some Bedouins about an Englishman having been held up somewhere by Arabs and forced to become a Moslem. He had rather a row with them, saying no Englishman would do that. But when he was back in Egypt he went flying into the Libyan desert, met another lot of Bedouins coming from the south, and came on precisely the same yarn, only more detailed, because they said it happened in Darfur, and they even had the man's name – Desert. Then, when he was up in Khartoum, Yule found it was common talk that young Desert had changed his religion. Naturally he put two and two together. But there's all the difference in the world, of course, between voluntarily swapping religions and doing it at the pistol's point. An Englishman who does that lets down the lot of us.'

Sir Lawrence, who during this recital had tried every motion for his monocle with which he was acquainted, dropped it and said: 'But, my dear Jack, if a man is rash enough to become a Mohammedan in a Mohammedan country, do you suppose for a minute that gossip won't say he was forced to?'

Yule, who had wriggled on to the very verge of his chair, said:

'*I* thought that; but the second account was extremely positive. Even to the month and the name of the Sheikh who forced the recantation; and I found that Mr Desert had in fact returned from Darfur soon after the month mentioned. There may be nothing in it; but whether there is or not, I needn't tell you that an undenied story of that kind grows by telling and does a lot of harm, not only to the man himself, but to our prestige. There seems to me a sort of obligation on one to let Mr Desert know what the Bedawi are spreading about him.'

'Well, he's over here,' said Sir Lawrence, gravely.

'I know,' said Jack Muskham, 'I saw him the other day, and he's a member of this Club.'

Through Sir Lawrence were passing waves of infinite dismay. What a sequel to Dinny's ill-starred announcement! To his ironic, detached personality, capricious in its likings, Dinny was precious. She embroidered in a queer way his plain-washed feelings about women; as a young man he might even have been in love with her, instead of being merely her uncle by marriage. During this silence he was fully conscious that both the other two were thoroughly uncomfortable. And the knowledge of their disquiet deepened the significance of the matter in an odd way.

At last he said: 'Desert was my boy's best man. I'd like to talk to Michael about it, Jack. Mr Yule will say nothing further at present, I hope.'

'Not on your life,' said Yule. 'I hope to God there's nothing in it. I like his verse.'

'And you, Jack?'

'I don't care for the look of him; but I'd refuse to believe that of an Englishman till it was plainer than the nose on my face, which is saying a good bit. You and I must be getting on, Yule, if we're to catch that train to Royston.'

This speech of Jack Muskham's further disturbed Sir Lawrence, left alone in his chair. It seemed so entirely to preclude leniency of judgment among the 'pukka sahibs' if the worst were true.

At last he rose, found a small volume, sat down again and turned its pages. The volume was Sir Alfred Lyall's *Verses Written in India*, and he looked for the poem called 'Theology in Extremis'.

He read it through, restored the volume, and stood rubbing his chin. Written, of course, more than forty years ago, and yet doubtful if its sentiments were changed by an iota! There was that poem, too, by Dogle, about the Corporal in the Buffs who, brought before a Chinese General and told to 'kow-tow' or die, said: 'We don't do that sort of thing in the Buffs,' and died. Well! That was the standard even today, among people of any caste or with any tradition. The war had thrown up innumerable instances. Could young Desert really have betrayed the tradition? It seemed improbable. And yet, in spite of his excellent war record, might there be a streak of yellow in him? Or was it, rather, that at times a flow of revolting bitterness carried him on to complete cynicism, so that he flouted almost for the joy of flouting?

With a strong mental effort Sir Lawrence tried to place himself in a like dilemma. Not being a believer, his success was limited to the thought: 'I should immensely dislike being dictated to in such a matter.' Aware that this was inadequate, he went down to the hall, shut himself up in a box, and rang up Michael's house. Then, feeling that if he lingered in the Club he might run into Desert himself, he took a cab to South Square.

Michael had just come in from the House; they met in the hall; and, with the instinct that Fleur, however acute, was not a fit person to share this particular consultation, Sir Lawrence demanded to be taken to his son's study. He commenced by announcing Dinny's engagement, which Michael heard with as strange a mixture of gratification and disquietude as could be seen on human visage.

'What a little cat, keeping it so dark!' he said. 'Fleur did say something about her being too limpid just now; but I never thought! One's got so used to Dinny being single. To Wilfrid, too? Well, I hope the old son has exhausted the East.'

'There's this question of his religion,' said Sir Lawrence gravely.

'I don't know why that should matter much; Dinny's not fervent. But I never thought Wilfrid cared enough to change his. It rather staggered me.'

'There's a story.'

When his father had finished, Michael's ears stood out and his face looked haggard.

'You know him better than anyone,' Sir Lawrence concluded: 'What do you think?'

'I hate to say it, but it might be true. It might even be natural for *him*; but no one would ever understand why. This is pretty ghastly, Dad, with Dinny involved.'

'Before we fash ourselves, my dear, we must find out if it's true. Could you go to him?'

'In old days – easily.'

Sir Lawrence nodded. 'Yes, I know all about that, but it's a long time ago.'

Michael smiled faintly. 'I never knew whether you spotted that, but I rather thought so. I've seen very little of Wilfrid since he went East. Still, I could—' He stopped, and added: 'If it *is* true, he must have told Dinny. He couldn't ask her to marry him with that untold.'

Sir Lawrence shrugged. 'If yellow in one way, why not in the other?'

'Wilfrid is one of the most perverse, complex, unintelligible natures one could come across. To judge him by ordinary standards is a wash-out. But if he *has* told Dinny, she'll never tell us.'

And they stared at each other.

'Mind you,' said Michael, 'there's a streak of the heroic in him. It comes out in the wrong places. That's why he's a poet.'

Sir Lawrence began twisting at an eyebrow, always a sign that he had reached a decision.

'The thing's got to be faced; it's not in human nature for a sleeping dog like that to be allowed to lie. I don't care about young Desert—'

'I do,' said Michael.

'It's Dinny I'm thinking of.'

'So am I. But there again, Dad, Dinny will do what she will do, and you needn't think we can deflect her.'

'It's one of the most unpleasant things,' said Sir Lawrence slowly, 'that I've ever come across. Well, my boy, are you going to see him, or shall I?'

'I'll do it,' said Michael, and sighed.

'Will he tell you the truth?'

'Yes. Won't you stay to dinner?'

Sir Lawrence shook his head.

'Daren't face Fleur with this on my mind. Needless to say, no one ought to know until you've seen him, not even she.'

'No. Dinny still with you?'

'She's gone back to Condaford.'

'Her people!' and Michael whistled.

Her people! The thought remained with him all through a dinner during which Fleur discussed the future of Kit. She was in favour of his going to Harrow, because Michael and his father had been at Winchester. He was down for both, and the matter had not yet been decided.

'All your mother's people,' she said, 'were at Harrow. Winchester seems to me so superior and dry. And they never get any notoriety. If you hadn't been at Winchester you'd have been a pet of the newspapers by now.'

'D'you want Kit to have notoriety?'

'Yes, the nice sort, of course, like your Uncle Hilary. You know, Michael, Bart's a dear, but I prefer the Cherrell side of your family.'

'Well, I was wondering,' said Michael, 'whether the Cherrell's weren't too straight-necked and servicey for anything,'

'Yes, they're that, but they've got a quirk in them, and they look like gentlemen.'

'I believe,' said Michael, 'that you really want Kit to go to Harrow because they play at Lords.'

Fleur straightened her own neck.

'Well, I do. I should have chosen Eton, only it's so obvious, and I hate light blue.'

'Well,' said Michael, 'I'm prejudiced in favour of my own school, so the choice is up to you. A school that produced Uncle Adrian will do for me, anyway.'

'No school produced your Uncle Adrian, dear,' said Fleur; 'he's palaeolithic. The Cherrells are the oldest strain in Kit's make-up, anyway, and I should like to breed to it, as Mr Jack Muskham would say. Which reminds me that when I saw him at Clare's wedding he wanted us to come down and see his stud farm at Royston. I should like to. He's like an advertisement for shooting capes – divine shoes and marvellous control of his facial muscles.'

Michael nodded.

'Jack's an example of so much stamp on the coin that there's hardly any coin behind it.'

'Don't you believe it, my dear. There's plenty of metal at the back.'

'The "pukka sahib",' said Michael. 'I never can make up my mind whether that article is to the good or to the bad. The Cherrells are the best type of it, because there's no manner to them as there is to Jack; but even with them I always have the feeling of too much in heaven and earth that isn't dreamed of in their philosophy.'

'We can't all have divine sympathy, Michael.'

Michael looked at her fixedly. He decided against malicious intent and went on: 'I never know where understanding and tolerance ought to end.'

'That's where men are inferior to us. We wait for the mark to fix itself; we trust our nerves. Men don't, poor things. Luckily you've a streak of woman in you, Michael. Give me a kiss. Mind Coaker, he's very sudden. It's decided, then: Kit goes to Harrow.'

'If there's a Harrow to go to by the time he's of age.'

'Don't be foolish. No constellations are more fixed than the public schools. Look at the way they flourished on the war.'

'They won't flourish on the next war.'

'There mustn't be one, then.'

'Under "pukka sahibism" it couldn't be avoided.'

'My dear, you don't suppose that keeping our word and all that was not just varnish? We simply feared German preponderance.'

Michael rumpled his hair.

'It was a good instance, anyway, of what I said about there being more things in heaven and earth than are dreamed of by the "pukka sahib"; yes, and of many situations that he's not adequate to handle.'

Fleur yawned.

'We badly want a new dinner service, Michael.'

Chapter Ten

After dinner Michael set forth, without saying where he was going. Since the death of his father-in-law, and the disclosure then made to him about Fleur and John Forsyte, his relations with her had been the same, with a slight but deep difference. He was no longer a tied but a free agent in his own house. Not a word had ever been spoken between them on a matter now nearly four years old, nor had there been in his mind any doubt about her since; the infidelity was scotched and buried. But, though outwardly the same, he was inwardly emancipated, and she knew it. In this matter of Wilfrid, for instance, his father's warning had not been needed. He would not have told her of it, anyway. Not because he did not trust her discretion – he could always trust that – but because he secretly felt that in a matter such as this he would not get any real help from her.

He walked. 'Wilfrid's in love,' he thought, 'so he ought to be in by ten, unless he's got an attack of verse; but even then you can't write poetry in this traffic or in a club, the atmosphere stops the flow.' He crossed Pall Mall and threaded the maze of narrow streets dedicated to unattached manhood till he came to Piccadilly, quiet before its storm of after-theatre traffic. Passing up a side street devoted to those male ministering angels – tailors, bookmakers and moneylenders – he rounded into Cork Street. It was ten o'clock exactly when he paused before the well-remembered house. Opposite was the gallery where he had first met Fleur, and he stood for a moment almost dizzy from past feelings. For three years, before Wilfrid's queer infatuation for Fleur had broken it all up, he had been Wilfrid's fidus Achates. 'Regular David and Jonathan stunt,' he thought, and all his old feelings came welling up as he ascended the stairs.

The monastic visage of the henchman Stack relaxed at sight of him.

'Mr Mont? Pleasure to see you, sir.'

'And how are you, Stack?'

'A little older, sir; otherwise in fine shape, thank you. Mr Desert *is* in.'

Michael resigned his hat, and entered.

Wilfrid, lying on the divan in a dark dressing-gown, sat up.

'Hallo!'

'How are you, Wilfrid?'

'Stack! Drinks!'

'Congratulations, old man!'

'I met her first at your wedding, you know.'

'Ten years ago, nearly. You've plucked the flower of our family, Wilfrid; we're all in love with Dinny.'

'I won't talk about her, but I think the more.'

'Any verse, old man?'

'Yes, a booklet going in tomorrow, same publisher. Remember the first?'

'Don't I? My only scoop.'

'This is better. There's one that *is* a poem.'

Stack re-entered with a tray.

'Help yourself, Michael.'

Michael poured out a little brandy and diluted it but slightly. Then with a cigarette he sat down.

'When's it to be?'

'Registrar's, as soon as possible.'

'Oh! And then?'

'Dinny wants to show me England. While there's any sun I suppose we shall hang around.'

'Going back to Syria?'

Desert wriggled on his cushions.

'I don't know: further afield, perhaps – she'll say.'

Michael looked at his feet, beside which on the Persian rug some cigarette ash had fallen.

'Old man,' he said.

'Well?'

'D'you know a bird called Telfourd Yule?'

'His name – writer of sorts.'

'He's just come back from Arabia and the Soudan; he brought a yarn with him.' Without raising his eyes, he was conscious that Wilfrid was sitting upright.

'It concerns you; and it's queer and damaging. He thinks you ought to know.'

'Well?'

Michael uttered an involuntary sigh.

'Shortly: The Bedouin are saying that your conversion to Islam was at the pistol's point. He was told the yarn in Arabia, and again in the Libyan desert, with the name of the Sheikh, and the place in Darfur, and the Englishman's name.' And, still without looking up, he knew that Wilfrid's eyes were fixed on him, and that there was sweat on his forehead.

'Well?'

'He wanted you to know, so he told my dad at the Club this afternoon, and Bart told me. I said I'd see you about it. Forgive me.'

Then, in the silence, Michael raised his eyes. What a strange, beautiful, tortured, compelling face!

'Nothing to forgive; it's true.'

'My dear old man!' The words burst from Michael, but no others would follow.

Desert got up, went to a drawer and took out a manuscript.

'Here, read this!'

During the twenty minutes Michael took to read the poem, there was not a sound, except from the sheets being turned. Michael put them down at last.

'Magnificent!'

'Yes, but *you'd* never have done it.'

'I haven't an idea what I should have done.'

'Oh, yes, you have. You'd never have let sophistication and God knows what stifle your first instinct, as I did. My first instinct was to say: "Shoot and be damned," and I wish to God I'd kept to it, then I shouldn't be here. The queer thing is, if he'd threatened torture I'd have stood out. Yet I'd much rather be killed than tortured.'

'Torture's caddish.'

'Fanatics aren't cads. I'd have sent him to hell, but he really hated shooting me; he begged me – stood there with the pistol and begged me not to make him. His brother's a friend of mine. Fanaticism's a rum thing! He stood there ready to loose off, begging me. Damned human. I can see his eyes. He was under a vow. I never saw a man so relieved.'

'There's nothing of that in the poem,' said Michael.

'Being sorry for your executioner is hardly an excuse. I'm not proud of it, especially when it saved my life. Besides, I don't know if that *was* the reason. Religion, if you haven't got it, is a fake. To walk out into everlasting dark for the sake of a fake! If I must die I want a reality to die for.'

'You don't think,' said Michael miserably, 'that you'd be justified in denying the thing?'

'I'll deny nothing. If it's come out, I'll stand by it.'

'Does Dinny know?'

'Yes. She's read the poem. I didn't mean to tell her, but I did. She behaved as people don't. Marvellous!'

'Yes. I'm not sure that you oughtn't to deny it for her sake.'

'No, but I ought to give her up.'

'She would have something to say about that. If Dinny's in love, it's over head and ears, Wilfrid.'

'Same here!'

Overcome by the bleakness of the situation, Michael got up and helped himself to more brandy.

'Exactly!' said Desert, following him with his eyes. 'Imagine if the Press gets hold of it!' and he laughed.

'I gather,' said Michael, with a spurt of cheerfulness, 'that it was only in the desert both times that Yule heard the story.'

'What's in the desert today is in the bazaars tomorrow. It's no use, I shall have to face the music.'

Michael put a hand on his shoulder. 'Count on me, anyway. I suppose the bold way is the only way. But I feel all you're up against.'

'Yellow. Labelled: "Yellow" – might give any show away. And they'll be right.'

'Rot!' said Michael.

Wilfrid went on without heeding: 'And yet my whole soul revolts against dying for a gesture that I don't believe in. Legends and superstitions – I hate the lot. I'd sooner die to give them a death-blow than to keep them alive. If a man tried to force me to torture an animal, to hang another man, to violate a woman, of course I'd die rather than do it. But why the hell should I die to gratify those whom I despise for believing outworn creeds that have been responsible for more misery in the world than any other mortal thing? Why? Eh?'

Michael had recoiled before the passion in this outburst, and was standing miserable and glum.

'Symbol,' he muttered.

'Symbol! For conduct that's worth standing for, honesty,

humanity, courage, I hope I'd stand; I went through with the war, anyway; but why should I stand for what I look on as dead wood?'

'It simply mustn't come out,' said Michael violently. 'I loathe the idea of a lot of swabs looking down their noses at you.'

Wilfrid shrugged. 'I look down my nose at myself, I assure you. Never stifle your instinct, Michael.'

'But what are you going to *do*?'

'What does it matter what I do? Things will be as they will be. Nobody will understand, or side with me if they did understand. Why should they? I don't even side with myself.'

'I think lots of people might nowadays.'

'The sort I wouldn't be seen dead with. No, I'm outcast.'

'And Dinny?'

'I'll settle that with her.'

Michael took up his hat.

'If there's anything I can do, count on me. Good-night, old man!'

'Good-night, and thanks!'

Michael was out of the street before any thinking power returned to him. Wilfrid had been caught, as it were, in a snare! One could see how his rebellious contempt for convention and its types had blinded him to the normal view. But one could not dissociate this or that from the general image of an Englishman: betrayal of one feature would be looked on as betrayal of the whole. As for that queer touch of compassion for his would-be executioner, who would see that who didn't know Wilfrid? The affair was bitter and tragic. The 'yellow' label would be stuck on indiscriminately for all eyes to see.

'Of course,' thought Michael, 'he'll have his supporters – egomaniacs, and Bolshies, and that'll make him feel worse than ever.' Nothing was more galling than to be backed up by people you didn't understand, and who didn't understand you. And how was support like that going to help Dinny, more detached from it even than Wilfrid? The whole thing was—!

And with that blunt reflection he crossed Bond Street and went down Hay Hill into Berkeley Square. If he did not see his father before he went home, he would not sleep.

At Mount Street his mother and father were receiving a special pale negus, warranted to cause slumber, from the hands of Blore.

'Catherine?' said Lady Mont: 'Measles?'

'No, Mother; I want to have a talk with Dad.'

'About that young man – changin' his religion. He always gave me a pain – defyin' the lightnin', and that.'

Michael stared. 'It *is* about Wilfrid.'

'Em,' said Sir Lawrence, 'this is dead private. Well, Michael?'

'The story's true; he doesn't and won't deny it. Dinny knows.'

'What story?' asked Lady Mont.

'He recanted to some fanatical Arabs on pain of death.'

'What a bore!'

Michael thought swiftly: 'My God! If only everyone would take that view!'

'D'you mean, then,' said Sir Lawrence, gravely, 'that I've got to tell Yule there's no defence?'

Michael nodded.

'But if so, dear boy, it won't stop there.'

'No, but he's reckless.'

'The lightnin',' said Lady Mont, suddenly.

'Exactly, Mother. He's written a poem on it, and a jolly good one it is. He's sending it in a new volume to his publisher tomorrow. But, Dad, at any rate, get Yule and Jack Muskham to keep their mouths shut. After all, what business is it of theirs?'

Sir Lawrence shrugged the thin shoulders which at seventy-two were only beginning to suggest age.

'There are two questions, Michael, and so far as I can see

they're quite separate. The first is how to muzzle club gossip. The second concerns Dinny and her people. You say Dinny knows; but her people don't, except ourselves; and as she didn't tell us, she won't tell them. Now that's not fair. And it's not wise,' he went on without waiting for an answer, 'because this thing's dead certain to come out later, and they'd never forgive Desert for marrying her without letting them know. I wouldn't myself, it's too serious.'

'Agitatin',' murmured Lady Mont. 'Ask Adrian.'

'Better Hilary,' said Sir Lawrence.

Michael broke in: 'That second question, Dad, seems to me entirely up to Dinny. She must be told that the story's in the wind, then either she or Wilfrid will let her people know.'

'If only she'd let him drop her! Surely he can't want to go on with it, with this story going about?'

'I don't see Dinny droppin' him,' murmured Lady Mont. 'She's been too long pickin' him up. Love's young dream.'

'Wilfrid said he knew he ought to give her up. Oh! damn!'

'Come back to question one, then, Michael. I can try, but I'm very doubtful, especially if this poem is coming out. What is it, a justification?'

'Or explanation.'

'Bitter and rebellious, like his early stuff?'

Michael nodded.

'Well, they might keep quiet out of charity, but they'll never stomach that sort of attitude, if I know Jack Muskham. He hates the bravado of modern scepticism like poison.'

'We can't tell what's going to happen in any direction, but it seems to me we ought all to play hard for delay.'

'Hope the Hermit,' murmured Lady Mont. 'Good-night, dear boy; I'm goin' up. Mind the dog – he's not been out.'

'Well, I'll do what I can,' said Sir Lawrence.

Michael received his mother's kiss, wrung his father's hand, and went.

He walked home, uneasy and sore at heart, for this concerned two people of whom he was very fond, and he could see no issue that was not full of suffering to both. And continually there came back to him the thought: 'What should I have done in Wilfrid's place?' And he concluded, as he walked, that no man could tell what he would do if he were in the shoes of another man. And so, in the spring wind of a night not devoid of beauty, he came to South Square and let himself in.

Chapter Eleven

Wilfrid sat in his rooms with two letters before him, one that he had just written to Dinny, and one that he had just received from her. He stared at the snapshots and tried to think clearly, and since he had been trying to think clearly ever since Michael's visit of the previous evening, he was the less successful. Why had he chosen this particular moment to fall really in love, to feel that he had found the one person with whom he could bear to think of permanent companionship? He had never intended to marry, he had never supposed he would feel towards women anything but a transient urge that soon died in satisfaction. Even at the height of his infatuation with Fleur he had never supposed it would last. On the whole he was as profoundly sceptical about women as about religion, patriotism, or the qualities popularly attributed to the Englishman. He had thought himself armoured in scepticism, but in his armour was a joint so weak that he had received a fatal thrust. With bitter amusement he perceived that the profound loneliness left by that experience in Darfur had started in him an involuntary craving for spiritual companionship of which Dinny had, as involuntarily, availed herself. The thing that should have kept them apart had brought them together.

After Michael had left he had spent half the night going over and over it, and always coming back to the crude thought that, when all was said and done, he would be set down as a coward. And yet, but for Dinny, would even that matter? What did he care for society and its opinion? What did he care for England and the English? Even if they had prestige, was it deserved, any more than the prestige of any other country? The war had shown all countries and their inhabitants to be pretty much alike, capable of the same heroisms, basenesses, endurance, and absurdities. The war had shown mob feeling in every country to be equally narrow, void of discrimination, and generally contemptible. He was a wanderer by nature, and even if England and the nearer East were closed to him, the world was wide, the sun shone in many places, the stars wheeled over one, books could be read, women had beauty, flowers scent, tobacco its flavour, music its moving power, coffee its fragrance, horses and dogs and birds were the same seductive creatures, and thought and feeling brought an urge to rhythmic expression, almost wherever one went. Save for Dinny he could strike his tent and move out, and let tongues wag behind him! And now he couldn't! Or could he? Was he not, indeed, in honour bound to? How could he saddle her with a mate at whom fingers were pointed? If she had inspired him with flaming desire, it would have been much simpler; they could have had their fling and parted, and no one the worse. But he had a very different feeling for her. She was like a well of sweet water met with in a desert; a flower with a scent coming up among the dry vegetation of the wilderness. She gave him the reverent longing that some tunes and pictures inspire; roused the same ache of pleasure as the scent of new-mown grass. She was a cool refreshment to a spirit sun-dried, wind-dried, and dark. Was he to give her up because of this damned business?

In the morning when he woke, the same confused struggle of feeling had gone on. He had spent the afternoon writing her a letter, and had barely finished it when her first love-letter came. And he sat now with the two before him.

'I can't send this,' he thought suddenly; 'it goes over and over and gets nowhere. Rotten!' He tore it up, and read her letter a third time.

'Impossible!' he thought; 'to go down there! God and the King and the rest of it. Impossible!' And seizing a piece of paper, he wrote:

Cork Street: Saturday.

Bless you for your letter. Come up here to lunch Monday. We must talk – WILFRID

Having sent Stack out with this missive, he felt a little more at peace . . .

Dinny did not receive this note till Monday morning, and was the more relieved to get it. The last two days had been spent by her in avoiding any mention of Wilfrid, listening to Hubert and Jean's account of their life in the Soudan, walking and inspecting the state of trees with her father, copying his income-tax return, and going to church with him and her mother. The tacit silence about her engagement was very characteristic of a family whose members were mutually devoted and accustomed to spare each other's feelings; it was all the more ominous.

After reading Wilfrid's note she said to herself blankly: 'For a love-letter it's not a love-letter.' And she said to her mother:

'Wilfrid's shy of coming, dear. I must go up and talk to him. If I can, I will bring him down with me. If I can't, I'll try and arrange for you to see him at Mount Street. He's lived alone so much that seeing people is a real strain.'

Lady Cherrell's answer was a sigh, but it meant more to Dinny than words; she took her mother's hand and said: 'Cheer up, Mother dear. It's something that I'm happy, isn't it?'

'That would be everything, Dinny.'

Dinny was too conscious of implications in the 'would be' to answer.

She walked to the station, reached London at noon, and set out for Cork Street across the Park. The day was fine, the sun shone; spring was established to the full, with lilac and with tulips, young green of plane-tree leaves, songs of birds, and the freshness of the grass. But though she looked in tune, she suffered from presentiment. Why she should feel so, going to a private lunch with her lover, she could not have explained. There could be but few people in all the great town at such an hour of day with prospect before them so closely joyful; but Dinny was not deceived: all was not well – she knew it. Being before her time, she stopped at Mount Street to titivate. According to Blore, Sir Lawrence was out, but his lady in. Dinny left the message that she might be in to tea.

Passing the pleasant smell at the corner of Burlington Street, she had that peculiar feeling, experienced by all at times, of having once been someone else which accounts for so much belief in the transmigration of souls.

'It only means,' she thought, 'something I've forgotten. Oh! here's the turning!' And her heart began to beat.

She was nearly breathless when Stack opened the door to her. 'Lunch will be ready in five minutes, miss.' His eyes, dark, prominent above his jutting nose, and yet reflective, and the curly benevolence of his lips always gave her the impression that he was confessing her before she had anything to confess. He opened the inner door, shut it behind her, and she was in Wilfrid's arms. That was a complete refutation of presentiment; the longest and most satisfactory moment of the sort she had yet experienced. So long that she was afraid he would not let her go in time. At last she said gently:

'Lunch has already been in a minute, darling, according to Stack.'

'Stack has tact.'

Not until after lunch, when they were alone once more with coffee, did discomfiture come with the suddenness of a thunderclap in a clear sky.

'That business has come out, Dinny.'

What! That? *That!* She mastered the rush of her dismay.

'How?'

'A man called Telfourd Yule has brought the story back with him. They talk of it among the tribes. It'll be in the bazaars by now, in the London clubs tomorrow. I shall be in Coventry in a few weeks' time. Nothing can stop a thing like that.'

Without a word Dinny got up, pressed his head against her shoulder, then sat down beside him on the divan.

'I'm afraid you don't understand,' he said gently.

'That this makes any difference? No, I don't. The only difference could have been when you told me yourself. That made none. How can this, then?'

'How can I marry you?'

'That sort of thing is only in books, Wilfrid. *We* won't have linkéd misery long drawn out.'

'False heroics are not in my line either; but I don't think you see yet.'

'I do. Now you can stand up straight again, and those who can't understand – well, they don't matter.'

'Then don't your people matter?'

'Yes, they matter.'

'But you don't suppose for a minute that they'll understand?'

'I shall make them.'

'My poor dear!'

It struck her, ominously, how quiet and gentle he was being. He went on:

'I don't know your people, but if they're the sort you've described – charm ye never so wisely – they won't rise. They can't, it's against their root convictions.'

'They're fond of me.'

'That will make it all the more impossible for them to see you tied to me.'

Dinny drew away a little and sat with her chin on her hands. Then, without looking at him, she said:

'Do you want to get rid of me, Wilfrid?'

'Dinny!'

'Yes, but do you?'

He drew her into his arms. Presently she said:

'I see. Then if you don't, you must leave this to me. And anyway it's no good going to meet trouble. It isn't known yet in London. We'll wait until it is. I know you won't marry me till then, so I *must* wait. After that it will be a clear issue, but you mustn't be heroic then, Wilfrid, because it'll hurt me too much – too much.' She clutched him suddenly; and he stayed silent.

With her cheek to his she said quietly:

'Do you want me to be everything to you before you marry me? If so, I can.'

'Dinny!'

'Very forward, isn't it?'

'No! But we'll wait. You make me feel too reverent.'

She sighed. 'Perhaps it's best.'

Presently she said: 'Will you leave it to me to tell my people everything or not?'

'I will leave anything to you.'

'And if I want you to meet any one of them, will you?'

Wilfrid nodded.

'I won't ask you to come to Condaford – yet. That's all settled, then. Now tell me exactly how you heard about this.'

When he had finished, she said reflectively:

'Michael and Uncle Lawrence. That will make it easier. Now, darling, I'm going. It'll be good for Stack, and I want to think. I can only think when I'm insulated from you.'

'Angel!'

She took his head between her hands. 'Don't be tragic, and I won't either. Could we go joy-riding on Thursday? Good! Foch at noon! I'm far from an angel, I'm your love.'

She went dizzily down the stairs, now that she was alone, terribly conscious of the ordeal before them. She turned suddenly towards Oxford Street. 'I'll go and see Uncle Adrian,' she thought.

Adrian's thoughts at his Museum had been troubled of late by the claim of the Gobi desert to be the cradle of Homo Sapiens. The idea had been patented and put on the market, and it bid fair to have its day. He was reflecting on the changeability of anthropological fashions, when Dinny was announced.

'Ah! Dinny! I've been in the Gobi desert all the afternoon, and was just thinking of a nice cup of "hot" tea. What do you say?'

'China tea always gives me an 'ick feeling, Uncle.'

'We don't go in for so-called luxuries. My duenna here makes good old Dover tea with leaves in it, and we have the homely bun.'

'Perfect! I came to tell you that I've given my young heart.'

Adrian stared.

'It's really rather a terrible tale, so can I take off my hat?'

'My dear,' said Adrian, 'take off anything. Have tea first. Here it is.'

While she was having tea Adrian regarded her with a rueful smile, caught, as it were, between his moustache and goatee. Since the tragic Ferse affair she had been more than ever his idea of a niece; and he perceived that she was really troubled.

Lying back in the only easy chair, with her knees crossed and the tips of her fingers pressed together, she looked, he thought, ethereal, as if she might suddenly float, and his eyes rested with comfort on the cap of her chestnut hair. But his face grew perceptibly longer while she was telling him her tale, leaving nothing out. She stopped at last and added:

'Uncle, please don't look like that!'

'Was I?'

'Yes.'

'Well, Dinny, is it surprising?'

'I want your "reaction", as they call it, to what he did.' And she looked straight into his eyes.

'My personal reaction? Without knowing him – judgment reserved.'

'If you wouldn't mind, you *shall* know him.'

Adrian nodded, and she said:

'Tell me the worst. What will the others who don't know him think and do?'

'What was your own reaction, Dinny?'

'I knew him.'

'Only a week.'

'And ten years.'

'Oh! don't tell me that a glimpse and three words at a wedding—'

'The grain of mustard-seed, dear. Besides, I'd read the poem, and knew from that all his feelings. He isn't a believer; it must have seemed to him like some monstrous practical joke.'

'Yes, yes, I've read his verse – scepticism and love of beauty. His type blooms after long national efforts, when the individual's been at a discount, and the State has exacted everything. Ego crops out and wants to kick the State and all its shibboleths. I understand all that. But – You've never been out of England, Dinny.'

'Only Italy, Paris, and the Pyrenees.'

'They don't count. You've never been where England has to have a certain prestige. For Englishmen in such parts of the world it's all for one and one for all.'

'I don't think he realised that at the time, Uncle.'

Adrian looked at her, and shook his head.

'I still don't,' said Dinny. 'And thank God he didn't, or I should never have known him. Ought one to sacrifice oneself for false values?'

'That's not the point, my dear. In the East, where religion still means everything, you can't exaggerate the importance attached to a change of faith. Nothing could so damage the Oriental's idea of the Englishman as a recantation at the pistol's point. The question before him was: Do I care enough for what is thought of my country and my people to die sooner than lower that conception? Forgive me, Dinny, but that was, brutally, the issue.'

She was silent for a minute and then said:

'I'm perfectly sure Wilfrid would have died sooner than do lots of things that would have lowered that conception; but he simply couldn't admit that the Eastern conception of an Englishman ought to rest on whether he's a Christian or not.'

'That's special pleading; he not only renounced Christianity, he accepted Islam – one set of superstitions for another.'

'But, can't you see, Uncle, the whole thing was a monstrous jest to him?'

'No, my dear, I don't think I can.'

Dinny leaned back, and he thought how exhausted she looked.

'Well, if *you* can't, no one else will. I mean no one of our sort, and that's what I wanted to know.'

A bad ache started in Adrian's midriff. 'Dinny, there's a fortnight of this behind you, and the rest of your life before you; you told me he'd give you up – for which I respect him. Now, doesn't it need a wrench, if not for your sake – for his?'

Dinny smiled.

'Uncle, you're so renowned for dropping your best pals when they're in a mess. And you know so little about love! You only waited eighteen years. Aren't you rather funny?'

'Admitted,' said Adrian. 'I suppose the word "Uncle" came over me. If I knew that Desert was likely to be as faithful as you, I should say: "Go to it and be damned in your own ways, bless you!"'

'Then you simply *must* see him.'

'Yes; but I've seen people seem so unalterably in love that they were divorced within the year. I knew a man so completely satisfied by his honeymoon that he took a mistress two months later.'

'We,' murmured Dinny, 'are not of that devouring breed. Seeing so many people on the screen examining each other's teeth has spiritualised me, I know.'

'Who has heard of this development?'

'Michael and Uncle Lawrence, possibly Aunt Em. I don't know whether to tell them at Condaford.'

'Let me talk to Hilary. He'll have another point of view; and it won't be orthodox.'

'Oh! Yes, I don't mind Uncle Hilary.' And she rose. 'May I bring Wilfrid to see you, then?'

Adrian nodded, and, when she had gone, stood again in front of a map of Mongolia, where the Gobi desert seemed to bloom like the rose in comparison with the wilderness across which his favourite niece was moving.

Chapter Twelve

Dinny stayed on at Mount Street for dinner to see Sir Lawrence.

She was in his study when he came in, and said at once: 'Uncle Lawrence, Aunt Em knows what you and Michael know, doesn't she?'

'She does, Dinny. Why?'

'She's been so discreet. I've told Uncle Adrian; he seems to think Wilfrid has lowered English prestige in the East. Just what is this English prestige? I thought we were looked on as a race of successful hypocrites. And in India as arrogant bullies.'

Sir Lawrence wriggled.

'You're confusing national with individual reputation. The things are totally distinct. The individual Englishman in the East is looked up to as a man who isn't to be rattled, who keeps his word, and sticks by his own breed.'

Dinny flushed. The implication was not lost on her.

'In the East,' Sir Lawrence went on, 'the Englishman, or rather the Briton, because as often as not he's a Scot or a Welshman or a North Irishman, is generally isolated: traveller, archæologist, soldier, official, civilian, planter, doctor, engineer, or missionary, he's almost always head man of a small separate show; he maintains himself against odds on the strength of the Englishman's reputation. If a single Englishman is found wanting, down goes the stock of all those other isolated Englishmen. People know that and recognise its importance. That's what you're up against, and it's no use underestimating. You can't expect Orientals, to whom religion means something, to understand that to some of us it means nothing. An Englishman to them is a believing Christian, and if he recants, he's understood as recanting his most precious belief.'

Dinny said drily: 'In fact, then, Wilfrid has no case in the eyes of our world.'

'In the eyes of the world that runs the Empire, I'm afraid – none, Dinny. Could it be otherwise? Unless there were complete mutual confidence between these isolated beings that none of them will submit to dictation, take a dare, or let the others down, the thing wouldn't work at all. Now would it?'

'I never thought about it.'

'Well, you can take it from me. Michael has explained to me how Desert's mind worked; and from the point of view of a disbeliever like myself, there's a lot to be said. I should intensely dislike being wiped out over such an issue. But it wasn't the real issue; and if you say: "He didn't see that," then I'm afraid my answer is he didn't because he has too much spiritual pride. And that won't help him as a defence, because spiritual pride is anathema to the Services, and indeed to the world generally. It's the quality, you remember, that got Lucifer into trouble.'

Dinny, who had listened with her eyes fixed on her uncle's twisting features, said:

'It's extraordinary the things one can do without.'

Sir Lawrence screwed in a puzzled eyeglass.

'Have you caught the jumping habit from your aunt?'

'If one can't have the world's approval, one can do without it.'

'"The world well lost for love," sounds gallant, Dinny, but it's been tried out and found wanting. Sacrifice on one side is the worst foundation for partnership, because the other side comes to resent it.'

'I don't expect more happiness than most people get.'

'That's not as much as I want for you, Dinny.'

'Dinner!' said Lady Mont, in the doorway: 'Have you a vacuum, Dinny? They use those cleaners,' she went on, as they went towards the dining room, 'for horses now.'

'Why not for human beings,' murmured Dinny, 'and clear out their fears and superstitions? Uncle wouldn't approve, though.'

'You've been talkin', then. Blore, go away!'

When he had gone, she added: 'I'm thinkin' of your father, Dinny.'

'So am I.'

'I used to get over him. But daughters! Still, he must.'

'Em!' said Sir Lawrence, warningly, as Blore came back.

'Well,' said Lady Mont, 'beliefs and that – too fatiguin'. I never liked christenin's – so unfeelin' to the baby; and puttin' it upon other people; only they don't bother, except for cups and Bibles. Why do they put fern leaves on cups? Or is that archery? Uncle Cuffs won a cup at archery when he was a curate. They used. It's all very agitatin'.'

'Aunt Em,' said Dinny, 'all I hope and want is that no one will agitate themselves over me and my small affair. If people won't agitate we can be happy.'

'So wise! Lawrence, tell Michael that. Blore! Give Miss Dinny some sherry.'

Dinny, putting her lips to the sherry, looked across at her aunt's face. It was comforting – slightly raised in the eyebrows, drooped in the lids, curved in the nose, and as if powdered in the hair above the comely neck, shoulders and bust.

In the taxi for Paddington she had such a vivid vision of Wilfrid, alone, with this hanging over him, that she very nearly leaned out to say: 'Cork Street.' The cab turned a corner. Praed

Street? Yes, it would be! All the worry in the world came from the conflict of love against love. If only her people didn't love her, and she them, how simple things would be!

A porter was saying: 'Any luggage, Miss?'

'None, thank you.' As a little girl she had always meant to marry a porter! That was before her music master came from Oxford. He had gone off to the war when she was ten. She bought a magazine and took her seat in the train. But she was very tired and lay back in her corner of the third-class carriage; railway travelling was a severe tax on her always slender purse. With head tilted, she went to sleep.

When she alighted from the train there was a nearly full moon, and the night was blowy and sweet-smelling. She would have to walk. It was light enough to take the short cut, and she climbed the first stile into the field path. She thought of the night, nearly two years ago, when she came back by this train with the news of Hubert's release and found her father sitting up, grey and worn, in his study, and how years had seemed to drop off him when she told him the good news. And now she had news that must grieve him. It was her father she really dreaded facing. Her mother, yes! Mother, though gentle, was stubborn; but women had not the same hard-and-fast convictions about what was not 'done' as men. Hubert? In old days she would have minded him most. Curious how lost he was to her! Hubert would be dreadfully upset. He was rigid in his views of what was 'the game'. Well! she could bear his disapproval. But Father! It seemed so unfair to him, after his forty years of hard service!

A brown owl floated from the hedge over to some stacks. These moony nights were owl-nights, and there would be the screams of captured victims, so dreadful in the night-time. Yet who could help liking owls, their blunt soft floating flight, their measured stirring calls? The next stile led her on to their own land. There was a linhay in this field where her father's old charger sheltered at night. Was it Plutarch or Pliny who had said: 'For my part I would not sell even an old ox who had laboured for me'? Nice man! Now that the sound of the train had died away it was very quiet: only the brushing of a little wind on young leaves, and the stamp of old Kismet's foot in the linhay. She crossed a second field and came to the narrow tree-trunk bridge. The night's sweetness was like the feeling always within her now. She crossed the plank and slipped in among the apple trees. They seemed to live brightly between her and the moving, moonlit, wind-brushed sky. They seemed to breathe, almost to be singing in praise at the unfolding of their blossoms. They were lit in a thousand shapes of whitened branches, and all beautiful, as if someone had made each with a rapt and moonstruck pleasure and brightened it with starshine. And this had been done in here each spring for a hundred years and more. The whole world seemed miraculous on a night like this, but always the yearly miracle of the apple blooming was to Dinny most moving of all. The many miracles of England thronged her memory, while she stood among the old trunks inhaling the lichen-bark-dusted air. Upland grass with larks singing; the stilly drip in coverts when sun came after rain; gorse on wind-blown commons; horses turning and turning at the end of the long mole-coloured furrows; river waters now bright, now green-tinged beneath the willows; thatch and its wood smoke; swathed hay meadows, tawnied cornfields; the bluish distances beyond; and the ever-changing sky – all these were as jewels in her mind, but the chief was this white magic of the spring. She became conscious that the long grass was drenched and her shoes and stockings wet through; there was light enough to see in that grass the stars of jonquil, grape hyacinth and the pale cast-out tulips; there would be polyanthus, too, bluebells and cowslips – a few. She slipped on upward, cleared the trees, and stood a moment to look back at the whiteness of the whole. 'It might have dropped from the moon,' she thought: 'My best stockings, too!'

Across the low-walled fruit garden and lawn she came to the terrace. Past eleven! Only her father's study window lighted on the ground floor! How like that other night!

'Shan't tell him,' she thought, and tapped on it.

He let her in.

'Hallo, Dinny, you didn't stop the night at Mount Street, then?'

'No, Dad, there's a limit to my powers of borrowing nightgowns.'

'Sit down and have some tea. I was just going to make some.'

'Darling, I came through the orchard, and I'm wet to the knees.'

'Take off your stockings; here's an old pair of slippers.'

Dinny stripped off the stockings and sat contemplating her legs in the lamplight, while the General lit the etna. He liked to do things for himself. She watched him bending over the tea-things, and thought how trim he still was, and how quick and precise his movements. His browned hands, with little dark hairs on them, had long, clever fingers. He stood up, motionless, watching the flame.

'Wants a new wick,' he said. 'There's going to be bad trouble in India, I'm afraid.'

'India seems to be getting almost more trouble than it's worth to us.'

The General turned his face with its high but small cheekbones; his eyes rested on her, and his thin lips beneath the close little grey moustache smiled.

'That often happens with trusts, Dinny. You've got very nice legs.'

'So I ought, dear, considering you and Mother.'

'Mine are all right for a boot – stringy. Did you ask Mr Desert down?'

'No, not today.'

The General put his hands into his side-pockets. He had taken off his dinner jacket and was wearing an old snuff-coloured shooting coat; Dinny noticed that the cuffs were slightly frayed, and one leather button missing. His dark, high-shaped eyebrows contracted till there were three ridges right in the centre of his forehead; he said gently:

'I don't understand that change of religion, you know, Dinny. Milk or lemon?'

'Lemon, please.'

She was thinking: 'Now is the moment, after all. Courage!'

'Two lumps?'

'Three, with lemon, Dad.'

The General took up the tongs. He dropped three lumps into the cup, then a slice of lemon, put back the tongs, and bent down to the kettle.

'Boiling,' he said, and filled up the cup; he put a covered spoonful of tea into it, withdrew the spoon and handed the cup to his daughter.

Dinny sat stirring the thin golden liquid. She took a sip, rested the cup on her lap, and turned her face up to him.

'I can explain it, Dad,' she said, and thought: 'It will only make him understand even less.'

The General filled his own cup, and sat down. Dinny clutched her spoon.

'You see, when Wilfrid was far out in Darfur he ran into a nest of fanatical Arabs, remaining from the Mahdi times. The chief of them had him brought into his tent and offered him his life if he would embrace Islam.'

She saw her father make a little convulsive movement, so that some of the tea was spilled into his saucer. He raised the cup and poured it back. Dinny went on:

'Wilfrid is like most of us nowadays about belief, only a great deal more so. It isn't only that he doesn't believe in Christianity, he actually hates any set forms of religion, he thinks they divide mankind and do more harm and bring more suffering than anything else. And then, you know – or you would if you'd read his poetry, Dad – the war left him very bitter about the way lives are thrown away, simply spilled out like water at the orders of people who don't know what they're about.'

Again the General made that slight convulsive movement.

'Yes, Dad, but I've heard Hubert talk in much the same way about that. Anyway, it has left Wilfrid with a horror of wasting life, and the deepest distrust of all shibboleths and beliefs. He only had about five minutes to decide in. It wasn't cowardice, it was just bitter scorn that men can waste each other's lives for beliefs that to him seem equally futile. And he just shrugged and accepted. Having accepted, he had to keep his word and go through the forms. Of course, you don't know him, so I suppose it's useless.' She sighed and drank thirstily.

The General had put his own cup down; he rose, filled a pipe, lit it, and stood by the hearth. His face was lined and dark and grave. At last he said:

'I'm out of my depth. Is the religion of one's fathers for hundreds of years to go for nothing, then? Is all that has made us the proudest people in the world to be chucked away at the bidding of an Arab? Have men like the Lawrences, John Nicholson, Chamberlayne, Sandeman, a thousand others, who spent and gave their lives to build up an idea of the English as brave men and true, to be knocked into a cocked hat by every Englishman who's threatened with a pistol?'

Dinny's cup clattered on its saucer.

'Yes, but if not by every Englishman, Dinny, why by one? Why by this one?'

Quivering all over, Dinny did not answer. Neither Adrian nor Sir Lawrence had made her feel like this – for the first time she had been reached and moved by the other side. Some age-long string had been pulled within her, or she was infected by the emotion of one whom she had always admired and loved, and whom she had hardly ever seen stirred to eloquence. She could not speak.

'I don't know if I'm a religious man,' the General went on; 'the faith of my fathers is enough for me' – and he made a gesture, as if adding, 'I leave myself aside' – 'but, Dinny, I could not take dictation of that sort; I could not, and I cannot understand how he could have.'

Dinny said, quietly: 'I won't try to make you, Dad; let's take it that you can't. Most people have done something in their lives that other people could not understand if it were known. The difference here is that this thing of Wilfrid's *is* known.'

'You mean the threat is known – the reason for the—?'

Dinny nodded.

'How?'

'A Mr Yule brought the story back from Egypt; Uncle Lawrence thinks it can't be scotched. I want you to know the worst.' She gathered her wet stockings and shoes in her hand. 'Would you mind telling Mother and Hubert for me, Dad?' And she stood up.

The General drew deeply at his pipe, which emitted a gurgling sound.

'Your pipe wants cleaning, dear. I'll do it tomorrow.'

'He'll be a pariah,' burst from the General, 'he'll be a pariah! Dinny, Dinny!'

No two words could have moved and disarmed her more. At one stroke they shifted his opposition from the personal to the altruistic.

She bit her lip and said:

'Dad, I shall pipe my eye if I stay down here with you. And my feet are very cold. Good-night, darling!'

She turned and went quickly to the door, whence she saw him standing like a horse that has just been harnessed.

She went up to her room and sat on her bed, rubbing her cold feet one against the other. It was done! Now she had only to confront the feeling that would henceforth surround her like a wall over which she must climb to the fulfilment of her love. And what surprised her most, while she rubbed and rubbed, was knowing that her father's words had drawn from her a secret endorsement which had not made the slightest inroad on her feeling for Wilfrid. Was love, then, quite detached from judgment? Was the old image of a blind God true? Was it even true that defects in the loved one made him the dearer? That seemed borne out, at all events, by the dislike one had for the too good people in books; one's revolt against the heroic figure; one's impatience at the sight of virtue rewarded.

'Is it that my family's standard,' she thought, 'is higher than mine, or simply that I want him close to me and don't care what he is or does so long as he comes?' And she had a strange and sudden feeling of knowing Wilfrid to the very core, with all his faults and shortcomings, and with a something that redeemed and made up for them and would keep her love alive, for in that, in that only, was an element mysterious to her. And she thought with a rueful smile: 'All evil I know by instinct; it's goodness, truth, beauty that keep me guessing!' And, almost too tired to undress, she got into bed.

Chapter Thirteen

'The Briery', Jack Muskham's residence at Royston, was old-fashioned and low, unpretentious without, comfortable within. It was lined with the effigies of racehorses and sporting prints. Only in one room, seldom used, was any sign of a previous existence. 'Here', as an American newspaper man put it, when he came to interview the 'last of the dandies' on the subject of bloodstock, 'here were evidences of this aristocrat's early life in our glorious South West. Here were specimens of Navaho rugs and silver work; the plaited horsehair from El Paso; the great cowboy hats; and a set of Mexican harness dripping with silver. I questioned my host about this phase in his career. "Oh! that," he said, in his Britisher's drawl, "I had five years cow-punchin' when I was a youngster. You see, I had only one thought – horses, and my father thought that might be better for me than ridin' steeplechases here."

'"Can I put a date to that?" I asked this long, lean patrician with the watchful eyes and the languid manner.

'"Why, yes, I came back in 1901, and except for the war I've been breedin' bloodstock ever since."

'"And in the war?" I queried.

'"Oh!" he answered; and I seemed to sense that I was intruding on him: "The usual thing. Yeomanry, cavalry, trenches, and that."

'"Tell me, Mr Muskham," I said: "Did you enjoy your life over with us out there?"'

'"Enjoy?" he said: "Rather, don't you know."'

The interview, produced in a Western paper, was baptised with the heading:

ENJOYED LIFE IN SOUTHLAND, SAYS BRITISH DANDY

The stud farm was fully a mile from Royston village, and at precisely a quarter to ten every day, when not away at races, bloodstock sales, or what not, Jack Muskham mounted his potter pony and ambled off to what the journalist had termed his 'equine nursery'. He was accustomed to point to this potter pony as an example of what horses become if never spoken to in any but a gentle voice. She was an intelligent little three-year-old, three-quarter-bred, with a fine mouse-coloured coat over which someone seemed to have thrown a bottle of ink and then imperfectly removed the splashes. Beyond a slightly ragged crescent on her forehead, she had no white at all; her mane was hogged, and her long tail banged just below her hocks. Her eyes were quiet and bright, and – for a horse – her teeth were pearly. She moved with a daisy-clipping action, quickly recovering from any stumble. Ridden with a single rein applied to her neck, her mouth was never touched. She was but fourteen-two, and Jack Muskham's legs, he using long stirrup leathers, came down very far. Riding her, as he said, was like sitting in a very easy chair. Besides himself, only one boy, chosen for the quietness of his voice, hands, nerves, and temper, was allowed to handle her.

Dismounting from this animal at the gate of the quadrangular yard which formed the stables, Jack Muskham would enter, smoking one of his special cigarettes in a short amber holder, and be joined on the central grass by his stud groom.

He would then put out his cigarette, and they would go round the boxes – where the foals would be with their mothers, and the yearlings – and have this and that one out to be led round the tan track which adjoined the boxes round the yard. After this inspection, they would pass under the archway opposite the entrance and go to the paddocks to see the mares, foals, and yearlings at grass. Discipline in his 'equine nursery' was perfect; to all seeming his employees were as quiet, as clean, as well-behaved as the horses they had charge of. From the moment of his entrance to the moment when he emerged and remounted his potter pony, his talk would be of horses – sparing and to the point. And, daily, there were so many little things to see and say that he was rarely back at the house till one o'clock. He never discussed breeding on its scientific side with his stud groom, in spite of that functionary's considerable knowledge, because, to Jack Muskham, the subject was as much a matter of high politics as the foreign relations of his country are to a Secretary for Foreign Affairs. His mating decisions were made in privacy, following the conclusions of close study welded to what he would have termed his 'flair' and others might have called his prejudices. Stars might come loose, Prime Ministers be knighted, Archdukes restored, towns swallowed up by earthquakes, together with all other forms of catastrophe, so long as Jack Muskham could blend St Simon on Speculum with the right dashes of Hampton and Bend Or; or, in accordance with a more original theory of his own, could get old Herod through Le Sancy at the extreme top and extreme bottom of a pedigree which had Carbine and Barcaldine blood in between. He was, in fact, an idealist. To breed the perfect horse was his ideal, as little realisable, perhaps, as the ideals of other men, and far more absorbing – in his view. Not that he ever mentioned it – one did not use such a word! Nor did he bet, so that he was never deflected in his judgments by earthly desires. Tall, in his cigar-brown overcoat, specially lined with camel's hair, and his fawn-coloured buckskin shoes and fawn-coloured face, he was probably the most familiar figure at Newmarket; nor was there any member of the Jockey Club, with the exception of three, whose dicta were more respected. He was in fact an outstanding example of the eminence in his walk of life that can be attained by a man who serves a single end with complete and silent fidelity. In truth, behind this ideal of the 'perfect horse' lay the shape of his own soul. Jack Muskham was a formalist, one of the few survivors in a form-shattering age; and that his formalism had pitched on the horse for its conspicuous expression was due in part to the completeness with which the racehorse was tied to the Stud Book, in part to the essential symmetry of that animal, and in part to the refuge the cult of it afforded from the whirr, untidiness, glare, blare, unending scepticism, and intrusive blatancy of what he termed 'this mongrel age'.

At 'The Briery' two men did all the work except scrubbing, for which a woman came in daily. But for that, there was no sign in all the house that women existed in this world. It was monastic as a club which has not succumbed to female service, and as much more comfortable as it was smaller. The rooms were low, and two wide staircases reached the only upper floor, where the rooms were lower still. The books, apart from endless volumes relating to the racehorse, were either works of travel or of history, or detective novels; other fiction, with its scepticism, slangy diction, descriptions, sentiment, and sensation, was absent, if an exception be made of complete sets of Surtees, Whyte-Melville, and Thackeray.

As, in the pursuit by men of their ideals, there is almost always some saving element of irony, so in the case of Jack Muskham. He, whose aim in life was the production of the perfect thoroughbred, was actually engaged in an attempt to cast the thoroughbred, as hitherto conceived, from muzzle to crupper, on to the scrap-heap, and substitute for it an animal with a cross of blood not as yet in the Stud Book!

Unconscious of this discrepancy, he was seated at lunch with Telfourd Yule, still discussing the transportation of Arab mares, when Sir Lawrence Mont was announced.

'Lunch, Lawrence?'

'I have lunched, Jack. But coffee would be the very thing; also some brandy.'

'Then let's go into the other room.'

'You have here,' said Sir Lawrence, 'what I never thought to see again, the bachelor's box of my youth. Jack is very remarkable, Mr Yule. A man who can afford to date in these days is a genius. Do I see Surtees and Whyte-Melville entire? Mr Yule, what did Mr Waffles say in Mr Sponge's *Sporting Tour* when they were holding Caingey up by the heels to let the water run out of his pockets and boots?'

Yule's humorous mug expanded, but he was silent.

'Exactly!' said Sir Lawrence: 'No one knows nowadays. He said: "Why, Caingey, old boy, you look like a boiled porpoise with parsley sauce." Yes, and what did Mr Sawyer answer in *Market Harboro*, when the Honourable Crasher drove at the turnpike gate, saying: "It's open, I think"?'

Yule's face, as of India rubber, expanded further, and he was still more silent.

'Dear, dear! Jack?'

'He said: "I think not".'

'Good!' Sir Lawrence sank into a chair. 'And was it? No. Well! Have you arranged to steal that mare? Fine! And when you get her over?'

'I shall put her to the most suitable sire standing. I shall mate the result with the most suitable sire or mare I can find. Then I shall match the result of that mating privately against the best of our present thoroughbreds of the same age. If I'm proved right I ought to be able to get my Arab mares entered in the Stud Book. I'm trying to get three mares, by the way.'

'How old are you, Jack?'

'Rising fifty-three.'

'I'm sorry. This is good coffee.'

After that the three sat silent, awaiting the real purpose of this visit.

'I've come, Mr Yule,' said Sir Lawrence, suddenly, 'about that affair of young Desert's.'

'Not true, I hope?'

'Unfortunately, yes. He makes no bones about it.' And, turning his monocle on Jack Muskham's face, he saw there exactly what he had expected.

'A man,' said Muskham slowly, 'ought to keep his form better than that, even if he *is* a poet.'

'We won't go into the rights and wrongs, Jack. Let it go at what you say. All the same' – and Sir Lawrence's manner acquired strange gravity – 'I want you two to keep mum. If it comes out, it can't be helped, but I beg that you'll neither of you say anything.'

'I don't like the look of the fellow,' said Muskham shortly.

'That applies to at least nine-tenths of the people we see about; the reason is not adequate.'

'He's one of those bitter, sceptical young moderns, with no real knowledge of the world and no reverence for anything.'

'I know you hold a brief for the past, Jack, but don't bring it into this.'

'Why not?'

'Well, I didn't want to mention it, but he's engaged to my favourite niece, Dinny Cherrell.'

'That nice girl!'

'Yes. We none of us like it, except my boy Michael, who still swears by Desert. But Dinny has got her teeth into it, and I don't think anything will budge her.'

'She can't be allowed to marry a man who's bound for Coventry the moment this comes out.'

'The more he's taboo, the closer she'll stick to him.'

'I like *that*,' said Muskham. 'What do you say, Yule?'

'It's no affair of mine. If Sir Lawrence wants me to say nothing, I shall say nothing.'

'Of course it's no affair of ours; all the same, if making it known would stop your niece, I'd do it. I call it a damned shame!'

'It would have just the opposite effect, Jack. Mr Yule, you know a lot about the Press. Suppose this story leaks into the Press, as it well may; what then?'

Yule's eyes snapped.

'First they'll tell it vaguely of a certain English traveller; then they'll find out whether it's denied by Desert; then they'll tell it of him, with a good many details wrong, but not so wrong as all that. If he admits it, he can't object. The Press is pretty fair, and damned inaccurate.'

Sir Lawrence nodded. 'If I knew anyone going in for journalism, I should say: "Be strictly accurate, and you will be unique." I have not read any absolutely accurate personal paragraphs in the papers since the war.'

'That's their dodge,' said Yule; 'they get a double shot – first the inaccurate report and then the correction.'

'I loathe the Press,' said Muskham. 'I had an American press-man here. There he sat, and short of kicking him out – I don't know what on earth he made of me.'

'Yes, you date, Jack. To you Marconi and Edison are the world's two greatest malefactors. Is it agreed, then, about young Desert?'

'Yes,' said Yule; and Muskham nodded.

Sir Lawrence passed swiftly from the subject.

'Nice country about here. Are you staying long, Mr Yule?'

'I go back to Town this afternoon.'

'Let me take you.'

'Willingly.'

Half an hour later they had started.

'My cousin Jack,' said Sir Lawrence, 'ought to be left to the nation. In Washington there's a museum with groups of the early Americans under glass smoking the communal pipe, holding tomahawks over each other, and that sort of thing. One might have Jack—' Sir Lawrence paused: 'That's the trouble! How could one have Jack preserved? It's so difficult to perpetuate the unemphatic. You can catch anything that jumps around; but when there's no attitude except a watchful languor – and yet a man with a God of his own.'

'Form, and Muskham is its prophet.'

'He might, of course,' murmured Sir Lawrence, 'be preserved in the act of fighting a duel. That's perhaps the only human activity formal enough.'

'Form's doomed,' said Yule.

'H'm! Nothing so hard to kill as the sense of shape. For what *is* life but the sense of shape, Mr Yule? Reduce everything to dead similarity, and still shape will "out".'

'Yes,' said Yule, 'but "form" is shape brought to perfection-point and standardised; and perfection bores our bright young things.'

'That nice expression. But do they exist outside books, Mr Yule?'

'Don't they! And yawn-making – as they'd call it! I'd sooner attend City dinners for the rest of my life than spend a week-end in the company of those bright young things.'

'I doubt,' said Sir Lawrence, 'whether I've come across them.'

'You should thank God. They never stop talking day or night, not even in their couplings.'

'You don't seem to like them.'

'Well,' said Yule, looking like a gargoyle, 'they can't stand me any more than I can stand them. A boring little crowd, but, luckily, of no importance.'

'I hope,' said Sir Lawrence, 'that Jack is not making the mistake of thinking young Desert is one.'

'Muskham's never met a bright young thing. No; what gets his goat about Desert is the look of his face. It's a deuced strange face.'

'Lost angel,' said Sir Lawrence. '"Spiritual pride, my buck!" Something fine about it.'

Yule nodded. 'I don't mind it myself; and his verse is good. But all revolt's anathema to Muskham. He likes mentality clipped, with its mane plaited, stepping delicately to the snaffle.'

'I don't know,' murmured Sir Lawrence, 'I think those two might like each other, if they could shoot each other first. Queer people, we English!'

Chapter Fourteen

When, about the same time that afternoon, Adrian entered his brother's parish and traversed the mean street leading to the Vicarage of St Augustine's-in-the-Meads, English people were being almost too well illustrated six doors round the corner.

An ambulance stood in front of a house without a future, and all who had something better to do were watching it. Adrian made one of the party. From the miserable edifice two men and a nurse were bearing the stretched-out body of a child, followed by a wailing, middle-aged, red-faced woman and a growling, white-faced man with a drooping moustache.

'What's up?' said Adrian to a policeman.

'The child's got to have an operation. You'd think she was goin' to be murdered, instead of havin' the best that care can give her. There's the Vicar. If he can't quiet 'em, no one can.'

Adrian saw his brother come out of the house and join the white-faced man. The growling ceased, but the woman's wails increased. The child was ensconced by now in the ambulance, and the mother made an unwieldly rush at its door.

'Where's their sense?' said the policeman, stepping forward.

Adrian saw Hilary put his hand on the woman's shoulder. She turned as if to deliver a wide-mouthed imprecation, but a mere whimper issued. Hilary put his arm through hers and drew her quietly back into the house. The ambulance drove away. Adrian moved up to the white-faced man and offered him a cigarette. He took it with a 'Thanks, mister,' and followed his wife.

All was over. The little crowd had gone. The policeman stood there alone.

'The Vicar's a wonder,' he said.

'My brother,' said Adrian.

The policeman looked at him more respectfully.

'A rare card, sir, the Vicar.'

'I quite agree. Was that child very bad?'

'Won't live the day out, unless they operate. Seems as if they'd saved it up to make a close run. Just an accident the Vicar happening on it. Some people'd rather die than go into 'ospitals, let alone their children.'

'Independence,' said Adrian. 'I understand the feeling.'

'Well, if you put it that way, sir, so do I. Still, they've got a wretched home in there, and everything of the best in the 'ospital.'

'"Be it never so humble—"' quoted Adrian.

'That's right. And in my opinion it's responsible for these slums. Very slummy round these parts, but try and move the people, and don't they let you know! The Vicar does good work, reconditionin' the 'ouses, as they call it. If you want him, I'll go and tell him.'

'Oh! I'll wait.'

'You'd be surprised,' said the policeman, 'the things people'll put up with sooner than be messed about. And you can call it what you like: Socialism, Communism, Government by the people for the people, all comes to that in the end, messin' you about. Here! You move on! No hawkin' in this street!'

A man with a barrow who had looked as if he had been going to cry 'Winkles!' altered the shape of his mouth.

Adrian, stirred by the confusion of the policeman's philosophy, waited in hopes of more, but at this moment Hilary emerged and came towards them.

'It won't be their fault if she lives,' he said, and, answering the policeman's salute, added: 'Are those petunias coming up, Bell?'

'They are, sir; my wife thinks no end of 'em.'

'Splendid! Look here! You'll pass the hospital on your way home, you might ask about that child for me; and ring me if the news is bad.'

'I will, Vicar; pleased to do it.'

'Thanks, Bell. Now, old man, let's go in and have some tea.'

Mrs Hilary being at a meeting, the brothers had tea by themselves.

'I've come about Dinny,' said Adrian, and unfolded her story.

Hilary lighted a pipe. 'That saying,' he said at last: '"Judge not that ye be not judged", is extraordinarily comforting, until you've got to do something about it. After that it appears to amount to less than nothing; all action is based on judgments, tacit or not. Is Dinny very much in love?'

Adrian nodded. Hilary drew deeply at his pipe.

'I don't like it a little bit, then. I've always wanted a clear sky for Dinny; and this looks to me like a sirocco. I suppose no amount of putting it to her from other people's points of view is any good?'

'I should say none.'

'Is there anything you want me to do?'

Adrian shook his head. 'I only wanted your reaction.'

'Just sorrow that Dinny's going to have a bad time. As to that recantation, my cloth rises on me, but whether it rises because I'm a parson, or a public-school Englishman, I don't know. I suspect the older Adam.'

'If Dinny means to stick to this,' said Adrian, 'one must

stick to her. I always feel that if a thing one hates has to happen to a person one loves, one can only help by swallowing the idea of it whole. I shall try to like him and see his point of view.'

'He probably hasn't one,' said Hilary. '*Au fond*, you know, like "Lord Jim", he just jumped; and he almost certainly knows it at heart.'

'The more tragic for them both; and the more necessary to stand by.'

Hilary nodded.

'Poor old Con will be badly hit. It gives such a chance to people to play the Pharisee. I can see the skirts being drawn aside.'

'Perhaps,' said Adrian, 'modern scepticism will just shrug its shoulders and say: "Another little superstition gone west!"'

Hilary shook his head.

'Human nature, in the large, will take the view that he kowtowed to save his life. However sceptical people are nowadays about religion, patriotism, the Empire, the word gentleman, and all that, they still don't like cowardice – to put it crudely. I don't mean to say that a lot of them aren't cowards, but they still don't like it in other people; and if they can safely show their dislike, they will.'

'Perhaps the thing won't come out.'

'Bound to, one way or another; and, for young Desert, the sooner the better. Give him a chance to captain his soul again. Poor little Dinny! This'll test her sense of humour. Oh! dear me! I feel older. What does Michael say?'

'Haven't seen him since.'

'Do Lawrence and Em know?'

'Probably.'

'Otherwise it's to be kept dark, eh?'

'Yes. Well, I must be getting on.'

'I,' said Hilary, 'shall carve my feelings into my Roman

galley; I shall get half an hour at it, unless that child has collapsed.'

Adrian strode on to Bloomsbury. And while he went he tried to put himself in the place of one threatened with sudden extinction. No future life, no chance of seeing again those he loved; no promise, assured or even vague, of future conscious experience analogous to that of this life!

'It's the sudden personal emergency coming out of the blue,' he thought, 'with no eyes on you, that's the acid test. Who among us knows how he'll come through it?'

His brothers, the soldier and the priest, would accept extinction as a matter of simple duty; even his brother the judge, though he would want to argue the point and might convert his executioner. 'But I?' he thought. 'How rotten to die like that for a belief I haven't got, in a remote corner of the earth, without even the satisfaction of knowing that my death was going to benefit anybody, or would ever even be known!' Without professional or official prestige to preserve, faced by such an issue, requiring immediate decision, one would have no time to weigh and balance; would be thrown back on instinct. One's temperament would decide. And if it were like young Desert's, judging from his verse; if he were accustomed to being in opposition to his fellows, or at least out of touch with them; scornful of convention and matter-of-fact English bull-doggedness; secretly, perhaps, more in sympathy with Arabs than with his own countrymen, would he not almost infallibly decide as Desert had? 'God knows how I should have acted,' thought Adrian, 'but I understand, and in a way I sympathise. Anyway, I'm with Dinny in this, and I'll see her through; as she saw me through that Ferse business.' And, having reached a conclusion, he felt better . . .

But Hilary carved away at his Roman galley. Those classical studies he had so neglected had led up to his becoming a parson, and he could no longer understand why. What sort of young man could he have been to think he was fit for it? Why had he not taken to forestry, become a cowboy, or done almost anything that kept him out of doors instead of in the slummy heart of a dim city? Was he or was he not based on revelation? And, if not, on what was he based? Planing away at an after-deck such as that whence those early plumbers, the Romans, had caused so many foreigners to perspire freely, he thought: 'I serve an idea, with a superstructure which doesn't bear examination.' Still, the good of mankind was worth working for! A doctor did it in the midst of humbug and ceremony. A statesman, though he knew that democracy, which made him a statesman, was ignorance personified. One used forms in which one didn't believe, and even exhorted others to believe in them. Life was a practical matter of compromise. 'We're all Jesuits,' he thought, 'using doubtful means to good ends. I should have had to die for my cloth, as a soldier dies for his. But that's neither here nor there!'

The telephone bell rang, and a voice said:

'The Vicar! . . . Yes, sir! . . . That girl. Too far gone to operate. So if you'd come, sir.'

Hilary put down the receiver, snatched his hat, and ran out of the house. Of all his many duties the deathbed was least to his taste, and, when he alighted from the taxi before the hospital, the lined mask of his face concealed real dread. Such a child! And nothing to be done except patter a few prayers and hold her hand. Criminal the way her parents had let it run on till it was too late. But to imprison them for it would be to imprison the whole British race, which never took steps to interfere with its independence till the last minute, and that too late!

'This way, sir,' said a nurse.

In the whiteness and order of a small preliminary room Hilary saw the little figure, white-covered, collapsed, and with a deathly face. He sat down beside it, groping for words with which to warm the child's last minutes.

'Shan't pray,' he thought, 'she's too young.'

The child's eyes, struggling out of their morphined immobility, flitted with terror round the room and fixed themselves, horror-stricken, first on the white figure of the nurse, then on the doctor in his overalls. Hilary raised his hand.

'D'you mind,' he said, 'leaving her with me a moment?'

They passed into an adjoining room.

'Loo!' said Hilary softly.

Recalled by his voice from their terrified wandering, the child's eyes rested on his smile.

'Isn't this a nice clean place? Loo! What d'you like best in all the world?'

The answer came almost inaudibly from the white puckered lips: 'Pictures.'

'That exactly what you're going to have, every day – twice a day. Think of that. Shut your eyes and have a nice sleep, and when you wake the pictures will begin. Shut your eyes! And I'll tell you a story. Nothing's going to happen to you. See! I'm here.'

He thought she had closed her eyes, but pain gripped her suddenly again; she began whimpering and then screamed.

'God!' murmured Hilary. 'Another touch, doctor, quick!'

The doctor injected morphia.

'Leave us alone again.'

The doctor slipped away, and the child's eyes came slowly back to Hilary's smile. He laid his fingers on her small emaciated hand.

'Now, Loo, listen!

'"The Walrus and the Carpenter were walking hand in hand.
They wept like anything to see such quantities of sand.
"If seven maids with seven brooms could sweep for half a year,
Do you suppose," the Walrus said, "that they could get it clear?"
"I doubt it," said the Carpenter, and shed a bitter tear!'

On and on went Hilary, reciting 'The Mad Hatter's Tea-party'. And, while he murmured, the child's eyes closed, the small hand lost warmth.

He felt its cold penetrating his own hand and thought: 'Now, God, if you are – give her pictures!'

Chapter Fifteen

When Dinny opened her eyes on the morning after she had told her father, she could not remember what her trouble was. Realisation caused her to sit up with a feeling of terror. Suppose Wilfrid ran away from it all, back to the East or further! He well might, and think he was doing it for her sake.

'I can't wait till Thursday,' she thought; 'I must go up. If only I had money, in case—!' She rummaged out her trinkets and took hasty stock of them. The two gentlemen of South Molton Street! In the matter of Jean's emerald pendant they had behaved beautifully. She made a little parcel of her pledgeable ornaments, reserving the two or three she normally wore. There were none of much value, and to get a hundred pounds on them, she felt, would strain benevolence.

At breakfast they all behaved as if nothing had happened. So then, they all knew the worst!

'Playing the angel!' she thought.

When her father announced that he was going up to Town, she said she would come with him.

He looked at her, rather like a monkey questioning man's right not to be a monkey too. Why had she never before noticed that his brown eyes could have that flickering mournfulness?

'Very well,' he said.

'Shall I drive you?' asked Jean.

'Thankfully accepted,' murmured Dinny.

Nobody said a word on the subject occupying all their thoughts.

In the opened car she sat beside her father. The may-blossom, rather late, was at its brightest, and its scent qualified the frequent drifts of petrol fume. The sky had the high brooding grey of rain withheld. Their road passed over the Chilterns, through Hampden, Great Missenden, Chalfont, and Chorley Wood; land so English that no one, suddenly awakened, could at any moment of the drive have believed he was in any other country. It was a drive Dinny never tired of; but today the spring green and brightness of the may and apple blossom, the windings and divings through old villages, could not deflect her attention from the impassive figure by whom she sat. She knew instinctively that he was going to try and see Wilfrid, and, if so – she was, too. But when he talked it was of India. And when she talked it was of birds. And Jean drove furiously and never looked behind her. Not till they were in the Finchley Road did the General say:

'Where d'you want to be set down, Dinny?'

'Mount Street.'

'You're staying up, then?'

'Yes, till Friday.'

'We'll drop you, and I'll go on to my Club. You'll drive me back this evening, Jean?'

Jean nodded without turning and slid between two vermilion-coloured buses, so that two drivers simultaneously used the same qualitative word.

Dinny was in a ferment of thought. Dared she telephone Stack to ring her up when her father came? If so, she could time her visit to the minute. Dinny was of those who at once establish liaison with 'staff'. She could not help herself to a potato without unconsciously conveying to the profferer that she was interested in his personality. She always said 'Thank you', and rarely passed from the presence without having made some remark which betrayed common humanity. She had only seen Stack three times, but she knew he felt that she was a human being, even if she did not come from Barnstaple. She mentally reviewed his no longer youthful figure, his monastic face, black-haired and large-nosed, with eyes full of expression, his curly mouth, at once judgmatic and benevolent. He moved upright and almost at a trot. She had seen him look at her as if saying to himself: 'If this is to be our fate, could I do with it? I could.' He was, she felt, permanently devoted to Wilfrid. She determined to risk it. When they drove away from her at Mount Street, she thought: 'I hope I shall never be a father!'

'Can I telephone, Blore?'

'Certainly, miss.'

She gave Wilfrid's number.

'Is that Stack? Miss Cherrell speaking . . . Would you do me a little favour? My father is going to see Mr Desert today, General Sir Conway Cherrell; I don't know at what time, but I want to come myself while he's there . . . Could you ring me up here as soon as he arrives? I'll wait in . . . Thank you so very much . . . Is Mr Desert well? . . . Don't tell him or my father, please, that I'm coming. Thank you ever so!'

'Now,' she thought, 'unless I've misread Dad! There's a picture gallery opposite, I shall be able to see him leave from the window of it.'

No call came before lunch, which she had with her aunt.

'Your uncle has seen Jack Muskham,' said Lady Mont, in the middle of lunch; 'Royston, you know; and he brought back the other one, just like a monkey – they won't say anything. But Michael says he mustn't, Dinny.'

'Mustn't what, Aunt Em?'

'Publish that poem.'

'Oh! but he will.'

'Why? Is it good?'

'The best he has ever written.'

'So unnecessary.'

'Wilfrid isn't ashamed, Aunt Em.'

'Such a bore for you, I do think. I suppose one of those companionable marriages wouldn't do, would it?'

'I've offered it, dear.'

'I'm surprised at you, Dinny.'

'He didn't accept it.'

'Thank God! I should hate you to get into the papers.'

'Not more than I should myself, Auntie.'

'Fleur got into the papers, libellin'.'

'I remember.'

'What's that thing that comes back and hits you by mistake?'

'A boomerang?'

'I knew it was Australian. Why do they have an accent like that?'

'Really I don't know, darling.'

'And marsupials? Blore, Miss Dinny's glass.'

'No more, thank you, Aunt Em. And may I get down?'

'Let's both get down'; and, getting up, Lady Mont regarded her niece with her head on one side. 'Deep breathin' and carrots to cool the blood. Why Gulf Stream, Dinny? What gulf is that?'

'Mexico, dear.'

'The eels come from there, I was readin'. Are you goin' out?'

'I'm waiting for a 'phone call.'

'When they say tr-r-roubled, it hurts my teeth. Nice girls, I'm sure. Coffee?'

'Yes, *please*!'

'It does. One comes together like a puddin' after it.'

Dinny thought: 'Aunt Em always sees more than one thinks.'

'Bein' in love,' continued Lady Mont, 'is worse in the country – there's the cuckoo. They don't have it in America, somebody said. Perhaps they don't fall in love there. Your Uncle'll know. He came back with a story about a poppa at Nooport. But that was years and years ago. I feel other people's insides,' continued her aunt, uncannily. 'Where's your father gone?'

'To his Club.'

'Did you tell him, Dinny?'

'Yes.'

'You're his favourite.'

'Oh, no! Clare is.'

'Fiddle!'

'Did the course of your love run smooth, Aunt Em?'

'I had a good figure,' replied her aunt; 'too much, perhaps; we had then. Lawrence was my first.'

'Really?'

'Except for choir-boys and our groom, and a soldier or two. There was a little captain with a black moustache. Inconsiderate, when one's fourteen.'

'I suppose your "wooing" was very decorous?'

'No; your uncle was passionate. 'Ninety-one. There'd been no rain for thirty years.'

'No such rain?'

'No! No rain at all – I forget where. There's the telephone!'

Dinny reached the 'phone just in front of the butler.

'It'll be for me, Blore, thank you.'

She took up the receiver with a shaking hand.

'Yes? . . . I see . . . thank you, Stack . . . thank you very much . . . Will you get me a taxi, Blore?'

She directed the taxi to the gallery opposite Wilfrid's rooms, bought a catalogue, and went upstairs to the window. Here, under pretext of minutely examining Number 35, called 'Rhythm', a misnomer so far as she could see, she kept watch on the door opposite. Her father could not already have left Wilfrid, for it was only seven minutes since the telephone call. Very soon, however, she saw him issuing from the door, and watched him down the street. His head was bent, and he shook it once or twice; she could not see his face, but she could picture its expression.

'Gnawing his moustache,' she thought; 'poor lamb!'

The moment he rounded the corner she ran down, slipped across the street and up the first flight. Outside Wilfrid's door she stood with her hand raised to the bell. Then she rang.

'Am I too late, Stack?'

'The General's just gone, Miss.'

'Oh! May I see Mr Desert? Don't announce me.'

'No, miss,' said Stack. Had she ever seen eyes more full of understanding?

Taking a deep breath, she opened the door. Wilfrid was standing at the hearth with his head bent down on his folded arms. She stole silently up, waiting for him to realise her presence.

Suddenly he threw his head up, and saw her.

'Darling!' said Dinny, 'so sorry for startling you!' And she tilted her head, with lips a little parted and throat exposed, watching the struggle on his face.

He succumbed and kissed her.

'Dinny, your father—'

'I know. I saw him go. "Mr Desert, I believe! My daughter has told me of an engagement, and – er – your position. I – er – have come about that. You have – er – considered what will happen when your – er – escapade out there becomes – er – known. My daughter is of age, she can please herself, but we are all extremely fond of her, and I think you will agree that in the face of such a – er – scandal it would be wholly wrong on your part – er – to consider yourself engaged to her at present."'

'Almost exact.'

'And you answered?'

'That I'd think it over. He's perfectly right.'

'He is perfectly wrong. I have told you before, "Love is not love which alters when it alteration finds." Michael thinks you ought not to publish "The Leopard".'

'I must. I want it off my chest. When I'm not with you I'm hardly sane.'

'I know! But, darling, those two are not going to say anything; need it ever come out? Things that don't come out quickly often don't come out at all. Why go to meet trouble?'

'It isn't that. It's some damned fear in me that I *was* yellow. I want the whole thing out. Then, yellow or not, I can hold my head up. Don't you see, Dinny?'

She did see. The look on his face was enough. 'It's my business,' she thought, 'to feel as he does, whatever I think; only so can I help him; perhaps only so can I keep him.'

'I understand, perfectly. Michael's wrong. We'll face the music, and our heads shall be "bloody but unbowed". But we won't be "captains of our souls", whatever happens.'

And, having got him to smile, she drew him down beside her. After that long close silence, she opened her eyes with the slow look all women know how to give.

'Tomorrow is Thursday, Wilfrid. Will you mind if we drop in on Uncle Adrian on the way home? He's on our side. And about our engagement, we can say we aren't engaged, and *be* all the same. Good-bye, my love!'

Down in the vestibule by the front door as she was opening it, Stack's voice said:

'Excuse me, miss.'

'Yes?'

'I've been with Mr Desert a long time, and I was thinking. You're engaged to him, if I don't mistake, miss?'

'Yes and no, Stack. I hope to marry him, however.'

'Quite, miss. And a good thing, too, if you'll excuse me. Mr Desert is a sudden gentleman, and I was thinking if we were in leeaison, as you might say, it'd be for his good.'

'I quite agree; that's why I rang you up this morning.'

'I've seen many young ladies in my time, but never one I'd rather he married, miss, which is why I've taken the liberty.'

Dinny held out her hand. 'I'm terribly glad you did; it's just what I wanted; because things are difficult, and going to be more so, I'm afraid.'

Having polished his hand, Stack took hers, and they exchanged a rather convulsive squeeze.

'I know there's something on his mind,' he said. 'That's not my business. But I have known him to take very sudden decisions. And if you were to give me your telephone numbers, miss, I might be of service to you both.'

Dinny wrote them down. 'This is the town one at my uncle, Sir Lawrence Mont's, in Mount Street; and this is my country one at Condaford Grange in Oxfordshire. One or the other is almost sure to find me. And thank you ever so. It takes a load off my mind.'

'And off mine, miss. Mr Desert has every call on me. And I want the best for him. He's not everybody's money, but he's mine.'

'And mine, Stack.'

'I won't bandy compliments, miss, but he'll be a lucky one, if you'll excuse me.'

Dinny smiled. 'No, I shall be the lucky one. Good-bye, and thank you again.'

She went away, treading, so to speak, on Cork Street. She had an ally in the lion's mouth; a spy in the friend's camp; a faithful traitor! Thus mixing her metaphors, she scurried back to her aunt's house. Her father would almost certainly go there before returning to Condaford.

Seeing his unmistakable old bowler in the hall, she took

the precaution of removing her own hat before going to the drawing room. He was talking to her aunt, and they stopped as she came in. Everyone would always stop now as she came in! Looking at them with quiet directness, she sat down.

The General's eyes met hers.

'I've been to see Mr Desert, Dinny.'

'I know, dear. He is thinking it over. We shall wait till everyone knows, anyway.'

The General moved uneasily.

'And if it is any satisfaction to you, we are not formally engaged.'

The General gave her a slight bow, and Dinny turned to her aunt, who was fanning a pink face with a piece of lilac-coloured blotting-paper.

There was a silence, then the General said:

'When are you going to Lippinghall, Em?'

'Next week,' replied Lady Mont, 'or is it the week after? Lawrence knows. I'm showing two gardeners at the Chelsea Flower Show. Boswell and Johnson, Dinny.'

'Oh! Are they still with you?'

'More so. Con, you ought to grow pestifera – no, that's not the name – that hairy anemone thing.'

'Pulsatilla, Auntie.'

'Charmin' flowers. They want lime.'

'We're short of lime at Condaford,' said the General, 'as you ought to know, Em.'

'Our azaleas were a dream this year, Aunt Em.'

Lady Mont put down the blotting-paper.

'I've been tellin' your father, Dinny, that it's no good fussin' you.'

Dinny, watching her father's glum face, said: 'Do you know that nice shop in Bond Street, Auntie, where they make animals? I got a lovely little vixen and her cubs there to make Dad like foxes better.'

'Huntin',' said Lady Mont, and sighed. 'When they get up chimneys, it's rather touchin'.'

'Even Dad doesn't like digging out, or stopping earths, do you, Dad?'

'N-no!' said the General, 'on the whole, no!'

'Bloodin' children, too,' said Lady Mont. 'I saw you blooded, Con.'

'Messy job, and quite unnecessary! Only the old raw-hide school go in for it now.'

'He looked so nasty, Dinny.'

'Yes, you haven't got the face for it, Dad. It wants one of those snub-nosed, red-haired, freckled boys, that like killing for the sake of killing.'

The General rose.

'I must be going back to the Club. Jean picks me up there. When shall we see you, Dinny? Your mother—' and he stopped.

'Aunt Em's keeping me till Saturday.'

The General nodded. He suffered his sister's and daughter's kiss with a face that seemed to say, 'Yes – but—'

From the window Dinny watched his figure moving down the street, and her heart twitched.

'Your father!' said her aunt's voice behind her. 'All this is very wearin', Dinny.'

'I think it's very dear of Dad not to have mentioned the fact that I'm dependent on him.'

'Con *is* a dear,' said Lady Mont; 'he said the young man was respectful. Who was it said: "Goroo – goroo"?'

'The old Jew in *David Copperfield*.'

'Well, it's what I feel.'

Dinny turned from the window.

'Auntie! I don't feel the same being at all as I did two weeks ago. I'm utterly changed. Then I didn't seem to have any desires; now I'm all one desire, and I don't seem to care whether I'm decent or not. Don't say Epsom salts!'

Lady Mont patted her arm.

'"Honour thy father and thy mother",' she said; 'but then there was "Forsake all and follow me", so you can't tell.'

'I can,' said Dinny. 'Do you know what I'm hoping now? That everything will come out tomorrow. If it did, we could be married at once.'

'Let's have some tea, Dinny. Blore, tea! Indian and rather strong!'

Chapter Sixteen

Dinny took her lover to Adrian's door at the museum the next day, and left him there. Looking round at his tall, hatless, girt-in figure, she saw him give a violent shiver. But he smiled, and even at that distance she felt warmed by his eyes.

Adrian, already notified, received the young man with what he stigmatised to himself as 'morbid curiosity', and placed him at once in mental apposition to Dinny. A curiously diverse couple they would make! Yet, with a perception not perhaps unconnected with the custody of skeletons, he had a feeling that his niece was not physically in error. This was a figure that could well stand or lie beside her. Its stringy grace and bony gallantry accorded with her style and slenderness; and the darkened face, with its drawn and bitter lines, had eyes which even Adrian, who had all the public-school-man's impatience of male film stars, could see would be attractive to the feminine gender. Bones broke the ice to some degree; and over the identity of a supposed Hittite in moderate preservation they became almost cordial. Places and people whom they had both seen in strange conditions were a further incentive to human feeling. But not till he had taken up his hat to go did Wilfrid say suddenly:

'Well, Mr Cherrell, what would *you* do?'

Adrian, who was looking up, halted and considered his questioner with narrowed eyes.

'I'm a poor hand at advice, but Dinny is a precious baggage—'

'She is.'

Adrian bent and shut the door of a cabinet.

'This morning,' he said, 'I watched a solitary ant in my bathroom trying to make its way and find out about things. I'm sorry to say I dropped some ashes from my pipe on it to see what it would do. Providence all over – always dropping ashes from its pipe on us to observe the result. I've been in several minds, but I've come to the conclusion that if you're really in love with Dinny—' a convulsive movement of Wilfrid's body ended in the tight clenching of his hands on his hat – 'as I see you are, and as I know her to be with you, then stand fast and work your way with her through the ashes. She'd rather be in the cart with you than in a Pullman with the rest of us. I believe' – and Adrian's face was illuminated by earnestness – 'that she is one of those of whom it is not yet written, "and they twain shall be one *spirit*".' The young man's face quivered.

'Genuine!' thought Adrian.

'So think first of her, but not in the "I love you so that nothing will induce me to marry you" fashion. Do what she wants – when she wants it – she's not unreasonable. And, honestly, I don't believe you'll either of you regret it.'

Desert took a step towards him, and Adrian could see that he was intensely moved. But he mastered all expression, save a little jerky smile, made a movement of one hand, turned, and went out.

Adrian continued to shut the doors of cupboards that contained bones. 'That,' he was thinking, 'is the most difficult, and in some ways the most beautiful face I've seen. The spirit walks upon its waters and is often nearly drowned. I wonder if that advice was criminal, because for some reason or other I believe he's going to take it.' And he returned to the reading of a geographical magazine which Wilfrid's visit had interrupted. It contained a spirited account of an Indian tribe on the Amazon which had succeeded, even without the aid of American engineers at capitalistic salaries, in perfecting the Communistic ideal. None of them, apparently, owned anything. Their whole lives, including the processes of nature, were passed in the public eye. They wore no clothes, they had no laws; their only punishment, something in connection with red ants, was inflicted for the only offence, that of keeping anything to themselves. They lived on the cassava root variegated with monkey, and were the ideal community!

'A wonderful instance,' thought Adrian, 'of how the life of man runs in cycles. For the last twenty thousand years or so we've been trying, as we thought, to improve on the principle which guides the life of these Indians, only to find it reintroduced as the perfect pattern.'

He sat for some time with a smile biting deep into the folds about his mouth. Doctrinaires, extremists! That Arab who put a pistol to young Desert's head was a symbol of the most mischievous trait in human nature! Ideas and creeds – what were they but half-truths, only useful in so far as they helped to keep life balanced? The geographical magazine slipped off his knee.

He stopped on the way home in the garden of his square to feel the sun on his cheek and listen to a blackbird. He had all he wanted in life: the woman he loved, fair health, a fair salary – seven hundred a year and the prospect of a pension – two adorable children, not his own, so that he was free from the misgivings of more normal parents; an absorbing job, a love of nature, and another thirty years, perhaps, before him. 'If at this moment,' he thought, 'someone put a pistol to my head and said: "Adrian Cherrell, renounce Christianity or out go your brains!" should I say with Clive in India: "Shoot and be damned!"?' And he could not answer. The blackbird continued to sing, the young leaves to twitter in the breeze, the sun to warm his cheek, and life to be desirable in the quiet of that one-time fashionable square . . .

Dinny, when she left those two on the verge of acquaintanceship, had paused, in two minds, and then gone north to St Augustine's-in-the-Meads. Her instinct was to sap the opposition of the outlying portions of her family, so as to isolate the defences of her immediate people. She moved towards the heart of practical Christianity with a certain rather fearful exhilaration.

Her Aunt May was in the act of dispensing tea to two young ex-Collegians before their departure to a club where they superintended the skittles, chess, draughts, and ping-pong of the neighbourhood.

'If you want Hilary, Dinny, he had two committees, but they might collapse, because he's almost the whole of both.'

'You and uncle know about me, I suppose?'

Mrs Hilary nodded. She was looking very fresh in a sprigged dress.

'Would you mind telling me what Uncle feels about it?'

'I'd rather leave that to him, Dinny. We neither of us remember Mr Desert very well.'

'People who don't know him well will always misjudge him. But neither you nor Uncle care what other people think.' She said this with a guileless expression which by no means deceived Mrs Hilary, accustomed to Women's Institutes.

'We're neither of us very orthodox, as you know, Dinny, but we do both of us believe very deeply in what Christianity stands for, and it's no good pretending we don't.'

Dinny thought a moment.

'Is that more than gentleness and courage and self-sacrifice, and must one be a Christian to have those?'

'I'd rather not talk about it. I should be sorry to say anything that would put me in a position different from Hilary's.'

'Auntie, how model of you!'

Mrs Hilary smiled. And Dinny knew that judgment in this quarter was definitely reserved.

She waited, talking of other things, till Hilary came in. He was looking pale and worried. Her aunt gave him tea, passed a hand over his forehead, and went out.

Hilary drank off his tea and filled his pipe with a knot of tobacco screwed up in a circular paper.

'Why corporations, Dinny? Why not three doctors, three engineers, three architects, an adding machine, and a man of imagination to work it and keep them straight?'

'Are you in trouble, Uncle?'

'Yes, gutting houses on an overdraft is ageing enough, without corporational red tape.'

Looking at his worn but smiling face, Dinny thought: 'I can't bother him with my little affairs.' 'You and Aunt May couldn't spare time, I suppose, to come to the Chelsea Flower Show on Tuesday?'

'My goodness!' said Hilary, sticking one end of a match into the centre of the knob and lighting the knob with the other end, 'how I would love to stand in a tent and smell azaleas!'

'We thought of going at one o'clock, so as to avoid the worst of the crush. Aunt Em would send for you.'

'Can't promise, so don't send. If we're not at the main entrance at one, you'll know that Providence has intervened. And now, what about you? Adrian has told me.'

'I don't want to bother you, Uncle.'

Hilary's shrewd blue eyes almost disappeared. He expelled a cloud of smoke.

'Nothing that concerns you will bother me, my dear, except in so far as it's going to hurt you. I suppose you *must*, Dinny?'

'Yes, I must.'

Hilary sighed.

'In that case it remains to make the best of it. But the world loves the martyrdom of others. I'm afraid he'll have a bad Press, as they say.'

'I'm sure he will.'

'I can only just remember him, as a rather tall, scornful young man in a buff waistcoat. Has he lost the scorn?'

Dinny smiled.

'It's not the side I see much of at present.'

'I sincerely trust,' said Hilary, 'that he has not what they call devouring passions.'

'Not so far as I have observed.'

'I mean, Dinny, that once that type has eaten its cake, it shows all the old Adam with a special virulence. Do you get me?'

'Yes. But I believe it's a "marriage of true minds" with us.'

'Then, my dear, good luck! Only, when people begin to throw bricks, don't resent it. You're doing this with your eyes open, and you'll have no right to. Harder to bear than having your own toe trodden on is seeing one you love batted over the head. So catch hold of yourself hard at the start, and go on catching hold, or you'll make it worse for him. If I'm not wrong, Dinny, you can get very hot about things.'

'I'll try not to. When Wilfrid's book of poems comes out, I want you to read one called "The Leopard"; it gives his state of mind about the whole thing.'

'Oh!' said Hilary blankly. 'Justification? That's a mistake.'

'That's what Michael says. I don't know whether it is or not; I think in the end – not. Anyway, it's coming out.'

'There beginneth a real dog-fight. "Turn the other cheek" and "too proud to fight" would have been better left unsaid. All the same, it's asking for trouble, and that's all about it.'

'I can't help it, Uncle.'

'I realise that, Dinny; it's when I think of the number of things you won't be able to help that I feel so blue. And what about Condaford? Is it going to cut you off from that?'

'People do come round, except in novels; and even there they have to in the end, or else die, so that the heroine may be happy. Will you say a word for us to Father if you see him, Uncle?'

'No, Dinny. An elder brother never forgets how superior he was to you when he was big and you were not.'

Dinny rose.

'Well, Uncle; thank you ever so for not believing in damnation, and even more for not saying so. I shall remember all you've said. Tuesday, one o'clock at the main entrance; and don't forget to eat something first; it's a very tiring business.'

When she had gone Hilary refilled his pipe.

'"And even more for not saying so!"' he repeated in thought. 'That young woman can be caustic. I wonder how often I say things I don't mean in the course of my professional duties.' And, seeing his wife in the doorway, he added:

'May, would you say I was a humbug – professionally?'

'Yes, dear. How could it be otherwise?'

'You mean, the forms a parson uses aren't broad enough to cover the variations of human nature? But I don't see how they could be. Would you like to go to the Chelsea Flower Show on Tuesday?'

Mrs Hilary, thinking: 'Dinny might have asked *me*,' replied cheerfully: 'Very much.'

'Let's try and arrange so that we can get there at one o'clock.'

'Did you talk to her about her affair?'

'Yes.'

'Is she immovable?'

'Quite.'

Mrs Hilary sighed. 'It's an awful pity. Do you think a man could ever live that down?'

'Twenty years ago I should have said "No". Now I'm not sure. It seems a queer thing to say, but it's not the really religious people who'll matter.'

'Why?'

'Because they won't come across them. It's the army, and Empire people, and Englishmen overseas, whom they will come across continually. The hub of unforgiveness is in her own family to start with. It's the yellow label. The gum they use putting that on is worse than the patent brand of any hotel that wants to advertise itself.'

'I wonder,' said Mrs Hilary, 'what the children would say about it?'

'Queer that we don't know.'

'We know less about our children than any of their friends do. Were we like that to our own elders, I wonder?'

'Our elders looked on us as biological specimens; they had us at an angle, and knew quite a lot about us. *We've* tried to put ourselves on a level with our youngsters, elder brother and sister business, and we don't know a thing. We've missed the one knowledge, and haven't got the other. A bit humiliating, but they're a decent crowd. It's not the young people I'm afraid of in Dinny's business, it's those who've had experience of the value of English prestige, and they'll be justified; and those who like to think he's done a thing they wouldn't have done themselves – and they won't be justified a bit.'

'I think Dinny's over-estimating her strength, Hilary.'

'No woman really in love could do otherwise. To find out whether she is or not will be her job. Well, she won't rust.'

'You speak as if you rather liked it.'

'The milk is spilled, and it's no good worrying. Let's get down to the wording of that new appeal. There's going to be a bad trade slump. Just our luck! All the people who've got money will be sticking to it.'

'I wish people wouldn't be less extravagant when times are

bad. It only means less work still. The shopkeepers are moaning about that already.'

Hilary reached for a notebook and began writing. His wife looked over his shoulder presently and read:

To all whom it may concern:

And whom does it not concern that there should be in our midst thousands of people so destitute from birth to death of the bare necessities of life that they don't know what real cleanliness, real health, real fresh air, real good food are?

'One "real" will cover the lot, dear.'

Chapter Seventeen

Arriving at the Chelsea Flower Show, Lady Mont said thoughtfully: 'I'm meetin' Boswell and Johnson at the calceolarias, Dinny. What a crowd!'

'Yes, and all plain. Do they come, Auntie, because they're yearning for beauty they haven't got?'

'I can't get Boswell and Johnson to yearn. There's Hilary! He's had that suit ten years. Take this and run for tickets, or he'll try and pay.'

With a five-pound note Dinny slid towards the wicket, avoiding her uncle's eyes. She secured four tickets, and turned smiling.

'I saw you being a serpent,' he said. 'Where are we going first? Azaleas? I like to be thoroughly sensual at a flower show.'

Lady Mont's deliberate presence caused a little swirl in the traffic, while her eyes from under slightly drooped lids took in the appearance of people selected, as it were, to show off flowers.

The tent they entered was warm with humanity and perfume, though the day was damp and cool. The ingenious beauty of each group of blossoms was being digested by variegated types of human being linked only through that mysterious air of kinship which comes from attachment to the same pursuit. This was the great army of flower-raisers

– growers of primulas in pots, of nasturtiums, gladioli and flags in London back gardens, of stocks, hollyhocks and sweet-williams in little provincial plots; the gardeners of larger grounds; the owners of hothouses and places where experiments are made – but not many of these, for they had already passed through or would come later. All moved with a prying air, as if marking down their own next ventures; and alongside the nurserymen would stop and engage as if making bets. And the subdued murmur of voices, cockneyfied, countrified, cultivated, all commenting on flowers, formed a hum like that of bees, if not so pleasing. This subdued expression of a national passion, walled-in by canvas, together with the scent of the flowers, exercised on Dinny an hypnotic effect, so that she moved from one brilliant planted posy to another, silent and with her slightly upturned nose twitching delicately.

Her aunt's voice roused her.

'There they are!' she said, pointing with her chin.

Dinny saw two men standing so still that she wondered if they had forgotten why they had come. One had a reddish moustache and sad cow-like eyes; the other looked like a bird with a game wing; their clothes were stiff with Sundays. They were not talking, nor looking at the flowers, but as if placed there by Providence without instructions.

'Which is Boswell, Auntie?'

'No moustache,' said Lady Mont; 'Johnson has the green hat. He's deaf. So like them.'

She moved towards them, and Dinny heard her say:

'Ah!'

The two gardeners rubbed their hands on the sides of their trousered legs, but did not speak.

'Enjoyin' it?' she heard her aunt say. Their lips moved, but no sound came forth that she could catch. The one she had called Boswell lifted his cap and scratched his head. Her aunt was pointing now at the calceolarias, and suddenly the one in the green hat began to speak. He spoke so that, as Dinny could see, not even her aunt could hear a word, but his speech went on and on and seemed to afford him considerable satisfaction. Every now and then she heard her aunt say: 'Ah!' But Johnson went on. He stopped suddenly, her aunt said 'Ah!' again and came back to her.

'What was he saying?' asked Dinny.

'No,' said Lady Mont, 'not a word. You can't. But it's good for him.' She waved her hand to the two gardeners, who were again standing without sign of life, and led the way.

They passed into the rose tent now, and Dinny looked at her watch. She had appointed to meet Wilfrid at the entrance of it.

She cast a hurried look back. There he was! She noted that Hilary was following his nose, Aunt May following Hilary, Aunt Em talking to a nurseryman. Screened by a prodigious group of 'K. of Ks.' she skimmed over to the entrance, and, with her hands in Wilfrid's, forgot entirely where she was.

'Are you feeling strong, darling? Aunt Em is here, and my Uncle Hilary and his wife. I should so like them to know you, because they all count in our equation.'

He seemed to her at that moment like a highly-strung horse asked to face something it has not faced before.

'If you wish, Dinny.'

They found Lady Mont involved with the representatives of 'Plantem's Nurseries'.

'That one – south aspect and chalk. The nemesias don't. It's cross-country – they do dry so. The phloxes came dead. At least they said so: you can't tell. Oh! Here's my niece! Dinny, this is Mr Plantem. He often sends – Oh! . . . ah! Mr Desert! How d'you do? I remember you holdin' Michael's arms up at his weddin'.' She had placed her hand in Wilfrid's and seemingly forgotten it, the while her eyes from under their raised brows searched his face with a sort of mild surprise.

'Uncle Hilary,' said Dinny.

'Yes,' said Lady Mont, coming to herself. 'Hilary, May – Mr Desert.'

Hilary, of course, was entirely his usual self, but Aunt May looked as if she were greeting a dean. And almost at once Dinny was tacitly abandoned to her lover.

'What do you think of Uncle Hilary?'

'He looks like a man to go to in trouble.'

'He is. He knows by instinct how not to run his head against brick walls, and yet he's always in action. I suppose that comes of living in a slum. He agrees with Michael that to publish "The Leopard" is a mistake.'

'Running my head against a brick wall – um?'

'Yes.'

'The die, as they say, is cast. Sorry if you're sorry, Dinny.'

Dinny's hand sought his. 'No. Let's sail under our proper colours – only, for my sake, Wilfrid, try to take what's coming quietly, and so will I. Shall we hide behind this firework of fuchsias and slip off? They'll expect it.'

Once outside the tent they moved towards the Embankment exit, past the rock gardens, each with its builder standing in the damp before it, as though saying: 'Look on this, and employ me!'

'Making nice things and having to cadge round to get people to notice them!' said Dinny.

'Where shall we go, Dinny?'

'Battersea Park?'

'Across this bridge, then.'

'You were a darling to let me introduce them, but you did so look like a horse trying to back through its collar. I wanted to stroke your neck.'

'I've got out of the habit of people.'

'It's nice not to be dependent on them.'

'The worst mixer in the world. But you, I should have thought—'

'I only want you; I think I must have a nature like a dog's. Without you, now, I should just be lost.'

The twitch of his mouth was better than an answer.

'Ever seen the Lost Dogs' Home? It's over there.'

'No. Lost dogs are dreadful to think about. Perhaps one ought to, though. Yes, let's!'

The establishment had its usual hospitalised appearance of all being for the best considering that it was the worst. There was a certain amount of barking and of enquiry on the faces of a certain number of dogs. Tails wagged as they approached. Such dogs as were of any breed looked quieter and sadder than the dogs that were of no breed, and those in the majority. A black spaniel was sitting in a corner of the wired enclosure, with head drooped between long ears. They went round to him.

'How on earth,' said Dinny, 'can a dog as nice as that stay unclaimed? He *is* sad!'

Wilfrid put his fingers through the wire. The dog looked up. They saw a little red under his eyes, and a wisp of hair loose and silky on his forehead. He raised himself slowly from off his haunches, and they could see him pant very slightly as though some calculation or struggle were going on in him.

'Come on, old boy!'

The dog came slowly, all black, foursquare on his feathered legs. He had every sign of breeding, making his forlorn position more mysterious than ever. He stood almost within reach; his shortened tail fluttered feebly, then came to a droop again, precisely as if he had said: 'I neglect no chance, but you are not.'

'Well, old fellow?' said Wilfrid.

Dinny bent down. 'Give me a kiss.'

The dog looked up at them. His tail moved once, and again drooped.

'Not a good mixer, either,' said Wilfrid.

'He's too sad for words.' She bent lower and this time got her hand through the wire.

'Come, darling!' The dog sniffed her glove. Again his tail fluttered feebly; a pink tongue showed for a moment as though to make certain of his lips. With a supreme effort Dinny's fingers reached his muzzle smooth as silk.

'He's awfully well bred, Wilfrid.'

'Stolen, I expect, and then got away. Probably from some country kennel.'

'I believe I could hang dog-thieves.'

The dog's dark-brown eyes had the remains of moisture in their corners. They looked back at Dinny, with suspended animation, as if saying: 'You are not my past, and I don't know if there is a future.'

She looked up. 'Oh, Wilfrid!'

He nodded and left her with the dog. She stayed stooped on her heels, slowly scratching behind the dog's ears, till Wilfrid, followed by a man with a chain and collar, came back.

'I've got him,' he said; 'he reached his time-limit yesterday, but they were keeping him another week because of his looks.'

Dinny turned her back, moisture was oozing from her eyes. She mopped them hastily, and heard the man say:

'I'll put this on, sir, before he comes out, or he might leg it; he's never taken to the place.'

Dinny turned round.

'If his owner turns up we'll give him back at once.'

'Not much chance of that, miss. In my opinion that's the dog of someone who's died. He slipped his collar, probably, and went out to find him, got lost, and no one's cared enough to send here and see. Nice dog, too. You've got a bargain. I'm glad. I didn't like to think of that dog being put away; young dog, too.'

He put the collar on, led the dog out to them, and transferred the chain to Wilfrid, who handed him a card.

'In case the owner turns up. Come on, Dinny; let's walk him a bit. Walk, boy!'

The nameless dog, hearing the sweetest word in his vocabulary, moved forward to the limit of the chain.

'That theory's probably right,' said Wilfrid, 'and I hope it is. We shall like this fellow.'

Once on grass they tried to get through to the dog's inner consciousness. He received their attentions patiently, without response, tail and eyes lowered, suspending judgment.

'We'd better get him home,' said Wilfrid. 'Stay here, and I'll bring up a cab.'

He wiped a chair with his handkerchief, transferred the chain to her, and swung away.

Dinny sat watching the dog. He had followed Wilfrid to the limit of the chain and then seated himself in the attitude in which they had first seen him.

What did dogs feel? They certainly put one and one together; loved, disliked, suffered, yearned, sulked, and enjoyed, like human beings; but they had a very small vocabulary and so – no ideas! Still, anything must be better than living in a wire enclosure with a lot of dogs less sensitive than yourself!

The dog came back to her side, but kept his head turned in the direction Wilfrid had taken, and began to whine.

A taxi cab drew up. The dog stopped whining, and began to pant.

'Master's coming!' The dog gave a tug at the chain.

Wilfrid had reached him. Through the slackened chain she could feel the disillusionment; then it tightened, and the wagging of the tail came fluttering down the links as the dog sniffed at the turn-ups of Wilfrid's trousers.

In the cab the dog sat on the floor with his chin hanging over Wilfrid's shoe. In Piccadilly he grew restless and ended with his chin on Dinny's knee. Between Wilfrid and the dog the drive was an emotional medley for her, and she took a deep breath when she got out.

'Wonder what Stack will say,' said Wilfrid. 'A spaniel in Cork Street is no catch.'

The dog took the stairs with composure.

'House-trained,' said Dinny thankfully.

In the sitting room the dog applied his nose to the carpet. Having decided that the legs of all the furniture were uninteresting and the place bereft of his own kind, he leaned his nose on the divan and looked out of the corners of his eyes.

'Up!' said Dinny. The dog jumped on to the divan.

'Jove! He does smell!' said Wilfrid.

'Let's give him a bath. While you're filling it, I'll look him over.'

She held the dog, who would have followed Wilfrid, and began parting his hair. She found several yellow fleas, but no other breed.

'Yes, you do smell, darling.'

The dog turned his head and licked her nose.

'The bath's ready, Dinny!'

'Only dog fleas.'

'If you're going to help, put on that bath gown, or you'll spoil your dress.'

Behind his back, Dinny slipped off her frock and put on the blue bath gown, half hoping he would turn, and respecting him because he didn't. She rolled up the sleeves and stood beside him. Poised over the bath, the dog protruded a long tongue.

'He's not going to be sick, is he?'

'No; they always do that. Gently, Wilfrid, don't let him splash – that frightens them. Now!'

Lowered into the bath, the dog, after a scramble, stood still with his head drooped, concentrated on keeping foothold of the slippery surface.

'This is hair shampoo, better than nothing. I'll hold him. You do the rubbing in.'

Pouring some of the shampoo on the centre of that polished black back, Dinny heaped water up the dog's sides and began to rub. This first domestic incident with Wilfrid was pure joy, involving no mean personal contact with him as well as with the dog. She straightened up at last.

'Phew! My back! Sluice him and let the water out. I'll hold him.'

Wilfrid sluiced, the dog behaving as if not too sorry for his fleas. He shook himself vigorously, and they both jumped back.

'Don't let him out,' cried Dinny; 'we must dry him in the bath.'

'All right. Put your hands round his neck and hold him still.'

Wrapped in a huge bath towel, the dog lifted his face to her; its expression was drooping and forlorn.

'Poor boy, soon over now, and you'll smell lovely.'

The dog shook himself.

Wilfrid withdrew the towel. 'Hold him a minute, I'll get an old blanket; we'll make him curl up till he's dry.'

Alone with the dog, who was now trying to get out of the bath, Dinny held him with his forepaws over the edge, and worked away at the accumulations of sorrow about his eyes.

'There! That's better!'

They carried the almost inanimate dog to the divan, wrapped in an old Guards' blanket.

'What shall we call him, Dinny?'

'Let's try him with a few names, we may hit on his real one.'

He answered to none. 'Well,' said Dinny, 'let's call him "Foch". But for Foch we should never have met.'

Chapter Eighteen

Feelings at Condaford, after the General's return, were vexed and uneasy. Dinny had said she would be back on Saturday, but it was now Wednesday and she was still in London. Her saying, 'We are not formally engaged,' had given little comfort, since the General had added, 'That was soft sawder.' Pressed by Lady Cherrell as to what exactly had taken place between him and Wilfrid, he was laconic.

'He hardly said a word, Liz. Polite and all that, and I must say he doesn't look like a fellow who'd quit. His record's very good, too. The thing's inexplicable.'

'Have you read any of his verse, Con?'

'No. Where is it?'

'Dinny has them somewhere. Very bitter. So many writers seem to be like that. But I could put up with anything if I thought Dinny would be happy.'

'Dinny says he's actually going to publish a poem about that business. He must be a vain chap.'

'Poets almost always are.'

'I don't know who can move Dinny. Hubert says he's lost touch with her. To begin married life under a cloud like that!'

'I sometimes think,' murmured Lady Cherrell, 'that living here, as we do, we don't know what will cause clouds and what won't.'

'There can't be a question,' said the General, with finality, 'among people who count.'

'Who does count, nowadays?'

The General was silent. Then he said shrewdly:

'England's still aristocratic underneath. All that keeps us going comes from the top. Service and tradition still rule the roost. The socialists can talk as they like.'

Lady Cherrell looked up, astonished at this flow.

'Well,' she said, 'what are we to do about Dinny?'

The General shrugged.

'Wait till things come to a crisis of some sort. Cut-you-off-with-a-shilling is out of date and out of question – we're too fond of her. You'll speak to her, Liz, when you get a chance, of course . . .'

Between Hubert and Jean discussion of the matter took a rather different line.

'I wish to God, Jean, Dinny had taken to your brother.'

'Alan's got over it. I had a letter from him yesterday. He's at Singapore now. There's probably somebody out there. I only hope it isn't a married woman. There are so few girls in the East.'

'I don't think he'd go for a married woman. Possibly a native; they say Malay girls are often pretty.'

Jean grimaced.

'A Malay girl instead of Dinny!'

Presently she murmured: 'I'd like to see this Mr Desert. I think I could give him an idea, Hubert, of what'll be thought of him if he carries Dinny into this mess.'

'You must be careful with Dinny.'

'If I can have the car I'll go up tomorrow and talk it over with Fleur. She must know him quite well; he was their best man.'

'I'd choose Michael of the two; but for God's sake take care, old girl.'

Jean, who was accustomed to carry out her ideas, slid away next day before the world was up and was at South Square, Westminster, by ten o'clock. Michael, it appeared, was down in his constituency.

'The safer his seat,' said Fleur, 'the more he thinks he has to see of them. It's the gratitude complex. What can I do for you?'

Jean slid her long-lashed eyes round from the Fragonard, which she had been contemplating as though it were too French, and Fleur almost jumped. Really, she *was* like a 'leopardess'!

'It's about Dinny and her young man, Fleur. I suppose you know what happened to him out there?'

Fleur nodded.

'Then can't something be done?'

Fleur's face became watchful. She was twenty-nine, Jean twenty-three; but it was no use coming the elder matron!

'I haven't seen anything of Wilfrid for a long time.'

'Somebody's got to tell him pretty sharply what'll be thought of him if he lugs Dinny into this mess.'

'I'm by no means sure there'll be a mess; even if his poem comes out. People like the Ajax touch.'

'You've not been in the East.'

'Yes, I have; I've been round the world.'

'That's not the same thing at all.'

'My dear,' said Fleur, 'excuse my saying so, but the Cherrells are about thirty years behind the times.'

'I'm not a Cherrell.'

'No, you're a Tasburgh, and, if anything, that's a little worse. Country rectories, cavalry, navy, Indian civil – how much d'you suppose all that counts nowadays?'

'It counts with those who belong to it; and he belongs to it, and Dinny belongs to it.'

'No one who's really in love belongs anywhere,' said Fleur.

'Did you care two straws when you married Hubert with a murder charge hanging over his head?'

'That's different. He'd done nothing to be ashamed of.'

Fleur smiled.

'True to type. Would it surprise you, as they say in the courts, if I told you that there isn't one in twenty people about town who'd do otherwise than yawn if you asked them to condemn Wilfrid for what he did? And there isn't one in forty who won't forget all about it in a fortnight.'

'I don't believe you,' said Jean flatly.

'You don't know modern Society, my dear.'

'It's modern Society,' said Jean, even more flatly, 'that doesn't count.'

'Well, I don't know that it does much; but then what does?'

'Where does he live?'

Fleur laughed.

'In Cork Street, opposite the Gallery. You're not thinking of bearding him, are you?'

'I don't know.'

'Wilfrid can bite.'

'Well,' said Jean, 'thanks. I must be going.'

Fleur looked at her with admiration. The girl had flushed, and that pink in her brown cheeks made her look more vivid than ever.

'Well, good-bye, my dear; and do come and tell me about it. I know you've the pluck of the devil.'

'I don't know that I'm going at all,' said Jean. 'Good-bye!'

She drove, rather angry, past the House of Commons. Her temperament believed so much in action that Fleur's worldly wisdom had merely irritated her. Still, it was not so easy as she had thought to go to Wilfrid Desert and say: 'Stand and deliver me back my sister-in-law.' She drove, however, to Pall Mall, parked her car near the Parthenaeum, and walked up to Piccadilly. People who saw her, especially men, looked back, because of the admirable grace of her limbs and the colour and light in her face. She had no idea where Cork Street was, except that it was near Bond Street. And, when she reached it, she walked up and down before locating the Gallery. 'That must be the door, opposite,' she thought. She was standing uncertainly in front of a door without a name, when a man with a dog on a lead came up the stairs and stood beside her.

'Yes, miss?'

'I am Mrs Hubert Cherrell. Does Mr Desert live here?'

'Yes, ma'am; but whether you can see him I don't know. Here, Foch, good dog! If you'll wait a minute I'll find out.'

A minute later Jean, swallowing resolutely, was in the presence. 'After all,' she was thinking, 'he can't be worse than a parish meeting when you want money from it.'

Wilfrid was standing at the window, with his eyebrows raised.

'I'm Dinny's sister-in-law,' said Jean. 'I beg your pardon for coming, but I wanted to see you.'

Wilfrid bowed.

'Come here, Foch.'

The spaniel, who was sniffing round Jean's skirt, did not respond until he was called again. He licked Wilfrid's hand and sat down behind him. Jean had flushed.

'It's frightful cheek on my part, but I thought you wouldn't mind. We've just come back from the Soudan.'

Wilfrid's face remained ironic, and irony always upset her. Not quite stammering, she continued:

'Dinny has never been in the East.'

Again Wilfrid bowed. The affair was not going like a parish meeting.

'Won't you sit down?' he said.

'Oh, thank you, no; I shan't be a minute. You see, what I wanted to say was that Dinny can't possibly realise what certain things mean out there.'

'D'you know, that's what occurred to me.'

'Oh!'

A minute of silence followed, while the flush on her face and the smile on Wilfrid's deepened. Then he said:

'Thank you so much for coming. Anything else?'

'Er – no! Good-bye!'

All the way downstairs she felt shorter than she had ever felt in her life. And the first man she passed in the street jumped, her eyes had passed through him like a magnetic shock. He had once been touched by an electric eel in Brazil, and preferred the sensation. Yet, curiously, while she retraced her steps towards her car, though worsted, she bore no grudge. Even more singularly, she had lost most of her feeling that Dinny was in danger.

Regaining her car, she had a slight altercation with a policeman and took the road for Condaford. Driving to the danger of the public all the way, she was home to lunch. All she said of her adventure was that she had been for a long drive. Only in the four-poster of the chief spare room did she say to Hubert:

'I've been up and seen him. D'you know, Hubert, I really believe Dinny will be all right. He's got charm.'

'What on earth,' said Hubert, turning on his elbow, 'has that to do with it?'

'A lot,' said Jean. 'Give me a kiss, and don't argue . . .'

When his strange young visitor had gone, Wilfrid flung himself on the divan and stared at the ceiling. He felt like a general who has won a 'victory' – the more embarrassed. Having lived for thirty-five years, owing to a variety of circumstances, in a condition of marked egoism, he was unaccustomed to the feelings which Dinny from the first had roused within him. The old-fashioned word 'worship' was hardly admissible, but no other adequately replaced it. When with her his sensations were so restful and refreshed that when not with her he felt like one who had taken off his soul and hung it up. Alongside this new beatitude was a growing sense that his own happiness would not be complete unless hers was too. She was always telling him that she was only happy in his presence. But that was absurd, he could never replace all the interests and affections of her life before the statue of Foch had made them acquainted. And, if not, for what was he letting her in? The young woman with the eyes, who had just gone, had stood there before him like an incarnation of this question. Though he had routed her, she had left the query printed on the air.

The spaniel, seeing the incorporeal more clearly than his master, was resting a long nose on his knee. Even this dog he owed to Dinny. He had got out of the habit of people. With this business hanging over him, he was quite cut off. If he married Dinny, he took her with him into isolation. Was it fair?

But, having appointed to meet her in half an hour, he rang the bell.

'I'm going out now, Stack.'

'Very good, sir.'

Leading the dog, he made his way to the Park. Opposite the Cavalry Memorial he sat down to wait for her, debating whether he should tell her of his visitor. And just then he saw her coming.

She was walking quickly from Park Lane, and had not yet seen him. She seemed to skim, straight, and – as those blasted novelists called it – 'willowy'! She had a look of spring, and was smiling as if something pleasant had just happened to her. This glimpse of her, all unaware of him, soothed Wilfrid. If she could look so pleased and carefree, surely he need not worry. She halted by the bronze horse which she had dubbed 'the jibbing barrel', evidently looking for him. Though she turned her head so prettily this way and that, her face had become a little anxious. He stood up. She waved her hand and came quickly across the drive.

'Been sitting to Botticelli, Dinny?'

'No – to a pawnbroker. If you ever want one I recommend Frewens of South Molton Street.'

'*You*, at a pawnbroker's?'

'Yes, darling. I've got more money of my own on me than I ever had in my life.'

'What do you want it for?'

Dinny bent and stroked the dog.

'Since I knew you I've grasped the real importance of money.'

'And what's that?'

'Not to be divided from you by the absence of it. The great open spaces are what we want now. Take Foch off the lead, Wilfrid; he'll follow, I'm sure.'

Chapter Nineteen

In a centre of literature such as London, where books come out by the half-dozen almost every day, the advent of a slender volume of poems is commonly of little moment. But circumstances combined to make the appearance of *The Leopard, and other Poems* a 'literary event'. It was Wilfrid's first production for four years. He was a lonely figure, marked out by the rarity of literary talent among the old aristocracy, by the bitter, lively quality of his earlier poems, by his Eastern sojourn and isolation from literary circles, and finally by the report that he had embraced Islam. Someone, on the appearance of his third volume four years ago, had dubbed him 'a sucking Byron'; the phrase had caught the ear. Finally, he had a young publisher who understood the art of what he called 'putting it over'. During the few weeks since he received Wilfrid's manuscript, he had been engaged in lunching, dining, and telling people to look out for 'The Leopard', the most sensation-making poem since 'The Hound of Heaven'. To the query 'Why?' he replied in nods and becks and wreathed smiles. Was it true that young Desert had become a Mussulman? Oh! Yes. Was he in London? Oh! yes, but, of course, the shyest and rarest bird in the literary flock.

He who was Compson Grice Ltd had from the first perceived

that in 'The Leopard' he had 'a winner' – people would not enjoy it, but they would talk about it. He had only to start the snowball rolling down the slope, and when moved by real conviction no one could do this better than he. Three days before the book came out he met Telfourd Yule by a sort of accidental prescience.

'Hallo, Yule, back from Araby?'

'As you see.'

'I say, I've got a most amazing book of poems coming out on Monday. *The Leopard*, by Wilfrid Desert. Like a copy? The first poem's a corker.'

'Oh!'

'Takes the wind clean out of that poem in Alfred Lyall's *Verses written in India*, about the man who died sooner than change his faith. Remember?'

'I do.'

'What's the truth about Desert taking to Islam?'

'Ask him.'

'That poem's so personal in feeling – it might be about himself.'

'Indeed?'

And Compson Grice thought, suddenly: 'If it were! What a stunt!'

'Do you know him, Yule?'

'No.'

'You must read the thing; I couldn't put it down.'

'Ah!'

'But would a man publish such a thing about his own experience?'

'Can't say.'

And, still more suddenly, Compson Grice thought: 'If it were, I could sell a hundred thousand!'

He returned to his office, thinking: 'Yule was deuced close. I believe I was right, and he knows it. He's only just back;

everything's known in the bazaars, they say. Now, let's see, where am I?'

Published at five shillings, on a large sale there would, after royalty paid, be a clear profit of sixpence a copy. A hundred thousand copies would be two thousand five hundred pounds, and about the same in royalties to Desert! By George! But, of course, loyalty to client first! And there came to him one of those inspirations which so often come to loyal people who see money ahead of them.

'I must draw his attention to the risk of people saying that it's his own case. I'd better do it the day after publication. In the meantime I'll put a second big edition in hand.'

On the day before publication, a prominent critic, Mark Hanna, who ran a weekly bell in the *Carillon*, informed him that he had gone all out for the poem. A younger man, well known for a certain buccaneering spirit, said no word, but wrote a criticism. Both critiques appeared on the day of publication. Compson Grice cut them out and took them with him to the 'Jessamine' restaurant, where he had bidden Wilfrid to lunch.

They met at the entrance and passed to a little table at the far end. The room was crowded with people who knew everybody in the literary, dramatic and artistic world. And Compson Grice waited, with the experience of one who had entertained many authors, until a bottle of Mouton Rothschild 1870 had been drunk to its dregs. Then, producing from his pocket the two reviews, he placed that of Mark Hanna before his guest, with the words: 'Have you seen this? It's rather good.'

Wilfrid read it.

The reviewer had indeed gone 'all out'. It was almost all confined to 'The Leopard', which it praised as the most intimate revelation of the human soul in verse since Shelley.

'Bunk! Shelley doesn't reveal except in his lyrics.'

'Ah! well,' said Compson Grice, 'they have to work in Shelley.'

The review acclaimed the poem as 'tearing away the last shreds of the hypocritical veil which throughout our literature has shrouded the muse in relation to religion'. It concluded with these words: 'This poem, indeed, in its unflinching record of a soul tortured by cruel dilemma, is the most amazing piece of imaginative psychology which has come our way in the twentieth century.'

Watching his guest lay down the cutting, Compson Grice said softly:

'Pretty good! It's the personal fervour of the thing that gets them.'

Wilfrid gave his queer shiver.

'Got a cigar-cutter?'

Compson Grice pushed one forward with the other review.

'I think you ought to read this in *The Daily Phase*.'

The review was headed: 'Defiance: Bolshevism and the Empire.'

Wilfrid took it up.

'Geoffrey Coltham?' he said. 'Who's he?'

The review began with some fairly accurate personal details of the poet's antecedents, early work and life, ending with the mention of his conversion to Islam. Then, after some favourable remarks about the other poems, it fastened on 'The Leopard', sprang, as it were, at the creature's throat, and shook it as a bulldog might. Then, quoting these lines:

> Into foul ditch each dogma leads.
> Cursed be superstitious creeds,
> In every driven mind the weeds!
> There's but one liquor for the sane—
> Drink deep! Let scepticism reign
> And its astringence clear the brain!

it went on with calculated brutality:

> The thin disguise assumed by the narrative covers a personal disruptive bitterness which one is tempted to connect with the wounded and overweening pride of one who has failed himself and the British world. Whether Mr Desert intended in this poem to reveal his own experience and feelings in connection with his conversion to Islam – a faith, by the way, of which, judging from the poor and bitter lines quoted above, he is totally unworthy – we cannot of course say, but we advise him to come into the open and let us know. Since we have in our midst a poet who, with all his undoubted thrust, drives at our entrails, and cuts deep into our religion and our prestige, we have the right to know whether or not he – like his hero – is a renegade.

'That, I think,' said Compson Grice, quietly, 'is libellous.'

Wilfrid looked up at him, so that he said afterwards: 'I never knew Desert had such eyes.'

'I *am* a renegade. I took conversion at the pistol's point, and you can let everybody know it.'

Smothering the words: 'Thank God!' Compson Grice reached out his hand. But Wilfrid had leaned back and veiled his face in the smoke of his cigar. His publisher moved forward on to the edge of his chair.

'You mean that you want me to send a letter to *The Daily Phase* to say that "The Leopard" is practically your own experience?'

'Yes.'

'My dear fellow, I think it's wonderful of you. That is courage, if you like.'

The smile on Wilfrid's face caused Compson Grice to sit back, swallow the words: 'The effect on the sales will be enormous,' and substitute:

'It will strengthen your position enormously. But I wish we could get back on that fellow.'

'Let him stew!'

'Quite!' said Compson Grice. He was by no means anxious to be embroiled, and have all his authors slated in the important *Daily Phase*.

Wilfrid rose. 'Thanks very much. I must be going.'

Compson Grice watched him leave, his head high and his step slow. 'Poor devil!' he thought. 'It *is* a scoop!'

Back in his office, he spent some time finding a line in Coltham's review which he could isolate from its context and use as advertisement. He finally extracted this: '*Daily Phase*: "No poem in recent years has had such power"' (the remaining words of the sentence he omitted because they were 'to cut the ground from under the feet of all we stand for'). He then composed a letter to the editor. He was writing – he said – at the request of Mr Desert, who, far from needing any challenge to come into the open, was only too anxious that everyone should know that 'The Leopard' was indeed founded on his personal experience. For his own part – he went on – he considered that this frank avowal was a more striking instance of courage than could be met with in a long day's march. He was proud to have been privileged to publish a poem which, in psychological content, quality of workmanship, and direct human interest, was by far the most striking of this generation.

He signed himself 'Your obedient servant, Compson Grice'. He then increased the size of the order for the second edition, directed that the words 'First edition exhausted; second large impression', should be ready for use immediately, and went to his club to play bridge.

His club was the Polyglot, and in the hall he ran on Michael. The hair of his erstwhile colleague in the publishing world was ruffled, the ears stood out from his head, and he spoke at once:

'Grice, what are you doing about that young brute Coltham?'

Compson Grice smiled blandly and replied:

'Don't worry! I showed the review to Desert, and he told me to draw its sting by complete avowal.'

'Good God!'

'Why? Didn't you know?'

'Yes, I knew, but—'

These words were balm to the ears of Compson Grice, who had been visited by misgiving as to the truth of Wilfrid's admission. Would a man really publish that poem if it were his own case; could he really want it known? But this was conclusive: Mont had been Desert's discoverer and closest friend.

'So I've written to *The Phase* and dealt with it.'

'Did Wilfrid tell you to do that?'

'He did.'

'To publish that poem was crazy. "Quem deus—"' He suddenly caught sight of the expression on Compson Grice's face. 'Yes,' he added, bitterly, 'you think you've got a scoop!'

Compson Grice said coldly:

'Whether it will do us harm or good remains to be seen.'

'Bosh!' said Michael. 'Everybody will read the thing now, blast them! Have you seen Wilfrid today?'

'He lunched with me.'

'How's he looking?'

Tempted to say 'Like Asrael!' Compson Grice substituted: 'Oh! all right – quite calm.'

'Calm as hell! Look here, Grice! If you don't stand by him and help him all you can through this, I'll never speak to you again.'

'My dear fellow,' said Compson Grice, with some dignity, 'what do you suppose?' And, straightening his waistcoat, he passed into the card room.

Michael, muttering, 'Cold-blooded fish!' hurried in the direction of Cork Street. 'I wonder if the old chap would like to see me,' he thought.

But at the very mouth of the street he recoiled and made for Mount Street instead. He was informed that both his father and mother were out, but that Miss Dinny had come up that morning from Condaford.

'All right, Blore. If she's in I'll find her.'

He went up and opened the drawing-room door quietly. In the alcove, under the cage of her aunt's parakeet, Dinny was sitting perfectly still and upright, like a little girl at a lesson, with her hands crossed on her lap and her eyes fixed on space. She did not see him till his hand was on her shoulder.

'Penny!'

'How does one learn not to commit murder, Michael?'

'Ah! Poisonous young brute! Have your people seen *The Phase*?'

Dinny nodded.

'What was the reaction?'

'Silence, pinched lips.'

Michael nodded.

'Poor dear! So you came up?'

'Yes, I'm going to the theatre with Wilfrid.'

'Give him my love, and tell him that if he wants to see me I'll come at any moment. Oh! and, Dinny, try to make him feel that we admire him for spilling the milk.'

Dinny looked up, and he was moved by the expression on her face.

'It wasn't all pride that made him, Michael. There's something egging him on, and I'm afraid of it. Deep down he isn't sure that it wasn't just cowardice that made him renounce. I know he can't get that thought out of his mind. He feels he's got to prove, not to others so much as to himself, that he isn't a coward. Oh! I know he isn't. But so long as he hasn't proved it to himself and everybody, I don't know what he might do.'

Michael nodded. From his one interview with Wilfrid he had formed something of the same impression.

'Did you know that he's told his publisher to make a public admission?'

'Oh!' said Dinny blankly. 'What then?'

Michael shrugged.

'Michael, will anyone grasp the situation Wilfrid was in?'

'The imaginative type is rare. I don't pretend *I* can grasp it. Can you?'

'Only because it happened to Wilfrid.'

Michael gripped her arm.

'I'm glad you've got the old-fashioned complaint, Dinny, not just this modern "physiological urge".'

Chapter Twenty

While Dinny was dressing her aunt came to her room.

'Your uncle read me that article, Dinny. I wonder!'

'What do you wonder, Aunt Em?'

'I knew a Coltham – but he died.'

'This one will probably die, too.'

'Where do you get your boned bodies, Dinny? So restful.'

'Harridge's.'

'Your uncle says he ought to resign from his club.'

'Wilfrid doesn't care two straws about his club; he probably hasn't been in a dozen times. But I don't think he'll resign.'

'Better make him.'

'I should never dream of "making" him do anything.'

'So awkward when they use black balls.'

'Auntie, dear, could I come to the glass?'

Lady Mont crossed the room and took up the slim volume from the bedside table.

'*The Leopard*! But he did change them, Dinny.'

'He did not, Auntie; he had no spots to change.'

'Baptism and that.'

'If baptism really meant anything, it would be an outrage on children till they knew what it was about.'

'Dinny!'

'I mean it. One doesn't commit people to things entirely without their consent; it isn't decent. By the time Wilfrid could think at all he had no religion.'

'It wasn't the givin' up, then, it was the takin' on.'

'He knows that.'

'Well,' said Lady Mont, turning towards the door, 'I think it served that Arab right; so intrudin'! If you want a latch-key, ask Blore.'

Dinny finished dressing quickly and ran downstairs. Blore was in the dining room.

'Aunt Em says I may have a key, Blore, and I want a taxi, please.'

Having telephoned to the cab-stand and produced a key, the butler said: 'What with her ladyship speaking her thoughts out loud, miss, I'm obliged to know, and I was saying to Sir Lawrence this morning: "If Miss Dinny could take him off just now, on a tour of the Scotch Highlands where they don't see the papers, it would save a lot of vexation." In these days, miss, as you'll have noticed, one thing comes on the top of another, and people haven't the memories they had. You'll excuse my mentioning it.'

'Thank you ever so, Blore. Nothing I'd like better; only I'm afraid he wouldn't think it proper.'

'In these days a young *lady* can do anything, miss.'

'But men still have to be careful, Blore.'

'Well, miss, of course, relatives are difficult; but it could be arranged.'

'I think we shall have to face the music.'

The butler shook his head.

'In my belief, whoever said that first is responsible for a lot of unnecessary unpleasantness. Here's your taxi, miss.'

In the taxi she sat a little forward, getting the air from both windows on her cheeks, which needed cooling. Even the anger and vexation left by that review were lost in this sweeter effervescence. At the corner of Piccadilly she read a newspaper poster:

'Derby horses arrive.' The Derby tomorrow! How utterly she had lost count of events! The restaurant chosen for their dinner was Blafard's in Soho, and her progress was impeded by the traffic of a town on the verge of national holiday. At the door, with the spaniel held on a leash, stood Stack. He handed her a note: 'Mr Desert sent me with this, miss. I brought the dog for a walk.'

Dinny opened the note with a sensation of physical sickness.

DINNY DARLING,

Forgive my failing you tonight. I've been in a torture of doubt all day. The fact is, until I know where I stand with the world over this business, I have an overwhelming feeling that I must not commit you to anything; and a public jaunt like this is just what I ought to avoid for you. I suppose you saw *The Daily Phase* – that is the beginning of the racket. I must go through this next week on my own, and measure up where I am. I won't run off, and we can write. You'll understand. The dog is a boon, and I owe him to you. Good-bye for a little, my dear love.

Your devoted

W.D.

It was all she could do not to put her hand on her heart under the driver's eyes. Thus to be shut away in the heat of the battle was what, she knew now, she had been dreading all along. With an effort she controlled her lips, said 'Wait a minute!' and turned to Stack.

'I'll take you and Foch back.'

'Thank you, miss.'

She bent down to the dog. Panic was at work within her breast! The dog! He was a link between them!

'Put him into the cab, Stack.'

On the way she said quietly:

'Is Mr Desert in?'

'No, miss, he went out when he gave me the note.'

'Is he all right?'

'A little worried, I think, miss. I must say I'd like to teach manners to that gentleman in *The Daily Phase*.'

'Oh! you saw that?'

'I did; it oughtn't to be allowed is what I say.'

'Free speech,' said Dinny. And the dog pressed his chin against her knee. 'Is Foch good?'

'No trouble at all, miss. A gentleman, that dog; aren't you, boy?'

The dog continued to press his chin on Dinny's knee; and the feel of it was comforting.

When the cab stopped in Cork Street, she took a pencil from her bag, tore off the empty sheet of Wilfrid's note, and wrote:

DARLING,

As you will. But by these presents know: I am yours for ever and ever. Nothing can or shall divide me from you, unless you stop loving.

Your devoted

DINNY

You won't do that, will you? Oh! don't!

Licking what was left of the gum on the envelope, she put her half sheet in and held it till it stuck. Giving it to Stack, she kissed the dog's head and said to the driver: 'The Park end of Mount Street, please. Good-night, Stack!'

'Good-night, miss!'

The eyes and mouth of the motionless henchman seemed to her so full of understanding that she turned her face away. And that was the end of the jaunt she had been so looking forward to.

From the top of Mount Street she crossed into the Park and sat on the seat where she had sat with him before, oblivious of the fact that she was unattached, without a hat, in evening dress, and that it was past eight o'clock. She sat with the collar of her cloak turned up to her chestnut-coloured hair, trying to see his point of view. She saw it very well. Pride! She had enough herself to understand. Not to involve others in one's troubles was elementary. The fonder one was, the less would one wish to involve them. Curiously ironical how love divided people just when they most needed each other! And no way out, so far as she could see. The strains of the Guards' band began to reach her faintly. They were playing – *Faust*? – no – *Carmen*! Wilfrid's favourite opera! She got up and walked over the grass towards the sound. What crowds of people! She took a chair some way off and sat down again, close to some rhododendrons. The Habanera! What a shiver its first notes always gave one! How wild, sudden, strange and inescapable was love! '*L'amour est enfant de Bohème*' . . . ! The rhododendrons were late this year. That deep rosy one! They had it at Condaford . . . Where was he – oh! where was he at this moment? Why could not love pierce veils, so that in spirit she might walk beside him, slip a hand into his! A spirit hand was better than nothing! And Dinny suddenly realised loneliness as only true lovers do when they think of life without the loved one. As flowers wilt on their stalks, so would she wilt – if she were cut away from him. 'See things through alone!' How long would he want to? For ever? At the thought she started up; and a stroller, who thought the movement meant for him, stood still and looked at her. Her face corrected his impression, and he moved on. She had two hours to kill before she could go in; she could not let them know that her evening had come to grief. The band was finishing off *Carmen* with the Toreador's song. A blot on the opera, its most popular tune! No, not a blot, for it was meant, of course, to blare above the desolation of that tragic end, as the world blared around the passion of lovers. The world was a heedless and a heartless stage for lives to strut across, or in dark corners join and cling together . . . How odd that clapping sounded in the open! She looked at her wrist watch. Half-past nine! An hour yet before it would be really dark. But there was a coolness now, a scent of grass and leaves; the rhododendrons were slowly losing colour, the birds had finished with song. People passed and passed her; she saw nothing funny about them, and they seemed to see nothing funny about her. And Dinny thought: 'Nothing seems funny any more, and I haven't had any dinner.' A coffee stall? Too early, perhaps, but there must be places where she could still get something! No dinner, almost no lunch, no tea – a condition appropriate to the love-sick! She began to move towards Knightsbridge, walking fast, by instinct rather than experience, for this was the first time she had ever wandered alone about London at such an hour. Reaching the gate without adventure, she crossed and went down Sloane Street. She felt much better moving, and chalked up in her mind the thought: 'For love-sickness, walking!' In this straight street there was practically nobody to notice her. The carefully closed and blinded houses seemed to confirm, each with its tall formal narrow face, the indifference of the regimented world to the longings of street-walkers such as she. At the corner of the King's Road a woman was standing.

'Could you tell me,' said Dinny, 'of any place close by where I could get something to eat?'

The woman addressed, she now saw, had a short face with high cheek-bones on which, and round the eyes, was a good deal of make-up. Her lips were good-natured, a little thick; her nose, too, rather thick; her eyes had the look which comes of having to be now stony and now luring, as if they had lost touch with her soul. Her dress was dark and fitted her curves, and she wore a large string of artificial pearls. Dinny could not help thinking she had seen people in Society not unlike her.

'There's a nice little place on the left.'

'Would you care to come and have something with me?' said Dinny, moved by impulse, or by something hungry in the woman's face.

'Why! I would,' said the woman. 'Fact is, I came out without anything. It's nice to have company, too.' She turned up the King's Road and Dinny turned alongside. It passed through her mind that if she met someone it would be quaint; but for all that she felt better.

'For God's sake,' she thought, 'be natural!'

The woman led her into a little restaurant, or rather public-house, for it had a bar. There was no one in the eating room, which had a separate entrance, and they sat down at a small table with a cruet-stand, a handbell, a bottle of Worcester sauce, and in a vase some failing pyrethrums which had never been fresh. There was a slight smell of vinegar.

'I *could* do with a cigarette,' said the woman.

Dinny had none. She tinkled the bell.

'Any particular sort?'

'Oh! Gaspers.'

A waitress appeared, looked at the woman, looked at Dinny, and said: 'Yes?'

'A packet of Players, please. A large coffee for me, strong

and fresh, and some cake or buns, or anything. What will you have?'

The woman looked at Dinny, as though measuring her capacity, looked at the waitress, and said, hesitating: 'Well, to tell the truth, I'm hungry. Cold beef and a bottle of stout?'

'Vegetables?' said Dinny: 'A salad?'

'Well, a salad, thank you.'

'Good! And pickled walnuts? Will you get it all as quickly as you can, please?'

The waitress passed her tongue over her lips, nodded, and went away.

'I say,' said the woman, suddenly, 'it's awful nice of you, you know.'

'It was so friendly of you to come. I should have felt a bit lost without you.'

'*She* can't make it out,' said the woman, nodding her head towards the vanished waitress. 'To tell you the truth, nor can I.'

'Why? We're both hungry.'

'No doubt about that,' said the woman; 'you're going to see me eat. I'm glad you ordered pickled walnuts, I never can resist a pickled onion, and it don't do.'

'I might have thought of cocktails,' murmured Dinny, 'but perhaps they don't make them here.'

'A sherry wouldn't be amiss. I'll get 'em.' The woman rose and disappeared into the bar.

Dinny took the chance to powder her nose. She also dived her hand down to the pocket in her 'boned body' where the spoils of South Molton Street were stored, and extracted a five-pound note. She was feeling a sort of sad excitement.

The woman came back with two glasses. 'I told 'em to charge it to our bill. The liquor's good here.'

Dinny raised her glass and sipped. The woman tossed hers off at a draught.

'I wanted that. Fancy a country where you couldn't get a drink!'

'But they can, of course, and do.'

'You bet. But they say some of the liquor's awful.'

Dinny saw that her gaze was travelling up and down her cloak and dress and face with insatiable curiosity.

'Pardon me,' said the woman, suddenly: 'You got a date?'

'No, I'm going home after this.'

The woman sighed. 'Wish she'd bring those bl-inkin' cigarettes.'

The waitress reappeared with a bottle of stout and the cigarettes. Staring at Dinny's hair, she opened the bottle.

'Coo!' said the woman, taking a long draw at her 'Gasper', 'I wanted that.'

'I'll bring you the other things in a minute,' said the waitress.

'I haven't seen you on the stage, have I?' said the woman.

'No, I'm not on the stage.'

The advent of food broke the ensuing hush. The coffee was better than Dinny had hoped and very hot. She had drunk most of it and eaten a large piece of plum cake before the woman, putting a pickled walnut in her mouth, spoke again.

'D'you live in London?'

'No. In Oxfordshire.'

'Well, I like the country, too; but I never see it now. I was brought up near Maidstone – pretty round there.' She heaved a sigh with a flavouring of stout. 'They say the Communists in Russia have done away with vice – isn't that a scream? An American journalist told me. Well! I never knew a budget make such a difference before,' she continued, expelling smoke as if liberating her soul: 'Dreadful lot of unemployment.'

'It does seem to affect everybody.'

'Affects me, I know,' and she stared stonily. 'I suppose you're shocked at that.'

'It takes a lot to shock people nowadays, don't you find?'

'Well, I don't mix as a rule with bishops.'

Dinny laughed.

'All the same,' said the woman, defiantly, 'I came across a parson who talked the best sense to me I ever heard; of course, I couldn't follow it.'

'I'll make you a bet,' said Dinny, 'that I know his name. Cherrell?'

'In once,' said the woman, and her eyes grew round.

'He's my uncle.'

'Coo! Well, well! It's a funny world! And not so large. Nice man he was,' she added.

'Still is.'

'One of the best.'

Dinny, who had been waiting for those inevitable words, thought: 'This is where they used to do the "My erring sister" stunt.'

The woman uttered a sigh of repletion.

'I've enjoyed that,' she said, and rose. 'Thank you ever so. I must be getting on now, or I'll be late for business.'

Dinny tinkled the bell. The waitress appeared with suspicious promptitude.

'The bill, please, and can you get me *that* changed?'

The waitress took the note with a certain caution.

'I'll just go and fix myself,' said the woman; 'see you in a minute.' She passed through a door.

Dinny drank up the remains of her coffee. She was trying to realise what it must be like to live like that. The waitress came back with the change, received her tip, said 'Thank you, miss,' and went. Dinny resumed the process of realisation.

'Well,' said the woman's voice behind her, 'I don't suppose I'll ever see you again. But I'd like to say I think you're a jolly good sort.'

Dinny looked up at her.

'When you said you'd come out without anything, did you mean you hadn't anything to come out with?'

'Sure thing,' said the woman.

'Then would you mind taking this change? It's horrid to have no money in London.'

The woman bit her lips, and Dinny could see that they were trembling.

'I wouldn't like to take your money,' she said, 'after you've been so kind.'

'Oh! bosh! Please!' And, catching her hand, she pressed the money into it. To her horror, the woman uttered a loud sniff. She was preparing to make a run for the door, when the woman said:

'D'you know what I'm going to do? I'm going home to have a sleep. My God, I am! I'm going home to have a sleep.'

Dinny hurried back to Sloane Street. Walking past the tall blinded houses, she recognised with gratitude that her love-sickness was much better. If she did not walk too fast, she would not be too soon at Mount Street. It was dark now, and in spite of the haze of city light the sky was alive with stars. She did not enter the Park again, but walked along its outside railings. It seemed an immense time since she had parted from Stack and the dog in Cork Street. Traffic was thickening as she rounded into Park Lane. Tomorrow all these vehicles would be draining out to Epsom Downs; the Town would be seeming almost empty. And, with a sickening sensation, it flashed on her how empty it would always feel without Wilfrid to see or look forward to.

She came to the gate by the 'jibbing barrel', and suddenly, as though all that evening had been a dream, she saw Wilfrid standing beside it. She choked and ran forward. He put out his arms and caught her to him.

The moment could hardly be prolonged, for cars and pedestrians were passing in and out; so arm-in-arm they moved towards Mount Street. Dinny just clung to him, and he seemed equally wordless; but the thought that he had come there to be near her was infinitely comforting.

They escorted each other back and forth past the house, like some footman and housemaid for a quarter of an hour off duty. Class and country, custom and creed, all were forgotten. And, perhaps, no two people in all its seven millions were in those few minutes more moved and at one in the whole of London.

At last the comic instinct woke.

'We can't see each other home all night, darling. So one kiss – and yet – one kiss – and yet – one kiss!'

She ran up the steps, and turned the key.

Chapter Twenty-one

Wilfrid's mood when he left his publisher at 'The Jessamine' was angry and confused. Without penetrating to the depths of Compson Grice's mental anatomy, he felt that he had been manipulated; and the whole of that restless afternoon he wandered, swung between relief at having burnt his boats and resentment at the irrevocable. Thus preoccupied, he did not really feel the shock his note would be to Dinny, and only when, returning to his rooms, he received her answer did his heart go out to her, and with it himself to where she had fortuitously found him. In the few minutes while they paraded Mount Street, silent and half-embraced, she had managed to pass into him her feeling that it was not one but two against the world. Why keep away and make her more unhappy than he need? And he sent her a note by Stack next morning asking her to go 'joy-riding'. He had forgotten the Derby, and their car was involved almost at once in a stream of vehicles.

'I've never seen the Derby,' said Dinny. 'Could we go?'

There was the more reason why they should go because there seemed to be no reasonable chance of not going.

Dinny was astonished at the general sobriety. No drinking and no streamers, no donkey-carts, false noses, badinage. Not a four-in-hand visible, not a coster nor a Kate; nothing but a wedged and moving stream of motor buses and cars mostly shut.

When, at last, they had 'parked' on the Downs, eaten their sandwiches and moved into the crowd, they turned instinctively toward the chance of seeing a horse.

Frith's 'Derby Day' seemed no longer true, if it ever was. In that picture people seemed to have lives and to be living them; in this crowd everybody seemed trying to get somewhere else.

In the paddock, which at first sight still seemed all people and no horses, Wilfrid said suddenly:

'This is foolish, Dinny; we're certain to be seen.'

'And if we are? Look, there's a horse!'

Quite a number of horses, indeed, were being led round in a ring. Dinny moved quickly towards them.

'They all look beautiful to me,' she said in a hushed voice, 'and just as good one as the other – except this one; I don't like his back.'

Wilfrid consulted his card. 'That's the favourite.'

'I still don't. D'you see what I mean? It comes to a point too near the tail, and then droops.'

'I agree, but horses run in all shapes.'

'I'll back the horse you fancy, Wilfrid.'

'Give me time, then.'

The people to her left and right kept on saying the horses' names as they passed. She had a place on the rail with Wilfrid standing close behind her.

'He's a pig of a horse,' said a man on her left, 'I'll never back the brute again.'

She took a glance at the speaker. He was broad and about five feet six, with a roll of fat on his neck, a bowler hat, and a cigar in his mouth. The horse's fate seemed to her the less dreadful.

A lady sitting on a shooting-stick to her right said:

'They ought to clear the course for the horses going out. That lost me my money two years ago.'

Wilfrid's hand rested on her shoulder.

'I like that one,' he said, 'Blenheim. Let's go and put our money on.'

They went to where people were standing in little queues before a row of what looked like pigeon-holes.

'Stand here,' he said. 'I'll lay my egg and come back to you.'

Dinny stood watching.

'How d'you do, Miss Cherrell?' A tall man in a grey top hat, with a very long case of field-glasses slung round him, had halted before her. 'We met at the Foch statue and your sister's wedding – remember?'

'Oh! yes. Mr Muskham.' Her heart was hurrying, and she restrained herself from looking towards Wilfrid.

'Any news of your sister?'

'Yes, we heard from Egypt. They must have had it terribly hot in the Red Sea.'

'Have you backed anything?'

'Not yet.'

'I shouldn't touch the favourite – he won't stay.'

'We thought of Blenheim.'

'Well, nice horse, and handy for the turns. But there's one more fancied in his stable. I take it you're a neophyte. I'll give you two tips, Miss Cherrell. Look for one or both of two things in a horse: leverage behind, and personality – not looks, just personality.'

'Leverage behind? Do you mean higher behind than in front?'

Jack Muskham smiled. 'That's about it. If you see that in a horse, especially where it has to come up a hill, back it.'

'But personality? Do you mean putting his head up and looking over the tops of people into the distance? I saw one horse do that.'

'By Jove, I should like you as a pupil! That's just about what I do mean.'

'But I don't know which horse it was,' said Dinny.

'That's awkward.' And then she saw the interested benevolence on his face stiffen. He lifted his hat and turned away. Wilfrid's voice behind her said:

'Well, you've got a tenner on.'

'Let's go to the Stand and see the race.' He did not seem to have seen Muskham; and, with his hand within her arm, she tried to forget the sudden stiffening of Jack Muskham's face. The crowd's multiple entreaty that she should have her 'fortune told' did its best to distract her, and she arrived at the Stand in a mood of indifference to all but Wilfrid and the horses. They found standing room close to the bookmakers near the rails.

'Green and chocolate – I can remember that. Pistache is my favourite chocolate filling. What shall I win if I do win, darling?'

'Listen!'

They isolated the words 'Eighteen to one Blenheim!'

'A hundred and eighty!' said Dinny. 'Splendid!'

'Well, it means that he's not fancied by the stable; they've got another running. Here they come! Two with chocolate and green. The second of them is ours.'

The parade, enchanting to all except the horses, gave her the chance to see the brown horse they had backed adorning its perched rider.

'How d'you like him, Dinny?'

'I love them nearly all. How can people tell which is the best by looking at them?'

'They can't.'

The horses were turning now and cantering past the Stand.

'Would you say Blenheim is higher behind than in front?' murmured Dinny.

'No. Very nice action. Why?'

But she only pressed his arm and gave a little shiver.

Neither of them having glasses, all was obscure to them when the race began. A man just behind kept saying: 'The favourite's leadin'! The favourite's leadin'!'

As the horses came round Tattenham Corner, the same man burbled: 'The Pasha – the Pasha'll win – no, the favourite – the favourite wins! – no, he don't – Iliad – Iliad wins.'

Dinny felt Wilfrid's hand grip her arm.

'Ours,' he said, 'on this side – look!'

Dinny saw a horse on the far side in pink and brown, and nearer her the chocolate and green. It was ahead, it was ahead! They had won!

Amidst the silence and discomfiture those two stood smiling at each other. It seemed an omen!

'I'll draw your money, and we'll go to the car and be off.'

He insisted on her taking all the money, and she ensconced it with her other wealth – so much more insurance against any sudden decision to deprive her of himself.

They drove again into Richmond Park on the way home, and sat a long time among the young bracken, listening to the cuckoos, very happy in the sunny, peaceful, whispering afternoon.

They dined together in a Kensington restaurant, and he left her finally at the top of Mount Street.

That night she slept unvisited by doubts or dreams, and went down to breakfast with clear eyes and a flush of sunburn on her cheeks. Her uncle was reading *The Daily Phase*. He put it down and said:

'When you've had your coffee, Dinny, you might glance at this. There is something about publishers,' he added, 'which makes one doubt sometimes whether they are men and brothers. And there is something about editors which makes it certain sometimes that they are not.'

Dinny read Compson Grice's letter, printed under the headlines:

MR DESERT'S APOSTASY.
OUR CHALLENGE TAKEN UP.
A CONFESSION.

Two stanzas from Sir Alfred Lyall's poem *Theology in Extremis* followed:

> Why? Am I bidding for glory's roll?
> I shall be murdered and clean forgot;
> Is it a bargain to save my soul?
> God, whom I trust in, bargains not.
> Yet for the honour of English race
> May I not live or endure disgrace . . .
>
> I must be gone to the crowd untold
> Of men by the Cause which they served
> unknown,
> Who moulder in myriad graves of old;
> Never a story and never a stone
> Tells of the martyrs who die like me,
> Just for the pride of the old countree.

And the pink of sunburn gave way to a flood of crimson.

'Yes,' murmured Sir Lawrence, watching her, '"the fat is in the fire", as old Forsyte would have said. Still, I was talking to a man last night who thought that nowadays nothing makes an indelible mark. Cheating at cards, boning necklaces – you go abroad for two years and it's all forgotten. As for sex abnormality, according to him it's no longer abnormal. So we must cheer up!'

Dinny said passionately: 'What I resent is that any worm will have the power to say what he pleases.'

Sir Lawrence nodded: 'The greater the worm, the greater the power. But it's not the worms we need bother about; it's the people with "pride of English race", and there are still a few about.'

'Uncle, is there any way in which Wilfrid can show publicly that he's not a coward?'

'He did well in the war.'

'Who remembers the war?'

'Perhaps,' muttered Sir Lawrence, 'we could throw a bomb at his car in Piccadilly, so that he could look at it over the side and light a cigarette. I can't think of anything more helpful.'

'I saw Mr Muskham yesterday.'

'Then you were at the Derby?' He took a very little cigar from his pocket. 'Jack takes the view that you are being victimised.'

'Oh! Why can't people leave one alone?'

'Attractive nymphs are never left alone. Jack's a misogynist.'

Dinny gave a little desperate laugh.

'I suppose one's troubles *are* funny.'

She got up and went to the window. It seemed to her that all the world was barking, like dogs at a cornered cat, and yet there was nothing in Mount Street but a van from the Express Dairy.

Chapter Twenty-two

Jack Muskham occupied a bedroom at Burton's Club when racing kept him overnight in town. Having read an account of the Derby in *The Daily Phase*, he turned the paper idly. The other features in 'that rag' were commonly of little interest to him. Its editing shocked his formalism, its news jarred his taste, its politics offended him by being so like his own. But his perusal was not perfunctory enough to prevent him from seeing the headline 'Mr Desert's Apostasy'. Reading the half column that followed it, he pushed the paper away and said: 'That fellow must be stopped.'

Glorying in his yellow streak, was he, and taking that nice girl with him to Coventry! Hadn't even the decency to avoid being seen with her in public on the very day when he was confessing himself as yellow as that rag!

In an age when tolerations and condonations seemed almost a disease, Jack Muskham knew and registered his own mind. He had disliked young Desert at first sight. The fellow's name suited him! And to think that this nice girl, who, without any training, had made those shrewd remarks about the racehorse, was to have her life ruined by this yellow-livered young braggart! It was too much! If it hadn't been for Lawrence, indeed, he would have done something about it before now. But there his mind stammered. What? . . . Here was the fellow publicly confessing his disgrace! An old dodge, that – taking the sting out of criticism! Making a virtue of necessity! Parading his desertion! That cock shouldn't fight, if he had his way! But once more his mind stammered . . . No outsider could interfere. And yet, unless there were some outward and visible sign condemning the fellow's conduct, it would look as if nobody cared.

'By George!' he thought. 'This Club, at least, can sit up and take notice. We don't want rats in Burton's!'

He brought the matter up in Committee meeting that very afternoon, and was astonished almost to consternation by the apathy with which it was received. Of the seven members present – 'the Squire', Wilfrid Bentworth, being in the Chair – four seemed to think it was a matter between young Desert and his conscience, and, besides, it looked like being a newspaper stunt. Times had changed since Lyall wrote that poem. One member went so far as to say he didn't want to be bothered, he hadn't read *The Leopard*, he didn't know Desert, and he hated *The Daily Phase*.

'So do I,' said Jack Muskham, 'but here's the poem.' He had sent out for it and spent an hour after lunch reading it. 'Let me read you a bit. It's poisonous.'

'For heaven's sake no, Jack!'

The fifth member, who had so far said nothing, supposed that if Muskham pressed it they must all read the thing.

'I do press it.'

'The Squire', hitherto square and silent, remarked: 'The secretary will get copies and send them round to the Committee. Better send them, too, a copy of today's *Daily Phase*. We'll discuss it at the meeting next Friday. Now about this claret?' And they moved to consideration of important matters.

It has been noticed that when a newspaper of a
type lights on an incident which enables it at onc
virtue and beat the drum of its own policy, it

incident, within the limits of the law of libel, without regard to the susceptibilities of individuals. Secured by the confession in Compson Grice's letter, *The Daily Phase* made the most of its opportunity, and in the eight days intervening before the next Committee meeting gave the Committeemen little chance of professing ignorance or indifference. Everybody, indeed, was reading and talking about *The Leopard* and, on the morning of the adjourned meeting, *The Daily Phase* had a long allusive column on the extreme importance of British behaviour in the East. It had also a large-type advertisement. '*The Leopard and other Poems*, by Wilfrid Desert: published by Compson Grice: 40,000 copies sold: Third Large Impression ready.'

A debate on the ostracism of a fellow-being will bring almost any man to a Committee meeting; and the attendance included some never before known to come.

A motion had been framed by Jack Muskham.

'That the Honourable Wilfrid Desert be requested, under Rule 23, to resign his membership of Burton's Club, because of conduct unbecoming to a member.'

He opened the discussion in these words:

'You've all had copies of Desert's poem 'The Leopard' and *The Daily Phase* of yesterday week. There's no doubt about the thing. Desert has publicly owned to having ratted from his religion at ... pistol's point, and I say he's no longer fit to be a ... f this Club. It was founded in memory of a ... who'd have dared Hell itself. We don't ... o don't act up to English traditions, and ... into the bargain.'

... ence, and then the fifth member of the ... us meeting remarked:

... n, all the same.'

... ho had once travelled in Turkey,

'Oughtn't he to have been asked to attend?'

'Why?' asked Jack Muskham. 'He can't say more than is said in that poem, or in that letter of his publisher's.'

The fourth member of the Committee at the previous meeting muttered: 'I don't like paying attention to *The Daily Phase*.'

'We can't help his having chosen that particular rag,' said Jack Muskham.

'Very distasteful,' continued the fourth member, 'diving into matters of conscience. Are we all prepared to say we wouldn't have done the same?'

There was a sound as of feet shuffling, and a wrinkled expert on the early civilisations of Ceylon murmured: 'To my mind, Desert is on the carpet – not for apostasy, but for the song he's made about it. Decency should have kept him quiet. Advertising his book! It's in a third edition, and everybody reading it. Making money out of it seems to me the limit.'

'I don't suppose,' said the fourth member, 'that he thought of that. It's the accident of the sensation.'

'He could have withdrawn the book.'

'Depends on his contract. Besides, that would look like running from the storm he's roused. As a matter of fact, I think it's rather fine to have made an open confession.'

'Theatrical!' murmured the K.C.

'If this,' said Jack Muskham, 'were one of the Service Clubs, they wouldn't think twice about it.'

An author of *Mexico Revisited* said drily:

'But it is not.'

'I don't know if you can judge poets like other people,' mused the fifth member.

'In matters of ordinary conduct,' said the expert on the civilisation of Ceylon, 'why not?'

A little man at the end of the table opposite the Chairman

remarked, '*The D-D-Daily Ph-Phase*,' as if releasing a small spasm of wind.

'Everybody's talking about the thing,' said the K.C.

'My young people,' put in a man who had not yet spoken, 'scoff. They say: "What does it matter what he did?" They talk about hypocrisy, laugh at Lyall's poem, and say it's good for the Empire to have some wind let out of it.'

'Exactly!' said Jack Muskham: 'That's the modern jargon. All standards gone by the board. Are we going to stand for that?'

'Anybody here know young Desert?' asked the fifth member.

'To nod to,' replied Jack Muskham.

Nobody else acknowledged acquaintanceship.

A very dark man with deep lively eyes said suddenly:

'All I can say is I trust the story has not got about in Afghanistan; I'm going there next month.'

'Why?' said the fourth member.

'Merely because it will add to the contempt with which I shall be regarded, anyway.'

Coming from a well-known traveller, this remark made more impression than anything said so far. Two members, who, with the Chairman, had not yet spoken, said simultaneously: 'Quite!'

'I don't like condemning a man unheard,' said the K.C.

'What about that, "Squire"?' asked the fourth member.

The Chairman, who was smoking a pipe, took it from his mouth.

'Anybody anything more to say?'

'Yes,' said the author of *Mexico Revisited*, 'let's put it on his conduct in publishing that poem.'

'You can't,' growled Jack Muskham; 'the whole thing's of a piece. The point is simply: Is he fit to be a member here or not? I ask the Chairman to put that to the meeting.'

But 'The Squire' continued to smoke his pipe. His experience of Committees told him that the time was not yet. Separate or 'knot' discussions would now set in. They led nowhere, of course, but ministered to a general sense that the subject was having justice done to it.

Jack Muskham sat silent, his long face impassive and his long legs stretched out. The discussion continued.

'Well?' said the member who had revisited Mexico, at last.

'The Squire' tapped out his pipe.

'I think,' he said, 'that Mr Desert should be asked to give us his reasons for publishing that poem.'

'Hear, hear!' said the K.C.

'Quite!' said the two members who had said it before.

'I agree,' said the authority on Ceylon.

'Anybody against that?' said 'The Squire'.

'I don't see the use of it,' muttered Jack Muskham. 'He ratted, and he's confessed it.'

No one else objecting, 'The Squire' continued:

'The Secretary will ask him to see us and explain. There's no other business, gentlemen.'

In spite of the general understanding that the matter was *sub judice*, these proceedings were confided to Sir Lawrence before the day was out by three members of the Committee, including Jack Muskham. He took the knowledge out with him to dinner at South Street.

Since the publication of the poems and Compson Grice's letter, Michael and Fleur had talked of little else, forced to by the comments and questionings of practically every acquaintance. They differed radically. Michael, originally averse to publication of the poem, now that it was out, stoutly defended the honesty and courage of Wilfrid's avowal. Fleur could not forgive what she called the 'stupidity of the whole thing'. If he had only kept quiet and not indulged his conscience or his pride, the matter would have blown over, leaving practically no mark. It was, she said, unfair to Dinny, and unnecessary so far as Wilfrid himself was concerned; but of course he had always been like that. She had not forgotten the uncompromising way in which eight years ago he had asked her to become his mistress, and the still more uncompromising way in which he had fled from her when she had not complied. When Sir Lawrence told them of the meeting at Burton's, she said simply:

'Well, what could he expect?'

Michael muttered:

'Why is Jack Muskham so bitter?'

'Some dogs attack each other at sight. Others come to it more meditatively. This appears to be a case of both. I should say Dinny is the bone.'

Fleur laughed.

'Jack Muskham and Dinny!'

'Sub-consciously, my dear. The workings of a misogynist's mind are not for us to pry into, except in Vienna. They can tell you everything there; even to the origin of hiccoughs.'

'I doubt if Wilfrid will go before the Committee,' said Michael, gloomily. Fleur confirmed him.

'Of course he won't, Michael.'

'Then what will happen?'

'Almost certainly he'll be expelled under rule whatever it is.'

Michael shrugged. 'He won't care. What's a Club more or less?'

'No,' said Fleur; 'but at present the thing is in flux – people just talk about it; but expulsion from his Club will be definite condemnation. It's just what's wanted to make opinion line up against him.'

'And *for* him.'

'Oh! for him, yes; but we know what that amounts to – the disgruntled.'

'That's all beside the point,' said Michael gruffly. 'I know what he's feeling: his first instinct was to defy that Arab, and he bitterly regrets that he went back on it.'

Sir Lawrence nodded.

'Dinny asked me if there was anything he could do to show publicly that he wasn't a coward. You'd think there might be, but it's not easy. People object to be put into positions of extreme danger in order that their rescuers may get into the papers. Van horses seldom run away in Piccadilly. He might throw someone off Westminster Bridge, and jump in after him; but that would merely be murder and suicide. Curious that, with all the heroism there is about, it should be so difficult to be deliberately heroic.'

'He ought to face the Committee,' said Michael; 'and I hope he will. There's something he told me. It sounds silly; but, knowing Wilfrid, one can see it made all the difference.'

Fleur had planted her elbows on the polished table and her chin on her hands. So, leaning forward, she looked like the girl contemplating a china image in her father's picture by Alfred Stevens.

'Well?' she said. 'What is it?'

'He said he felt sorry for his executioner.'

Neither his wife nor his father moved, except for a slight raising of the eyebrows. He went on defiantly:

'Of course, it sounds absurd, but he said the fellow begged him not to make him shoot – he was under a vow to convert the infidel.'

'To mention that to the Committee,' Sir Lawrence said slowly, 'would certainly be telling it to the marines.'

'He's not likely to,' said Fleur; 'he'd rather die than be laughed at.'

'Exactly! I only mentioned it to show that the whole thing's not so simple as it appears to the pukka sahib.'

'When,' murmured Sir Lawrence, in a detached voice, 'have

I heard anything so nicely ironical? But all this is not helping Dinny.'

'I think I'll go and see him again,' said Michael.

'The simplest thing,' said Fleur, 'is for him to resign at once.'

And with that common-sense conclusion the discussion closed.

Chapter Twenty-three

Those who love, when the object of their love is in trouble, must keep sympathy to themselves and yet show it. Dinny did not find this easy. She watched, lynx-eyed, for any chance to assuage her lover's bitterness of soul; but though they continued to meet daily, he gave her none. Except for the expression of his face when he was off guard, he might have been quite untouched by tragedy. Throughout that fortnight after the Derby she came to his rooms, and they went joy-riding, accompanied by the spaniel Foch; and he never mentioned that of which all more or less literary and official London was talking. Through Sir Lawrence, however, she heard that he had been asked to meet the Committee of Burton's Club and had answered by resignation. And, through Michael, who had been to see him again, she heard that he knew of Jack Muskham's part in the affair. Since he so rigidly refused to open out to her, she, at great cost, tried to surpass him in obliviousness of purgatory. His face often made her ache, but she kept that ache out of her own face. And all the time she was in bitter doubt whether she was right to refrain from trying to break through to him. It was a long and terrible lesson in the truth that not even real love can reach and anoint deep spiritual sores. The other half of her trouble, the unending quiet pressure of her family's sorrowful alarm, caused her an irritation of which she was ashamed.

And then occurred an incident which, however unpleasant and alarming at the moment, was almost a relief because it broke up that silence.

They had been to the Tate Gallery and, walking home, had just come up the steps leading to Carlton House Terrace. Dinny was still talking about the pre-Raphaelites, and saw nothing till Wilfrid's changed expression made her look for the cause. There was Jack Muskham, with a blank face, formally lifting a tall hat as if to someone who was not there, and a short dark man removing a grey felt covering, in unison. They passed, and she heard Muskham say:

'That I consider the limit.'

Instinctively her hand went out to grasp Wilfrid's arm, but too late. He had spun round in his tracks. She saw him, three yards away, tap Muskham on the shoulder, and the two face each other, with the little man looking up at them like a terrier at two large dogs about to fight. She heard Wilfrid say in a low voice:

'What a coward and cad you are!'

There followed an endless silence, while her eyes flitted from Wilfrid's convulsed face to Muskham's, rigid and menacing, and the terrier man's black eyes snapping up at them. She heard him say: 'Come on, Jack!' saw a tremor pass through the length of Muskham's figure, his hands clench, his lips move:

'You heard that, Yule?'

The little man's hand, pushed under his arm, pulled at him; the tall figure turned; the two moved away; and Wilfrid was back at her side.

'Coward and cad!' he muttered: 'Coward and cad! Thank God I've told him!' He threw up his head, took a gulp of air, and said: 'That's better! Sorry, Dinny!'

In Dinny feeling was too churned up for speech. The moment had been so savagely primitive; and she had the horrid fear that it could not end there; an intuition, too, that she was the cause, the hidden reason of Muskham's virulence. She remembered Sir Lawrence's words: 'Jack thinks you are being victimised.' What if she were! What business was it of that long, lounging man who hated women! Absurd! She heard Wilfrid muttering:

'"The limit!" He might know what one feels!'

'But, darling, if we all knew what other people felt, we should be seraphim, and he's only a member of the Jockey Club.'

'He's done his best to get me outed, and he couldn't even refrain from *that*.'

'It's I who ought to be angry, not you. It's I who force you to go about with me. Only, you see, I like it so. But, darling, I don't shrink in the wash. What *is* the use of my being your love if you won't let yourself go with me?'

'Why should I worry you with what can't be cured?'

'I exist to be worried by you. *Please* worry me!'

'Oh! Dinny, you're an angel!'

'I repeat it is not so. I really have blood in my veins.'

'It's like earache; you shake your head, and shake your head, and it's no good. I thought publishing *The Leopard* would free me, but it hasn't. Am I "yellow", Dinny – am I?'

'If you were yellow I should not have loved you.'

'Oh! I don't know. Women can love anything.'

'Proverbially we admire courage before all. I'm going to be brutal. Has doubt of your courage anything to do with your ache? Isn't it just due to feeling that other people doubt?'

He gave a little unhappy laugh. 'I don't know; I only know it's there.'

Dinny looked up at him.

'Oh! darling, don't ache! I do so hate it for you.'

They stood for a moment looking deeply at each other, and a vendor of matches, without the money to indulge in spiritual trouble, said:

'Box o' lights, sir?' . . .

Though she had been closer to Wilfrid that afternoon than perhaps ever before, Dinny returned to Mount Street oppressed by fears. She could not get the look on Muskham's face out of her head, nor the sound of his: 'You heard that, Yule?'

It was silly! Out of such explosive encounters nothing but legal remedies came nowadays; and of all people she had ever seen, she could least connect Jack Muskham with the Law. She noticed a hat in the hall, and heard voices, as she was passing her uncle's study. She had barely taken off her own hat when he sent for her. He was talking to the little terrier man, who was perched astride of a chair, as if riding a race.

'Dinny, Mr Telfourd Yule; my niece Dinny Cherrell.'

The little man bowed over her hand.

'Yule has been telling me,' said Sir Lawrence, 'of that encounter. He's not easy in his mind.'

'Neither am I,' said Dinny.

'I'm sure Jack didn't mean those words to be heard, Miss Cherrell.'

'I don't agree; I think he did.'

Yule shrugged. The expression on his face was rueful, and Dinny liked its comical ugliness.

'Well, he certainly didn't mean *you* to hear them.'

'He ought to have, then. Mr Desert would prefer not to be seen with me in public. It's I who make him.'

'I came to your Uncle because when Jack won't talk about a thing, it's serious. I've known him a long time.'

Dinny stood silent. The flush on her cheeks had dwindled to two red spots. And the two men stared at her, thinking, perhaps, that, with her cornflower-blue eyes, slenderness, and that hair, she looked unsuited to the matter in hand. She said quietly: 'What can I do, Uncle Lawrence?'

'I don't see, my dear, what anyone can do at the moment. Mr Yule says that he left Jack going back to Royston. I thought possibly I might take you down to see him tomorrow. He's a queer fellow; if he didn't date so, I shouldn't worry. Such things blow over, as a rule.'

Dinny controlled a sudden disposition to tremble.

'What do you mean by "date"?'

Sir Lawrence looked at Yule and said: 'We don't want to seem absurd. There's been no duel fought between Englishmen, so far as I know, for seventy or eighty years; but Jack is a survival. We don't quite know what to think. Horse-play is not in his line; neither is a law court. And yet we can't see him taking no further notice.'

'I suppose,' said Dinny, with spirit, 'he won't see, on reflection, that he's more to blame than Wilfrid?'

'No,' said Yule, 'he won't. Believe me, Miss Cherrell, I am deeply sorry about the whole business.'

Dinny bowed. 'I think it was very nice of you to come; thank you!'

'I suppose,' said Sir Lawrence, doubtfully, 'you couldn't get Desert to send him an apology?'

'So *that*,' she thought, 'is what they wanted me for.' 'No, Uncle, I couldn't – I couldn't even ask him. I'm quite sure he wouldn't.'

'I see,' said Sir Lawrence glumly.

Bowing to Yule, Dinny turned towards the door. In the hall she seemed to be seeing through the wall behind her the renewed shrugging of their shoulders, the ruefulness on their glum faces, and she went up to her room. Apology! Thinking of Wilfrid's badgered, tortured face, the very idea of it offended her. Stricken to the quick already on the score of personal courage, it was the last thing he would dream of. She wandered unhappily about her room, then took out his photograph. The face she loved looked back at her with the sceptical indifference of an effigy. Wilful, sudden, proud, self-centred, deeply dual; but cruel, no, and cowardly – *no*!

'Oh! my darling!' she thought, and put it away.

She went to her window and leaned out. A beautiful evening – the Friday of Ascot week, the first of those two weeks when in England fine weather is almost certain! On Wednesday there had been a deluge, but today had the feel of real high summer. Down below a taxi drew up – her uncle and aunt were going out to dinner. There they came, with Blore putting them in and standing to look after them. Now the staff would turn on the wireless. Yes! Here it was! She opened her door. Grand opera! *Rigoletto*! The twittering of those tarnished melodies came up to her in all the bravura of an age which knew better than this, it seemed, how to express the emotions of wayward hearts.

The gong! She did not want to go down and eat, but she must, or Blore and Augustine would be upset. She washed hastily, compromised with her dress, and went down.

But while she ate she grew more restless, as if sitting still and attending to a single function were sharpening the edge of her anxiety. A duel! Fantastic, in these days! And yet – Uncle Lawrence was uncanny, and Wilfrid in just the mood to do anything to show himself unafraid. Were duels illegal in France? Thank heaven she had all that money. No! It was absurd! People had called each other names with impunity for nearly a century. No good to fuss; tomorrow she would go with Uncle Lawrence and see that man. It was all, in some strange way, on her account. What would one of her own people do if called a coward and a cad – her father, her brother, Uncle Adrian? What *could* they do? Horsewhips, fists, law courts – all such hopeless, coarse, ugly remedies! And she felt for the first time that Wilfrid had been wrong to use such words. Ah! But was he not entitled to hit back? Yes, indeed! She could see again his head jerked up and hear his: 'Ah! That's better!'

Swallowing down her coffee, she got up and sought the

drawing room. On the sofa was her aunt's embroidery thrown down, and she gazed at it with a feeble interest. An intricate old French design needing many coloured wools – grey rabbits looking archly over their shoulders at long, curious, yellow dogs seated on yellower haunches, with red eyes and tongues hanging out; leaves and flowers, too, and here and there a bird, all set in a background of brown wool. Tens of thousands of stitches, which, when finished, would lie under glass on a little table, and last till they were all dead and no one knew who had wrought them. *Tout lasse, tout passe!* The strains of *Rigoletto* still came floating from the basement. Really Augustine must have drama in her soul, to be listening to a whole opera.

'*La Donna è mobile!*'

Dinny took up her book, the *Memoirs of Harriette Wilson*; a tome in which no one kept any faith to speak of except the authoress, and she only in her own estimation; a loose, bright, engaging, conceited minx, with a good heart and one real romance among a peck of love affairs.

'*La Donna è mobile!*' It came mocking up the stairs, fine and free, as if the tenor had reached his Mecca. *Mobile!* No! That was more true of men than of women! Women did not change. One loved – one lost, perhaps! She sat with closed eyes till the last notes of that last act had died away, then went up to bed. She passed a night broken by dreams, and was awakened by a voice saying:

'Someone on the telephone for you, Miss Dinny.'

'For me? Why! What time is it?'

'Half-past seven, miss.'

She sat up startled.

'Who is it?'

'No name, miss; but he wants to speak to you special.'

With the thought 'Wilfrid!' she jumped up, put on a dressing-gown and slippers, and ran down.

'Yes. Who is it?'

'Stack, miss. I'm sorry to disturb you so early, but I thought it best. Mr Desert, miss, went to bed as usual last night, but this morning the dog was whining in his room, and I went in, and I see he's not been in bed at all. He must have gone out very early, because I've been about since half-past six. I shouldn't have disturbed you, miss, only I didn't like the look of him last night . . . Can you hear me, miss?'

'Yes. Has he taken any clothes or anything?'

'No, miss.'

'Did anybody come to see him last night?'

'No, miss. But a letter came by hand about half-past nine. I noticed him distraight, miss, when I took the whisky in. Perhaps it's nothing, but being so sudden, I . . . Can you hear me, miss?'

'Yes. I'll dress at once and come round. Stack, can you get me a taxi, or, better, a car, by the time I'm there?'

'I'll get a car, miss.'

'Is there any service to the Continent he could have caught?'

'Nothing before nine o'clock.'

'I'll be round as quick as I can.'

'Yes, miss. Don't you worry, miss; he might be wanting exercise or something.'

Dinny replaced the receiver and flew upstairs.

Chapter Twenty-four

Wilfrid's taxi-cab, whose tank he had caused to be filled to the brim, ground slowly up Haverstock Hill towards the Spaniard's Road. He looked at his watch. Forty miles to Royston – even in this growler he would be there by nine! He took out a letter and read it through once more.

Liverpool Street Station: Friday.

SIR,

You will agree that the matter of this afternoon cannot rest there. Since the Law denies one decent satisfaction, I give you due notice that I shall horsewhip you publicly whenever and wherever I first find you unprotected by the presence of a lady.

Yours faithfully,

J. MUSKHAM

The Briery, Royston.

'Whenever and wherever I first find you unprotected by the presence of a lady!' That would be sooner than the swine thought! A pity the fellow was so much older than himself.

The cab had reached the top now, and was speeding along the lonely Spaniard's Road. In the early glistening morning the view was worth a poet's notice, but Wilfrid lay back in the cab, unseeing, consumed by his thoughts. Something to hit at. This chap, at any rate, should no longer sneer at him! He had no plan except to be publicly on hand at the first possible moment after reading those words: 'Unprotected by the presence of a lady!' Taken as sheltering behind a petticoat? Pity it was not a real duel! The duels of literature jigsawed in his brain – Bel Ami, Bazarov, Dr Slammer, Sir Lucius O'Trigger, D'Artagnan, Sir Toby, Winkle – all those creatures of fancy who had endeared the duel to readers. Duels and runs on banks, those two jewels in the crown of drama – gone! Well, he had shaved – with cold water! – and dressed with as much care as if he were not going to a vulgar brawl. The dandified Jack Muskham and a scene of low violence! Very amusing! The cab ground and whirred its way on through the thin early traffic of market and milk carts; and Wilfrid sat drowsing after his almost sleepless night. Barnet he passed, and Hatfield, and the confines of Welwyn Garden City, then Knebworth, and the long villages of Stevenage, Graveley and Baldock. Houses and trees seemed touched by unreality in the fine haze. Postmen, and maids on doorsteps, boys riding farm horses, and now and then an early cyclist, alone inhabited the outdoor world. And, with that wry smile on his lips and his eyes half closed, he lay back, his feet pressed against the seat opposite. He had not to stage the scene, nor open the brawl. He had but to deliver himself, as it were registered, so that he could not be missed.

The cab slowed up.

'We're gettin' near Royston, governor; where d'you want to go?'

'Pull up at the inn.'

The cab resumed its progress. The morning light hardened. All, now, was positive, away to the round, high-lying clumps of beeches. On the grassy slope to his right he saw a string of sheeted racehorses moving slowly back from exercise. The cab entered a long village street, and near its end stopped at an hotel. Wilfrid got out.

'Garage your cab. I'll want you to take me back.'

'Right, governor.'

He went in and asked for breakfast. Just nine o'clock! While eating he enquired of the waiter where the Briery was.

'It's the long low 'ouse lying back on the right, sir; but if you want Mr Muskham, you've only to stand in the street outside 'ere. 'E'll be passing on his pony at five past ten; you can set your watch by him going to his stud farm when there's no racing.'

'Thank you, that will save me trouble.'

At five minutes before ten, smoking a cigarette, he took his position at the hotel gate. Girt-in, and with that smile, he stood motionless, and through his mind passed and repassed the scene between Tom Sawyer and the boy in the too-good clothes, walking round each other with an elaborate ritual of insults before the whirlwind of their encounter. There would be no ritual today! 'If I can lay him out,' he thought, 'I will!' His hands, concealed in the pockets of his jacket, kept turning into fists; otherwise he stood, still as the gatepost against which he leaned, his face veiled in the thin fume rising from his cigarette. He noticed with satisfaction his cabman talking to another chauffeur outside the yard, a man up the street opposite cleaning windows, and a butcher's cart. Muskham could not pretend this was not a public occasion. If they had neither of them boxed since schooldays, the thing would be a crude mix-up; all the more chance of hurting or being hurt! The sun topped some trees on the far side and shone on his face. He moved a pace or two to get the full of it. The sun – all good in life came from the sun! And suddenly he thought of Dinny. The sun to her was not what it was to him. Was he in a dream – was she real? Or, rather, were she and all this English business some rude interval of waking? God knew! He stirred and looked at his watch. Three minutes past ten, and there, sure enough, as the waiter had said, coming up the street was a rider, unconcerned, sedate, with a long easy seat on a small well-bred animal. Closer and closer, unaware! Then the rider's eyes came round, there was a movement of his chin. He raised a hand to his hat, checked the pony, wheeled it and cantered back.

'H'm!' thought Wilfrid. 'Gone for his whip!' And from the stump of his cigarette he lighted another. A voice behind him said:

'What'd I tell you, sir? That's Mr Muskham.'

'He seems to have forgotten something.'

'Ah!' said the waiter, 'he's regular as a rule. They say at the stud he's a Turk for order. Here he comes again; not lost much time, 'as 'e?'

He was coming at a canter. About thirty yards away he reined up and got off. Wilfrid heard him say to the pony, 'Stand, Betty!' His heart began to beat, his hands in his pockets were clenched fast; he still leaned against the gate. The waiter had withdrawn, but with the tail of his eye Wilfrid could see him at the hotel door, waiting as if to watch over the interview he had fostered. His cabman was still engaged in the endless conversation of those who drive cars; the shopman still cleaning his windows; the butcher's man rejoining his cart. Muskham came deliberately, a cut-and-thrust whip in his hand.

'Now!' thought Wilfrid.

Within three yards Muskham stopped. 'Are you ready?'

Wilfrid took out his hands, let the cigarette drop from his lips, and nodded. Raising the whip, the long figure sprang. One blow fell, then Wilfrid closed. He closed so utterly that the whip was useless and Muskham dropped it. They swayed back clinched together against the gate; then, both, as if struck by the same idea, unclinched and raised their fists. In a moment it was clear that neither was any longer expert. They drove at each other without science, but with a sort of fury, length and weight on one side, youth and agility on the other. Amidst the scrambling concussions of this wild encounter, Wilfrid was conscious of a little crowd collecting – they had become a street show! Their combat was so breathless, furious and silent, that its nature seemed to infect that gathering, and from it came nothing but a muttering. Both were soon cut on the mouth and bleeding, both were soon winded and half dazed. In sheer breathlessness they clinched again and stood swaying, striving to get a grip of each other's throats.

'Go it, Mr Muskham!' cried a voice.

As if encouraged, Wilfrid wrenched himself free and sprang; Muskham's fist thumped into his chest as he came on, but his outstretched hands closed round his enemy's neck. There was a long stagger, and then both went crashing to the ground. There, again as if moved by the same thought, they unclinched and scrambled up. For a moment they stood panting, glaring at each other for an opening. For a second each looked round him. Wilfrid saw Muskham's blood-stained face change and become rigid, his hands drop and hide in his pockets; saw him turn away. And suddenly he realised why. Standing up in an open car, across the street, was Dinny, with one hand covering her lips and the other shading her eyes.

Wilfrid turned as abruptly and went into the hotel.

Chapter Twenty-five

While Dinny dressed and skimmed along the nearly empty streets, she had been thinking hard. That letter brought last night by hand surely meant that Muskham was the cause of Wilfrid's early sortie. Since he had slipped like a needle into a bundle of hay, her only chance was to work from the other end. No need to wait for her uncle to see Jack Muskham. She could see him alone just as well as, perhaps better. It was eight o'clock when she reached Cork Street, and she at once said: 'Has Mr Desert a revolver, Stack?'

'Yes, miss.'

'Has he taken it?'

'No.'

'I ask because he had a quarrel yesterday.'

Stack passed his hand over his unshaven chin. 'Don't know where you're going, miss, but would you like me to come with you?'

'I think it would be better if you'd go and make sure he isn't taking a boat train.'

'Certainly, miss. I'll take the dog, and do that.'

'Is that car outside for me?'

'Yes, miss. Would you like it opened?'

'I would; the more air, the better.'

The henchman nodded, his eyes and nose seeming to Dinny unusually large and intelligent.

'If I run across Mr Desert first, where shall I get in touch with you, miss?'

'I'll call at Royston post-office for any telegram. I'm going to see a Mr Muskham there. The quarrel was with him.'

'Have you had anything to eat, miss? Let me get you a cup of tea.'

'I've had one, thank you.' It saved time to say what was not true.

That drive, on an unknown road, seemed interminable to her, haunted by her uncle's words: 'If Jack didn't date so, I shouldn't worry . . . He's a survival.' Suppose that, even now, in some enclosure – Richmond Park, Ken Wood, where not – they were playing the old-fashioned pranks, of honour! She conjured up the scene – Jack Muskham, tall, deliberate; Wilfrid, girt-in, defiant, trees around them, wood-pigeons calling, their hands slowly rising to the level—! Yes, but who would give the word? And pistols! People did not go about with duelling pistols nowadays. If that had been suggested, Wilfrid would surely have taken his revolver! What should she say if, indeed, she found Muskham at home? 'Please don't mind being called a cad and coward! They are really almost terms of endearment.' Wilfrid must never know that she had tried to mediate. It would but wound his pride still further. Wounded pride! Was there any older, deeper, more obstinate cause of human trouble, or any more natural and excusable! The consciousness of having failed oneself! Overmastered by the attraction that knows neither reason nor law, she loved Wilfrid none the less for having failed himself; but she was not blind to that failure. Ever since her father's words 'by any Englishman who's threatened with a pistol' had touched some nerve in the background of her being, she had realised that she was divided by her love from her instinctive sense of what was due from Englishmen.

The driver stopped to examine a back tyre. From the hedge a drift of elderflower scent made her close her eyes. Those flat white scented blossoms! The driver remounted and started the car with a jerk. Was life always going to jerk her away from love? Was she never to rest drugged and happy in its arms?

'Morbid!' she thought. 'I ought to be keying my pitch to the Jockey Club.'

Royston began, and she said: 'Stop at the post-office, please.'

'Right, lady!'

There was no telegram for her, and she asked for Muskham's house. The post-mistress looked at the clock.

'Nearly opposite, miss; but if you want Mr Muskham, I saw him pass riding just now. He'll be going to his stud farm – that'll be through the town and off to the right.'

Dinny resumed her seat, and they drove slowly on.

Afterwards she did not know whether her instinct or the driver's stopped the car. For when he turned round and said: 'Appears like a bit of a mix-up, miss,' she was already standing, to see over the heads of that ring of people in the road. She saw only too well the stained, blood-streaked faces, the rain of blows, the breathless, swaying struggle. She had opened the door, but with the sudden thought: 'He'd never forgive me!' banged it to again, and stood, with one hand shading her eyes, the other covering her lips, conscious that the driver, too, was standing.

'Something like a scrap!' she heard him say admiringly.

How strange and wild Wilfrid looked! But with only fists they could not kill each other! And mixed with her alarm was a sort of exultation. He had come down to seek battle! Yet every blow seemed falling on her flesh, each clutch and struggling movement seemed her own.

'Not a blasted bobby!' said her driver, carried away. 'Go it! I back the young 'un.'

Dinny saw them fall apart, then Wilfrid rushing with outstretched hands; she heard the thump of Muskham's fist on his chest, saw them clinch, stagger, and fall; then rise and stand gasping, glaring. She saw Muskham catch sight of her, then Wilfrid; saw them turn away; and all was over. The driver said: 'Now, that's a pity!' Dinny sank down on the car seat, and said quietly:

'Drive on, please.'

Away! Just away! Enough that they had seen her – more than enough, perhaps!

'Drive on a little, then turn and go back to Town.' They wouldn't begin again!

'Neither of 'em much good with 'is 'ands, miss, but a proper spirit.'

Dinny nodded. Her hand was still over her mouth, for her lips were trembling. The driver looked at her.

'You're a bit pale, miss – too much blood! Why not stop somewhere and 'ave a drop o' brandy?'

'Not here,' said Dinny, 'the next village.'

'Baldock. Right-o!' And he put the car to speed.

The crowd had disappeared as they repassed the hotel. Two dogs, a man cleaning windows, and a policeman were the only signs of life.

At Baldock she had some breakfast. Conscious that she ought to feel relieved, now that the explosion had occurred, she was surprised by the foreboding which oppressed her. Would he not resent her having come as if to shield him? Her accidental presence had stopped the fight, and she had seen them disfigured, blood-stained, devoid of their dignities. She decided to tell no one where she had been, or what she had seen – not even Stack or her uncle.

Such precautions are of small avail in a country so civilised. An able, if not too accurate, description of the 'Encounter at Royston between that well-known breeder of bloodstock,

Mr John Muskham – cousin to Sir Charles Muskham, Bart – and the Hon. Wilfrid Desert, second son of Lord Mullyon, author of "The Leopard", which has recently caused such a sensation,' appeared in that day's last edition of the *Evening Sun*, under the heading, 'Fisticuffs in High Quarters'. It was written with spirit and imagination, and ended thus: 'It is believed that the origin of the quarrel may be sought in the action which it is whispered was taken by Mr Muskham over Mr Desert's membership of a certain Club. It seems that Mr Muskham took exception to Mr Desert continuing a member after his public acknowledgment that "The Leopard" was founded on his own experience. The affair, no doubt, was very high-spirited, if not likely to improve the plain man's conception of a dignified aristocracy.'

This was laid before Dinny at dinner-time by her uncle without comment. It caused her to sit rigid, till his voice said: 'Were you there, Dinny?'

'Uncanny, as usual,' she thought; but, though by now habituated to the manipulation of truth, she was not yet capable of the lie direct, and she nodded.

'What's that?' said Lady Mont.

Dinny pushed the paper over to her aunt, who read, screwing up her eyes, for she had long sight.

'Which won, Dinny?'

'Neither. They just stopped.'

'Where is Royston?'

'In Cambridgeshire.'

'Why?'

Neither Dinny nor Sir Lawrence knew.

'He didn't take you on a pillion, Dinny?'

'No, dear. I just happened to drive up.'

'Religion is very inflamin',' murmured Lady Mont.

'It is,' said Dinny bitterly.

'Did the sight of you stop them?' said Sir Lawrence.

'Yes.'

'I don't like that. It would have been better if a bobby or a knock-out blow—'

'I didn't want them to see me.'

'Have you seen him since?'

Dinny shook her head.

'Men are vain,' said her aunt.

That closed the conversation.

Stack telephoned after dinner that Wilfrid had returned; but instinct told her to make no attempt to see him.

After a restless night she took the morning train to Condaford. It was Sunday, and they were all at church. She seemed strangely divided from her family. Condaford smelled the same, looked the same, and the same people did the same things; yet all was different! Even the Scottish terrier and the spaniels sniffed her with doubting nostrils, as if uncertain whether she belonged to them any more.

'And do I?' she thought. 'The scent is not there when the heart is away!'

Jean was the first to appear, Lady Cherrell having stayed to Communion, the General to count the offertory and Hubert to inspect the village cricket pitch. She found Dinny sitting by an old sundial in front of a bed of delphiniums. Having kissed her sister-in-law, she stood and looked at her for quite a minute, before saying: 'Take a pull, my dear, or you'll be going into a decline, whatever that is.'

'I only want my lunch,' said Dinny.

'Same here. I thought my dad's sermons were a trial even after I'd censored them; but your man here!'

'Yes, one *can* "put him down".'

Again Jean paused, and her eyes searched Dinny's face.

'Dinny, I'm all for you. Get married at once, and go off with him.'

Dinny smiled.

'There are two parties to every marriage.'

'Is that paragraph in this morning's paper correct, about a fight at Royston?'

'Probably not.'

'I mean was there one?'

'Yes.'

'Who began it?'

'I did. There's no other woman in the case.'

'Dinny, you're very changed.'

'No longer sweet and disinterested.'

'Very well!' said Jean. 'If you want to play the love-lorn female, play it!'

Dinny caught her skirt. Jean knelt down and put her arms round her.

'You were a brick to me when I was up against it.'

Dinny laughed.

'What are my father and Hubert saying now?'

'Your father says nothing and looks glum. Hubert either says: "Something must be done", or "It's the limit".'

'Not that it matters,' said Dinny suddenly; 'I'm past all that.'

'You mean you're not sure what *he'll* do? But, of course, he must do what you want.'

Again Dinny laughed.

'You're afraid,' said Jean, with startling comprehension, 'that he might run off and leave you?' And she subsided on to her hams the better to look up into Dinny's face. 'Of course he might. You know I went to see him?'

'Oh?'

'Yes; he got over me. I couldn't say a word. Great charm, Dinny.'

'Did Hubert send you?'

'No. On my own. I was going to let him know what would be thought of him if he married you, but I couldn't. I should have imagined he'd have told you about it. But I suppose he knew it would worry you.'

'I don't know,' said Dinny; and did not. It seemed to her at that moment that she knew very little.

Jean sat silently pulling an early dandelion to pieces.

'If I were you,' she said at last, 'I'd vamp him. If you'd once belonged to him, he couldn't leave you.'

Dinny got up. 'Let's go round the gardens and see what's out.'

Chapter Twenty-six

Since Dinny said no further word on the subject occupying every mind, no word was said by anyone; and for this she was truly thankful. She spent the next three days trying to hide the fact that she was very unhappy. No letter had come from Wilfrid, no message from Stack; surely, if anything had happened, *he* would have let her know. On the fourth day, feeling that she could bear the suspense no longer, she telephoned to Fleur and asked if she might come up to them.

The expressions on her father's and her mother's faces when she said she was going affected her as do the eyes and tails of dogs whom one must leave. How much more potent was the pressure put by silent disturbance than by nagging!

Panic assailed her in the train. Had her instinct to wait for Wilfrid to make the first move been wrong? Ought she not to have gone straight to him? And on reaching London she told her driver: 'Cork Street.'

But he was out, and Stack did not know when he would be in. The henchman's demeanour seemed to her strangely different, as if he had retreated to a fence and were sitting on it. Was Mr Desert well? Yes. And the dog? Yes, the dog was well. Dinny drove away disconsolate. At South Square again no one was in; it seemed as if the world were in conspiracy to make her feel deserted. She had forgotten Wimbledon, the Horse Show, and other activities of the time of year. All such demonstrations of interest in life were, indeed, so far from her present mood that she could not conceive people taking part in them.

She sat down in her bedroom to write to Wilfrid. There was no longer any reason for silence, for Stack would tell him she had called.

She wrote:

South Square, Westminster.

Ever since Saturday I've been tortured by the doubt whether to write, or wait for you to write to me. Darling, I never meant to interfere in any way. I had come down to see Mr Muskham and tell him that it's I only who was responsible for what he so absurdly called the limit. I never expected you to be there. I didn't really much hope even to find him. Please let me see you.

Your unhappy

DINNY

She went out herself to post it. On the way back she came on Kit, with his governess, the dog, and the two youngest of her Aunt Alison's children. They seemed entirely happy; she was ashamed not to seem so too, so they all went together to Kit's schoolroom to have tea. Before it was over Michael came in. Dinny, who had seldom seen him with his little son, was fascinated by the easy excellence of their relationship. It was, perhaps, a little difficult to tell which was the elder, though a certain difference in size and the refusal of a second helping of strawberry jam seemed to favour Michael. That hour, in fact, brought her the nearest approach to happiness she had known since she left Wilfrid five days ago. After it was over she went with Michael to his study.

'Anything wrong, Dinny?'

Wilfrid's best friend, and the easiest person in the world to confide in, and she did not know what to say! And then suddenly she began to talk, sitting in his armchair, her elbows on her knees, her chin in her hands, staring not at him, but at her future. And Michael sat on the window-sill, his face now rueful, now whimsical, making little soothing sounds. Nothing would matter, she said, neither public opinion, the Press, nor even her family, if only there were not in Wilfrid himself this deep bitter unease, this basic doubt of his own conduct, this permanent itch to prove to others, and, above all, to himself, that he was not 'yellow'. Now that she had given way, it poured out of her, all that bottled-up feeling that she was walking on a marsh, where at any moment she might sink in some deep, unlooked-for hole thinly covered by specious surface. She ceased and lay back in the chair exhausted.

'But, Dinny,' said Michael, gently, 'isn't he really fond of you?'

'I don't know, Michael; I thought so – I don't know. Why should he be? I'm an ordinary person, he's not.'

'We all seem ordinary to ourselves. I don't want to flatter you, but you seem to me less ordinary than Wilfrid.'

'Oh, no!'

'Poets,' said Michael gloomily, 'give a lot of trouble. What are we going to do about it?'

That evening after dinner he went forth, ostensibly to the House, in fact to Cork Street.

Wilfrid was not in, so he asked Stack's permission to wait. Sitting on the divan in that unconventional, dimly-lighted room, he twitted himself for having come. To imply that he came from Dinny would be worse than useless. Besides, he hadn't. No! He had come to discover, if he could, whether Wilfrid really was in love with her. If not, then – well, then the sooner she was out of her misery the better. It might half break her heart, but that was better than pursuing a substance which wasn't there. He knew, or thought he knew, that Wilfrid was the last person to endure a one-sided relationship. The worst of all disasters for Dinny would be to join herself to him under a misconception of his feelings for her. On a little table close to the divan, with the whisky, were the night's letters – only two, one of them, he could see, from Dinny herself. The door was opened slightly and a dog came in. After sniffing at Michael's trousers, it lay down with its head on its paws and its eyes fixed on the door. He spoke to it, but it took no notice – the right sort of dog. 'I'll give him till eleven,' thought Michael. And almost immediately Wilfrid came. He had a bruise on one cheek and some plaster on his chin. The dog fluttered round his legs.

'Well, old man,' said Michael, 'that must have been a hearty scrap.'

'It was. Whisky?'

'No, thanks.'

He watched Wilfrid take up the letters and turn his back to open them.

'I ought to have known he'd do that,' thought Michael; 'there goes my chance! He's bound to pretend to be in love with her!'

Before turning round again Wilfrid made himself a drink and finished it. Then, facing Michael, he said: 'Well?'

Disconcerted by the abruptness of that word, and by the knowledge that he had come to pump his friend, Michael did not answer.

'What d'you want to know?'

Michael said abruptly: 'Whether you're in love with Dinny.'

Wilfrid laughed. 'Really, Michael!'

'I know. But things can't go on like this. Damn it! Wilfrid, you ought to think of her.'

'I do.' He said it with a face so withdrawn and unhappy that Michael thought: 'He means that.'

'Then for God's sake,' he said, 'show it! Don't let her eat her heart out like this!'

Wilfrid had turned to the window. Without looking round he said:

'You've never had occasion to try and prove yourself the opposite of yellow. Well, don't! You won't find the chance. It comes when you don't want it, not when you do.'

'Naturally! But, my dear fellow, that's not Dinny's fault.'

'Her misfortune.'

'Well, then?'

Wilfrid wheeled round.

'Oh! damn you, Michael! Go away! No one can interfere in this. It's much too intimate.'

Michael rose and clutched his hat. Wilfrid had said exactly what he himself had really been thinking ever since he came.

'You're quite right,' he said humbly. 'Good-night, old man! That's a nice dog.'

'I'm sorry,' said Wilfrid; 'you meant well, but you can't help. No one can. Good-night!'

Michael got out, and all the way downstairs he looked for the tail between his legs.

When he reached home Dinny had gone up, but Fleur was waiting down for him. He had not meant to speak of his visit, but, after looking at him keenly, she said:

'You haven't been to the House, Michael. You've been to see Wilfrid.'

Michael nodded.

'Well?'

'No go!'

'I could have told you that. If you come across a man and woman quarrelling in the street, what do you do?'

'Pass by on the other side, if you can get there in time.'

'Well?'

'They're *not* quarrelling.'

'No, but they've got a special world no one else can enter.'

'That's what Wilfrid said.'

'Naturally.'

Michael stared. Yes, of course. She had once had her special world, and not with – him!

'It was stupid of me. But I *am* stupid.'

'No, not stupid; well-intentioned. Are you going up?'

'Yes.'

As he went upstairs he had the peculiar feeling that it was she who wanted to go to bed with him rather than he with her. And yet, once in bed, that would all change, for of such was the nature of man!

Dinny, in her room above theirs, through her open window could hear the faint murmur of their voices, and, bowing her face on her hands, gave way to a feeling of despair. The stars in their courses fought against her! External opposition one could cut through or get round; but this deep spiritual unease in the loved one's soul, that – ah! that – one could not reach; and the unreachable could not be pushed away, cut through, or circumvented. She looked up at the stars that fought against her. Did the ancients really believe that, or was it, with them, as with her, just a manner of speaking? Did those bright wheeling jewels on the indigo velvet of all space really concern themselves with little men, the lives and loves of human insects, who, born from an embrace, met and clung and died and became dust? Those candescent worlds, circled by little off-split planets – were their names taken in vain, or were they really in their motions and their relative positions the writing on the wall for men to read?

No! That was only human self-importance! To his small wheel man bound the Universe. Swing low, sweet chariots! But they didn't! Man swung with them – in space . . .

Chapter Twenty-seven

Two days later the Cherrell family met in conclave because of a sudden summons received by Hubert to rejoin his regiment in the Soudan. He wished to have something decided about Dinny before he left. The four Cherrell brothers, Sir Lawrence, Michael, and himself, gathered, therefore, in Adrian's room at the Museum after Mr Justice Charwell's Court had risen. They all knew that the meeting might be futile, because, as even Governments find, to decide is useless if decision cannot be carried out.

Michael, Adrian, and the General, who had been in personal touch with Wilfrid, were the least vocal, Sir Lawrence and the Judge the most vocal; Hubert and Hilary were now vocal and now dumb.

Starting from the premise, which nobody denied, that the thing was a bad business, two schools of thought declared themselves – Adrian, Michael, and to some extent Hilary believed there was nothing to be done but wait and see; the rest thought there was much to be done, but what – they could not say.

Michael, who had never seen his four uncles so close together before, was struck by the resemblance in the shape and colouring of their faces, except that the eyes of Hilary and Lionel were blue and grey, and of the General and Adrian brown and hazel. They all, notably, lacked gesture, and had a lean activity of figure. In Hubert these characteristics were accentuated by youth, and his hazel eyes at times looked almost grey.

'If only,' Michael heard his father say, 'you could injunct her, Lionel?' and Adrian's impatient:

'We must let Dinny alone; trying to control her is absurd. She's got a warm heart, an unselfish nature, and plenty of sense.' Then Hubert's retort:

'We know all that, Uncle, but the thing will be such a disaster for her, we must do what we can.'

'Well, what *can* you do?'

'Exactly!' thought Michael, and said: 'Just now she doesn't know how she stands.'

'You couldn't get her to go out with you to the Soudan, Hubert?' said the Judge.

'I've lost all touch with her.'

'If someone wanted her badly—' began the General, and did not finish.

'Even then,' murmured Adrian, 'only if she were quite sure Desert didn't want her more.'

Hilary took out his pipe. 'Has anyone tried Desert?'

'I have,' said the General.

'And I, twice,' muttered Michael.

'Suppose,' said Hubert gloomily, 'I had a shot.'

'Not, my dear fellow,' put in Sir Lawrence, 'unless you can be quite certain of keeping your temper.'

'I never can be certain of that.'

'Then don't!'

'Would *you* go, Dad?' asked Michael.

'I?'

'He used to respect you.'

'Not even a blood relation!'

'You might take a chance, Lawrence,' said Hilary.

'But why?'

'None of the rest of us can, for one reason or another.'

'Why shouldn't *you*?'

'In a way I agree with Adrian; it's best to leave it all alone.'

'What exactly is the objection to Dinny's marrying him?' asked Adrian. The General turned to him abruptly.

'She'd be marked out for life.'

'So was that fellow who stuck to his wife when she was convicted. Everybody respected him the more.'

'There's no such sharp hell,' said the Judge, 'as seeing fingers pointed at your life's partner.'

'Dinny would learn not to notice them.'

'Forgive me, but you're missing the point,' muttered Michael. 'The point is Wilfrid's own feeling. If he remains bitter about himself and marries her – that'll be hell for her, if you like. And the fonder she is of him, the worse it'll be.'

'You're right, Michael,' said Sir Lawrence unexpectedly. 'I'd think it well worth while to go if I could make him see that.'

Michael sighed.

'Whichever way it goes, it's hell for poor Dinny.'

'"Joy cometh in the morning",' murmured Hilary through a cloud of smoke.

'Do you believe that, Uncle Hilary?'

'Not too much.'

'Dinny's twenty-six. This is her first love. If it goes wrong – what then?'

'Marriage.'

'With somebody else?'

Hilary nodded.

'Lively!'

'Life is lively.'

'Well, Lawrence?' asked the General, sharply: 'You'll go?'

Sir Lawrence studied him for a moment, and then replied: 'Yes.'

'Thank you!'

It was not clear to any of them what purpose would be

served, but it was a decision of sorts, and at least could be carried out . . .

Wilfrid had lost most of his bruise and discarded the plaster on his chin when Sir Lawrence, encountering him on the stairs at Cork Street that same late afternoon, said:

'D'you mind if I walk a little way with you?'

'Not at all, sir.'

'Any particular direction?'

Wilfrid shrugged, and they walked side by side, till at last Sir Lawrence said:

'Nothing's worse than not knowing where you're going!'

'You're right.'

'Then why go, especially if in doing it you take someone with you? Forgive my putting things crudely, but, except for Dinny, would you be caring a hang about all this business? What other ties have you got here?'

'None. I don't want to discuss things. If you'll forgive me, I'll branch off.'

Sir Lawrence stopped. 'Just one moment, and then I'll do the branching. Have you realised that a man who has a quarrel with himself is not fit to live with until he's got over it? That's all I wanted to say; but it's a good deal. Think it over!' And, raising his hat, Sir Lawrence turned on his heel. By George! He was well out of that! What an uncomfortable young man! And, after all, one had said all one had come to say! He walked towards Mount Street, reflecting on the limitations imposed by tradition. But for tradition, would Wilfrid mind being thought 'yellow'? Would Dinny's family care? Would Lyall have written his confounded poem? Would not the Corporal in the Buffs have kowtowed? Was a single one of the Cherrells, met in conclave, a real believing Christian? Not even Hilary – he would bet his boots! Yet not one of them could stomach this recantation. Not religion, but the refusal to take the 'dare'! That was the rub to them. The imputation of cowardice, or at least of not caring for the good name of one's country. Well! About a million British had died for that good name in the war; had they all died for a futility? Desert himself had nearly died for it, and got the M.C., or D.S.O., or something! All very contradictory! People cared for their country in a crowd, it seemed, but not in a desert; in France, but not in Darfur.

He heard hurrying footsteps, and, turning round, saw Desert behind him. Sir Lawrence had almost a shock looking at his face, dry, dark, with quivering lips and deep suffering eyes.

'You were quite right,' he said; 'I thought I'd let you know. You can tell her family I'm going away.'

At this complete success of his mission Sir Lawrence experienced dismay.

'Be careful!' he said: 'You might do her a great injury.'

'I shall do her that, anyway. Thank you for speaking to me. You've made me see. Good-bye!' He turned and was gone.

Sir Lawrence stood looking after him, impressed by his look of suffering. He turned in at his front door doubtful whether he had not made bad worse. While he was putting down his hat and stick, Lady Mont came down the stairs.

'I'm so bored, Lawrence. What have you been doin'?'

'Seeing young Desert; and, it seems, I've made him feel that until he can live on good terms with himself he won't be fit to live with at all.'

'That's wicked.'

'How?'

'He'll go away. I always knew he'd go away. You must tell Dinny at once what you've done.' And she went to the telephone.

'Is that you, Fleur? . . . Oh! Dinny . . . This is Aunt Em! . . . Yes . . . Can you come round here? . . . Why not? . . . That's not a reason . . . But you must! Lawrence wants to speak to you . . . At once? Yes. He's done a very stupid thing . . . What? . . . No! . . . He wants to explain. In ten minutes . . . very well.'

'My God!' thought Sir Lawrence. He had suddenly realised that to deaden feeling on any subject one only needed to sit in conclave. Whenever the Government got into trouble, they appointed a Commission. Whenever a man did something wrong, he went into consultation with solicitor and counsel. If he himself hadn't been sitting in conclave, would he ever have gone to see Desert and put the fat into the fire like this? The conclave had dulled his feelings. He had gone to Wilfrid as some juryman comes in to return his verdict after sitting in conclave on a case for days. And now he had to put himself right with Dinny, and how the deuce would he do that? He went into his study, conscious that his wife was following.

'Lawrence, you must tell her exactly what you've done, and how he took it. Otherwise it may be too late. And I shall stay until you've done it.'

'Considering, Em, that you don't know what I said, or what he said, that seems superfluous.'

'No,' said Lady Mont, 'nothing is, when a man's done wrong.'

'I was charged to go and see him by your family.'

'You ought to have had more sense. If you treat poets like innkeepers, they blow up.'

'On the contrary, he thanked me.'

'That's worse. I shall have Dinny's taxi kept at the door.'

'Em,' said Sir Lawrence, 'when you want to make your will, let me know.'

'Why?'

'Because of getting you consecutive before you start.'

'Anything I have,' said Lady Mont, 'is to go to Michael, to be kept for Catherine. And if I'm dead when Kit goes to Harrow, he's to have my grandfather's "stirrup-cup" that's in the armoire in my sittin'room at Lippin'hall. But he's not to take it to school with him, or they'll melt it, or drink boiled peppermints out of it, or something. Is that clear?'

'Perfectly.'

'Then,' said Lady Mont, 'get ready and begin at once when Dinny comes.'

'Quite!' said Sir Lawrence meekly. 'But how the deuce am I to put it to Dinny?'

'Just put it, and don't invent as you go along.'

Sir Lawrence played a tune with his fingers on the window-pane. His wife stared at the ceiling. They were like that when Dinny came.

'Keep Miss Dinny's taxi, Blore.'

At the sight of his niece Sir Lawrence perceived that he had indeed lost touch with feeling. Her face, under its chestnut-coloured hair, was sharpened and blanched, and there was a look in her eyes that he did not like.

'Begin,' said Lady Mont.

Sir Lawrence raised one high thin shoulder as if in protection.

'My dear, your brother has been recalled, and I was asked whether I would go and see young Desert. I went. I told him that if he had a quarrel with himself he would not be fit to live with till he'd made it up. He said nothing and turned off. Afterwards he came up behind me in this street, and said that I was right. Would I tell your family that he was going away. He looked very queer and troubled. I said: "Be careful! You might do her a great injury." "I shall do her that, anyway," he said. And he went off. That was about twenty minutes ago.'

Dinny looked from one to the other, covered her lips with her hand, and went out.

A moment later they heard her cab move off.

Chapter Twenty-eight

Except for receiving a little note in answer to her letter, which relieved her not at all, Dinny had spent these last two days in distress of mind. When Sir Lawrence made his communication, she felt as if all depended on whether she could get to Cork Street before he was back there, and in her taxi she sat with hands screwed tight together in her lap and her eyes fixed on the driver's back, a back, indeed, so broad that it was not easy to fix them elsewhere. Useless to think of what she was going to say – she must say whatever came into her head when she saw him. His face would give her a lead. She realised that if he once got away from England it would be as if she had never seen him. She stopped the cab in Burlington Street and walked swiftly to his door. If he had come straight home, he must be in! In these last two days she had realised that Stack had perceived some change in Wilfrid and was conforming to it, and when he opened the door she said:

'You mustn't put me off, Stack, I *must* see Mr Desert.' And, slipping past, she opened the door of the sitting room. Wilfrid was pacing up and down.

'Dinny!'

She felt that if she said the wrong thing it might be, then and there, the end; and she only smiled. He put his hands over his eyes; and, while he stood thus blinded, she stole up and put her arms round his neck.

Was Jean right? Ought she to—?

Then, through the opened door Foch came in. He slid the velvet of his muzzle under her hand, and she sank on her knees to kiss him. When she looked up, Wilfrid had turned away. Instantly she scrambled up, and stood, as it were, lost. She did not know of what, if of anything, she thought, not even whether she were feeling. All seemed to go blank within her. He had thrown the window open and was leaning there holding his hands to his head. Was he going to throw himself out? She made a violent effort to control her nerves, and said very gently: 'Wilfrid!' He turned and looked at her, and she thought: 'My God! He hates me!' Then his expression changed, and became the one she knew; and she was aware once more of how at sea one is with wounded pride – so multiple and violent and changing in its moods!

'Well?' she said. 'What do you wish me to do?'

'I don't know. The whole thing is mad. I ought to have buried myself in Siam by now.'

'Would you like me to stay here tonight?'

'Yes! No! I don't know.'

'Wilfrid, why take it so hard? It's as if love were nothing to you. Is it nothing?'

For answer he took out Jack Muskham's letter.

'Read this!'

She read it. 'I see. It was doubly unfortunate that I came down.'

He threw himself down again on the divan, and sat there looking up at her.

'If I do go,' thought Dinny, 'I shall only begin tearing to get back again.' And she said: 'What are you doing for dinner?'

'Stack's got something, I believe.'

'Would there be enough for me?'

'Too much, if you feel as I do.'

She rang the bell.

'I'm staying to dinner, Stack. I only want about a pin's head of food.'

And, craving for a moment in which to recover her balance, she said: 'May I have a wash, Wilfrid?'

While she was drying her face and hands, she took hold of herself with all her might, and then as suddenly relaxed. Whatever she decided would be wrong, painful, perhaps impossible. Let it go!

When she came back to the sitting room he was not there. The door into his bedroom was open, but it was empty. Dinny rushed to the window. He was not in the street. Stack's voice said.

'Excuse me, miss: Mr Desert was called out. He told me to say he would write. Dinner will be ready in a minute.'

Dinny went straight up to him.

'Your first impression of me was the right one, Stack: not your second. I am going now. Mr Desert need have no fear of me. Tell him that, please.'

'Miss,' said Stack, 'I told you he was very sudden; but this is the most sudden thing I've ever known him do. I'm sorry, miss. But I'm afraid it's a case of cutting your losses. If I can be of service to you, I will.'

'If he leaves England,' said Dinny, 'I should like to have Foch.'

'If I know Mr Desert, miss, he means to go. I've seen it coming on him ever since he had that letter the night before you came round in the early morning.'

'Well,' said Dinny, 'shake hands, and remember what I said.'

They exchanged a hand-grip, and, still unnaturally steady, she went out and down the stairs. She walked fast, giddy and strange in her head, and nothing but the word: So! recurring in her mind. All that she had felt, all that she had meant to feel, compressed into that word of two letters. In her life she had never felt so withdrawn and tearless, so indifferent as to where she went, what she did, or whom she saw. The world might well be without end, for its end had come. She did not believe that he had designed this way of breaking from her. He had not enough insight into her for that. But, in fact, no way could have been more perfect, more complete. Drag after a man! Impossible! She did not even have to form that thought, it was instinctive.

She walked and walked for three hours about the London streets, and turned at last towards Westminster with the feeling that if she didn't she would drop. When she went in at South Square, she summoned all that was left in her to a spurt of gaiety; but, when she had gone up to her room, Fleur said:

'Something very wrong, Michael.'

'Poor Dinny! What the hell has he done now?'

Going to the window, Fleur drew aside the curtain. It was not yet quite dark. Except for two cats, a taxi to the right, and a man on the pavement examining a small bunch of keys, there was nothing to be seen.

'Shall I go up and see if she'll talk?'

'No. If Dinny wants us, she'll let us know. If it's as you think, she'll want no one. She's proud as the devil when her back's to the wall.'

'I hate pride,' said Fleur; and, closing the curtain, she went towards the door. 'It comes when you don't want it, and does you down. If you want a career, don't have pride.' She went out.

'I don't know,' thought Michael, 'if I have pride, but I haven't got a career.' He followed slowly upstairs, and for some little time stood in the doorway of his dressing room. But no sound came from upstairs . . .

Dinny, indeed, was lying on her bed, face down. So this was the end! Why had the force called love exalted and tortured her, then thrown her, used and exhausted, quivering, longing, wounded, startled, to eat her heart out in silence and grief? Love and pride, and the greater of these is pride! So the saying seemed to go within her, and to be squeezed into her pillow. Her love against his pride! Her love against her own pride! And the victory with pride! Wasteful and bitter! Of all that evening only one moment now seemed to her real: when he had turned from the window, and she had thought: 'He hates me!' Of course he hated her, standing like the figure of his wounded self-esteem; the one thing that prevented him from crying out: 'God damn you all! Good-bye!'

Well, now he could cry it and go! And she – suffer, suffer – and slowly get over it. No! Lie on it, keep it down, keep it silent, press it into her pillows. Make little of it, make nothing of it, while inside her it swelled and ravaged her. The expression of instinct is not so clear as that; but behind all formless throbbing there is meaning; and that was the meaning within Dinny's silent and half-smothered struggle on her bed. How could she have acted differently? Not her fault that Muskham had sent the letter with that phrase about the protection of a woman! Not her fault that she had rushed down to Royston! What had she done wrong? The whole thing arbitrary, gratuitous! Perhaps love in its courses was always so! It seemed to her that the night ticked while she lay there; the rusty ticking of an old clock. Was it the night, or her own life, abandoned and lying on its face?

Chapter Twenty-nine

Wilfrid had obeyed impulse when he ran down into Cork Street. Ever since the sudden breaking off of that fierce undignified scuffle at Royston, and the sight of Dinny standing in the car covering her eyes with a hand, his feelings towards her had been terribly confused. Now at the sudden sight, sound, scent of her, warmth had rushed up in him and spent itself in kisses; but the moment she left him his insane feeling had returned and hurled him down into a London where at least one could walk and meet no one. He went south and became involved with a queue of people trying to get into 'His Majesty's'. He stood among them thinking: 'As well in here as anywhere.' But, just as his turn came, he broke away and branched off eastward; passed through Covent Garden, desolate and smelling of garbage; and came out into Ludgate Hill. Hereabouts he was reminded by scent of fish that he had eaten nothing since breakfast. And, going into a restaurant, he drank a cocktail and ate some *hors-d'oeuvre*. Asking for a sheet of paper and envelope, he wrote:

'I had to go. If I had stayed, you and I would have been one. I don't know what I'm going to do – I may finish in the river tonight, or go abroad, or come back to you. Whatever I do, forgive, and believe that I have loved you. Wilfrid.'

He addressed the envelope and thrust it into his pocket.

But he did not post it. He felt he could never express what he was feeling. Again he walked east. Through the City zone, deserted as if it had been mustard-gassed, he was soon in the cheerier Whitechapel Road. He walked, trying to tire himself out and stop the whirling of his thoughts. He moved northwards now, and towards eleven was nearing Chingford. All was moonlit and still when he passed the hotel and went on towards the Forest. One car, a belated cyclist, a couple or two, and three tramps were all he met before he struck off the road in among the trees. Daylight was gone, and the moon was silvering the leaves and branches. Thoroughly exhausted, he lay down on the beech mast. The night was an unwritten poem – the gleam and drip of light like the play of an incoherent mind, fluttering, slipping in and out of reality; never at rest; never the firm silver of true metal; burnished and gone like a dream. Up there were the stars he had travelled by times without number, the Wain, and all the others that seemed meaningless, if not nameless, in this town world.

He turned over and lay on his face, pressing his forehead to the ground. And suddenly he heard the drone of a flying machine. But through the heavily-leafed boughs he could see no gliding, sky-scurrying shape. Some night-flier to Holland; some English airman pricking out the lighted shape of London, or practising flight between Hendon and an East Coast base. After flying in the war he had never wished to fly again. The very sound of it brought back still that sick, fed-up feeling from which the Armistice had delivered him. The drone passed on and away. A faint rumbling murmur came from London, but here the night was still and warm, with only a frog croaking, a bird cheeping feebly once, two owls hooting against each other. He turned again on to his face, and fell into an uneasy sleep.

When he woke light was just rifting the clear darkness. A heavy dew had fallen; he felt stiff and chilled, but his mind was clear. He got up and swung his arms, lit a cigarette, and drew the smoke deep in. He sat with his arms clasped round his knees, smoking his cigarette to its end without ever moving it from his lips, and spitting out the stub with its long ash just before it burned his mouth. Suddenly he began to shiver. He got up to walk back to the road. Stiff and sore, he made poor going. It was full dawn by the time he reached the road, and then, knowing that he ought to go towards London, he went in the opposite direction. He plodded on, and every now and then shivered violently. At last he sat down and, bowed over his knees, fell into a sort of coma. A voice saying: 'Hi!' roused him. A fresh-faced young man in a small car had halted alongside. 'Anything wrong?'

'Nothing,' muttered Wilfrid.

'You appear to be in poor shape, all the same. D'you know what time it is?'

'No.'

'Get in here, and I'll run you to the hotel at Chingford. Got any money?'

Wilfrid looked at him grimly and laughed.

'Yes.'

'Don't be touchy! What you want is a sleep and some strong coffee! Come on!'

Wilfrid got up. He could hardly stand. He lay back in the little car, huddled beside the young man, who said: 'Now we shan't be long.'

In ten minutes, which to a blurred and shivering consciousness might have been five hours, they were in front of the hotel.

'I know the "boots" here,' said the young man; 'I'll put you in charge of him. What's your name?'

'Hell!' muttered Wilfrid.

'Hi! George! I found this gentleman on the road. He seems to have gone a bit wonky. Put him into some decent bedroom.

Heat him up a good hot bottle, and get him into bed with it. Brew him some strong coffee, and see that he drinks it.'

The boots grinned. 'That all?'

'No; take his temperature, and send for a doctor. Look here, sir,' the young man turned to Wilfrid, 'I recommend this chap. He can polish boots with the best. Just let him do for you, and don't worry. I must get on. It's six o'clock.' He waited a moment, watching Wilfrid stagger into the hotel on the arm of the 'boots', then sped away.

The 'boots' assisted Wilfrid to a room. 'Can you undress, governor?'

'Yes,' muttered Wilfrid.

'Then I'll go and get you that bottle and the coffee. Don't be afraid, we don't 'ave damp beds 'ere. Were you out all night?'

Wilfrid sat on the bed and did not answer.

''Ere!' said the 'boots': 'give us your sleeves!' He pulled Wilfrid's coat off, then his waistcoat and trousers. 'You've got a proper chill, it seems to me. Your underthings are all damp. Can you stand?'

Wilfrid shook his head.

The 'boots' stripped the sheets off the bed, pulled Wilfrid's shirt over his head; then with a struggle wrenched off vest and drawers, and wrapped him in a blanket.

'Now, governor, a good pull and a pull altogether.' He forced Wilfrid's head on to the pillow, heaved his legs on to the bed, and covered him with two more blankets.

'You lie there; I won't be gone ten minutes.'

Wilfrid lay, shivering so that his thoughts would not join up, nor his lips make consecutive sounds owing to the violent chattering of his teeth. He became conscious of a chamber-maid, then of voices.

'His teeth'll break it. Isn't there another place?'

'I'll try under his arm.'

A thermometer was pressed under his arm and held there.

'You haven't got yellow fever, have you, sir?'

Wilfrid shook his head.

'Can you raise yourself, governor, and drink this?'

Robust arms raised him, and he drank.

'One 'undred and four.'

'Gawd! 'Ere, pop this bottle to his feet, I'll 'phone the Doc.'

Wilfrid could see the maid watching him, as if wondering what sort of fever she was going to catch.

'Malaria,' he said, suddenly, 'not infectious. Give me a cigarette! In my waistcoat.'

The maid put a cigarette between his lips and lit it. Wilfrid took a long pull.

'A-again!' he said.

Again she put it between his lips, and again he took a pull.

'They say there's mosquitoes in the forest. Did you find any last night, sir?'

'In the sys-system.'

Shivering a little less now, he watched her moving about the room, collecting his clothes, drawing the curtains so that they shaded the bed. Then she approached him, and he smiled up at her.

'Another nice drop of hot coffee?'

He shook his head, closed his eyes again, and shivered deep into the bed, conscious that she was still watching him, and then again of voices.

'Can't find a name, but he's some sort of nob. There's money and this letter in his coat. The doctor'll be here in five minutes.'

'Well, I'll wait till then, but I've got my work to do.'

'Same 'ere. Tell the missus when you call her.'

He saw the maid stand looking at him with a sort of awe. A stranger and a nob, with a curious disease, interesting to a simple mind. Of his face, pressed into the pillow, she couldn't see much – one dark cheek, one ear, some hair, the screwed-up eye under the brow. He felt her touch his forehead timidly with a finger. Burning hot, of course!

'Would you like your friends written to, sir?'

He shook his head.

'The doctor'll be here in a minute.'

'I'll be like this two days – nothing to be done – quinine – orange juice—' Seized by a violent fit of shivering, he was silent. He saw the doctor come in; and the maid still leaning against the chest of drawers, biting her little finger. She took it from her mouth, and he heard her say: 'Shall I stay, sir?'

'Yes, you can stay.'

The doctor's fingers closed on his pulse, raised his eyelid, pushed his lips apart.

'Well, sir? Had much of this?'

Wilfrid nodded.

'All right! You'll stay where you are, and shove in quinine, and that's all I can do for you. Pretty sharp bout.'

Wilfrid nodded.

'There are no cards on you. What's your name?'

Wilfrid shook his head.

'All right! Don't worry! Take this.'

Chapter Thirty

Stepping from an omnibus, Dinny walked into the large of Wimbledon Common. After a nearly sleepless night, she had slipped out, leaving a note to say she would be away all day. She hurried over the grass into a birch grove, and lay down. The high moving clouds, the sunlight striking in and out of the birch-tree branches, the water wagtails, the little dry patches of sand, and that stout wood-pigeon, undismayed by her motionless figure, brought her neither peace nor the inclination to think of Nature. She lay on her back, quivering and dry-eyed, wondering for whose inscrutable delight she was thus suffering. The stricken do not look for outside help, they seek within. To go about exuding tragedy was abhorrent to her. She would not do that! But the sweetness of the wind, the moving clouds, the rustle of the breeze, the sound of children's voices, brought no hint of how she was to disguise herself and face life afresh. The isolation in which she had been ever since the meeting with Wilfrid under Foch's statue now showed nakedly. All her eggs had been in one basket, and the basket had fallen. She dug with her fingers at the sandy earth; and a dog, seeing a hole, came up and sniffed it. She had begun to live, and now she was dead. 'No flowers by request!'

So sharp had been her realisation of finality yesterday

evening that she did not even consider the possibility of tying up the broken thread. If he had pride, so had she! Not the same sort, but as deep in her marrow. No one had any real need of her! Why not go away? She had nearly three hundred pounds. The notion gave her neither exhilaration nor any real relief; but it would save her from making herself a nuisance to those who would expect her to be her old cheerful self. She thought of the hours she had spent with Wilfrid in places like this. So sharp was her memory that she had to cover her lips to prevent anguish welling out of them. Until she met him she had never felt alone. And now – she *was* alone! Chill, terrifying, endless! Remembering how she had found swift motion good for heartache, she got up and crossed the road where the Sunday stream of cars was already flowing out of town. Uncle Hilary had once exhorted her not to lose her sense of humour. But had she ever had one? At the end of Barnes Common she climbed on to a bus and went back to London. She must have something to eat, or she would be fainting. She got down near Kensington Gardens and went into an hotel.

After lunch she sat some time in the Gardens, and then walked to Mount Street. No one was in, and she sank down on the sofa in the drawing room. Thoroughly exhausted, she fell asleep. Her aunt's entrance woke her, and, sitting up, she said:

'You can all be happy about me, Aunt Em. It's finished.'

Lady Mont stared at her niece sitting there with such a ghostly little smile, and two tears, starting not quite together, ran down her cheeks.

'I didn't know you cried at funerals, too, Aunt Em.'

She got up, went over to her aunt, and with her handkerchief removed the marks the tears had made.

'There!'

Lady Mont got up. 'I *must* howl,' she said, 'I simply must.' And she swayed rapidly out of the room.

Dinny sat on, that ghost of a smile still on her face. Blore brought in the tea-things, and she talked to him of Wimbledon, and his wife. He did not seem to know which of the two was in worse shape, but, as he was going out, he turned and said:

'And if I might suggest, Miss Dinny, a little sea air for you.'

'Yes, Blore, I was thinking of it.'

'I'm glad, miss; one overdoes it at this time of year.'

He, too, seemed to know that her course was run. And, feeling suddenly that she could not go on thus attending her own funeral, she stole to the door, listened for sounds, then slipped down the stairs and away.

But she was so physically exhausted that she could scarcely drag herself as far as St James's Park. There she sat down by the water. People, sunbeams, and ducks, shading leaves, spiky reeds, and this sirocco within her! A tall man walking from the Whitehall end made a little convulsive movement, as if to put his hand to his hat, corrected it at sight of her face, and lounged on. Realising what her face must be expressing, she got up, and, trailing on to Westminster Abbey, went in and sat down in a pew. There, bent forward, with her face resting on her arms, she stayed quite half an hour. She had not prayed, but she had rested, and the expression on her face had changed. She felt more fit to face people and not show so much.

It was past six, and she went on to South Square. Getting unseen to her room, she had a long hot bath, put on a dinner frock, and resolutely went down. Only Fleur and Michael were there, and neither of them asked her any questions. It was clear to her that they knew. She got through the evening somehow. When she was going up, both of them kissed her, and Fleur said:

'I've told them to put you a hot-water bottle; stuck against your back, it helps you to sleep. Good-night, bless you!'

Again Dinny had the feeling that Fleur had once suffered

as she was suffering now. She slept better than she could have hoped.

With her early tea she received a letter with the heading of an hotel at Chingford.

> MADAM,
>
> The enclosed letter addressed to you was found in the pocket of a gentleman who is lying here with a very sharp attack of malaria. I am posting it on to you, and am
>
> Truly yours,
>
> ROGER QUEAL, M.D.

She read the letter . . . 'Whatever I do, forgive, and believe that I have loved you. Wilfrid.' And he was ill! All the impulses which sprang up she instantly thrust back. Not a second time would she rush in where angels feared to tread! But, hurrying down, she telephoned to Stack the news that he was lying at the Chingford hotel with an attack of malaria.

'He'll want his pyjamas and his razors, then, miss. I'll take 'em down to him.'

Forcing back the words: 'Give him my love,' she said instead, 'He knows where I am if there is anything I can do.'

The blacker bitterness of her mood was gone; yet she was as cut off from him as ever! Unless he came or sent for her she could make no move; and deep down she seemed to know that he would neither come nor send. No! He would strike his tent and flit away from where he had felt too much.

Towards noon Hubert came to say good-bye. It was at once clear to her that he, too, knew. He was coming back for the rest of his leave in October, he said. Jean was to stay at Condaford till after her child was born in November. She had been ordered to be out of the summer heat. He seemed to

Dinny that morning like the old Hubert again. He dwelt on the advantage of being born at Condaford. And, endeavouring to be sprightly, she said:

'Quaint to find you talking like that, Hubert. You never used to care about Condaford.'

'It makes a difference to have an heir.'

'Oh! It'll be an heir, will it?'

'Yes, we've made up our minds to a boy.'

'And will there be a Condaford by the time he comes into it?'

Hubert shrugged. 'We'll have a try at keeping it. Things don't last unless you set yourself to keep them.'

'And not always then,' murmured Dinny.

Chapter Thirty-one

Wilfrid's words: 'You can tell her family I'm going away', and Dinny's: 'It's finished', had travelled, if not like wildfire, throughout the Cherrell family. There was no rejoicing as over a sinner that repenteth. All were too sorry for her, with a sorrow nigh unto dismay. Each wanted to show sympathy, none knew how. Sympathy smelling of sympathy was worse than none. Three days passed, during which not one member of the family succeeded in expressing anything. Then Adrian had a brainwave: He would ask her to eat something with him, though why food should be regarded as consolatory neither he nor anyone else had ever known. He appointed a café which had perhaps more repute than merit.

Since Dinny was not of those young women who make the ravages of life into an excuse for French-varnishing their surfaces, he had every opportunity to note her pallor. He forbore to comment. Indeed, he found it difficult to talk at all, for he knew that, though men, when enthralled by women, remain devoted to their mental mainsprings, women, less bodily enthralled, stay mentally wrapped up in the men they love. He began, however, to tell her how someone had tried to 'sell him a pup'.

'He wanted five hundred pounds, Dinny, for a Cromagnon skull found in Suffolk. The whole thing looked extraordinarily genuine. But I happened to see the county archaeologist. "Oh!" he said: "So he's been trying to palm that off on you, has he? That's the well-known 'pup'. He's dug it up at least three times. The man ought to be in gaol. He keeps it in a cupboard and every five or six years digs a hole, puts it in, takes it out, and tries to sell it. It possibly *is* a Cromagnon skull, but he picked it up in France, about twenty years ago. It would be unique, of course, as a British product." Thereon I went off to have another look at where it was found last time. And it was plain enough, when you already knew it, that he'd put the thing in. There's something about antiques that saps what the Americans call one's *moral*.'

'What sort of man was he, Uncle?'

'An enthusiastic-looking chap, rather like my hairdresser.'

Dinny laughed. 'You ought to do something, or he *will* sell it next time.'

'The depression is against him, my dear. Bones and first editions are extraordinarily sensitive. He'll have to live a good ten years to get anything like a price.'

'Do many people try to palm things off on you?'

'Some succeed, Dinny. I regret that "pup", though; it was a lovely skull. There aren't many as good nowadays.'

'We English certainly are getting uglier.'

'Don't you believe it. Put the people we meet in drawing-rooms and shops into cassocks and cowls, armour and jerkins, and you'll have just the faces of the fourteenth and fifteenth centuries.'

'But we do despise beauty, Uncle. We connect it with softness and immorality.'

'Well, it makes people happy to despise what they haven't got. We're only about the third – no, the fourth – plainest people in Europe. But take away the Celtic infusions, and I admit we'd be the first.'

Dinny looked round the café. Her survey added nothing to

her conclusions, partly because she took but little in, and partly because the lunchers were nearly all Jews or Americans.

Adrian watched her with an ache. She looked so bone-listless.

'Hubert's gone, then?' he said.

'Yes.'

'And what are you going to do, my dear?'

Dinny sat looking at her plate. Suddenly she raised her head and said:

'I think I shall go abroad, Uncle.'

Adrian's hand went to his goatee.

'I see,' he said, at last. 'Money?'

'I have enough.'

'Where?'

'Anywhere.'

'By yourself?'

Dinny nodded.

'The drawback to going away,' murmured Adrian, 'is the having to come back.'

'There doesn't seem to be anything much for me to do just now. So I think I'll cheer people up by not seeing them for a bit.'

Adrian debated within himself.

'Well, my dear, only you can decide what's best for you. But if you felt like a long travel, it strikes me that Clare might be glad to see you in Ceylon.'

Seeing by the surprised movement of her hands that the idea was new to her, he went on:

'I have a feeling that she may not be finding life very easy.'

Her eyes met his.

'That's what I thought at the wedding, Uncle; I didn't like his face.'

'You have a special gift for helping others, Dinny; and whatever's wrong about Christianity, it's not the saying "To give is more blessed than to receive".'

'Even the Son of Man liked His little joke, Uncle.'

Adrian looked at her hard, and said:

'Well, if you do go to Ceylon, mind you eat your mangoes over a basin.'

He parted from her a little later and, too much out of mood to go back to work, went to the Horse Show instead.

Chapter Thirty-two

At South Square *The Daily Phase* was among those journals which politicians take lest they should miss reading correctly the temperature of Fleet Street. Michael pushed it over to Fleur at breakfast.

During the six days since Dinny's arrival neither of them had said a word to her on the subject of Wilfrid; and it was Dinny who now said: 'May I see that?'

Fleur handed her the paper. She read, gave a little shudder, and went on with her breakfast. Kit broke the ensuing hush by stating Hobbs's average. Did Aunt Dinny think he was as great as W. G. Grace?

'I never saw either of them, Kit.'

'Didn't you see W. G.?'

'I think he died before I was born.'

Kit scrutinised her doubtfully.

'Oh!'

'He died in 1915,' said Michael: 'You'd have been eleven.'

'But haven't you really seen Hobbs, Auntie?'

'No.'

'*I've* seen him three times. I'm practising his hook to leg. *The Daily Phase* says Bradman is the best batsman in the world now. Do you think he's better than Hobbs?'

'Better news than Hobbs.'

Kit stared.

'What is "news"?'

'What newspapers are for.'

'Do they make it up?'

'Not always.'

'What news were you reading just now?'

'Nothing that would interest you.'

'How do you know?'

'Kit, don't worry!' said Fleur.

'May I have an egg?'

'Yes.'

The hush began again, till Kit stopped his eggspoon in midair and isolated a finger:

'Look! The nail's blacker than it was yesterday. Will it come off, Auntie?'

'How did you do that?'

'Pinched it in a drawer. I didn't cry.'

'Don't boast, Kit.'

Kit gave his mother a clear upward look and resumed his egg.

Half an hour later, when Michael was just settling down to his correspondence, Dinny came into his study.

'Busy, Michael?'

'No, my dear.'

'That paper! Why can't they leave him alone?'

'You see *The Leopard* is selling like hot cakes. Dinny, how do things stand now?'

'I know he's been having malaria, but I don't even know where or how he is.'

Michael looked at her face, masked in its desperate little smile, and said, hesitatingly:

'Would you like me to find out?'

'If he wants me, he knows where I am.'

'I'll see Compson Grice. I'm not lucky with Wilfrid himself.'

When she was gone he sat staring at the letters he had not

begun to answer, half dismayed, half angered. Poor dear Dinny! What a shame! Pushing the letters aside, he went out.

Compson Grice's office was near Covent Garden, which, for some reason still to be discovered, attracts literature. When Michael reached it, about noon, that young publisher was sitting in the only well-furnished room in the building, with a newspaper cutting in his hand and a smile on his lips. He rose and said: 'Hallo, Mont! Seen this in *The Phase*?'

'Yes.'

'I sent it round to Desert, and he wrote that at the top and sent it back. Neat, eh!'

Michael read in Wilfrid's writing:

'Whene'er the lord who rules his roosts
Says: "Bite!" he bites, says: "Boost!" he boosts.'

'He's in town, then?'

'Was half an hour ago.'

'Have you seen him at all?'

'Not since the book came out.'

Michael looked shrewdly at that comely fattish face. 'Satisfied with the sales?'

'We're in the forty-first thousand, and going strong.'

'I suppose you don't know whether Wilfrid is returning to the East?'

'Haven't the least little idea.'

'He must be pretty sick with the whole thing.'

Compson Grice shrugged.

'How many poets have ever made a thousand pounds out of a hundred pages of verse?'

'Small price for a soul, Grice.'

'It'll be two thousand before we've done.'

'I always thought it a mistake to print "The Leopard". Since he did it I've defended it, but it was a fatal thing to do.'

'I don't agree.'

'Obviously. It's done you proud.'

'You can sneer,' said Grice, with some feeling, 'but he wouldn't have sent it to me if he hadn't wished it to come out. I am not my brother's keeper. The mere fact that it turns out a scoop is nothing to the point.'

Michael sighed.

'I suppose not; but this is no joke for him. It's his whole life.'

'Again, I don't agree. That happened when he recanted to save himself being shot. This is expiation, and damned good business into the bargain. His name is known to thousands who'd never heard of it.'

'Yes,' said Michael, brooding, 'there is that, certainly. Nothing like persecution to keep a name alive. Grice, will you do something for me? Make an excuse to find out what Wilfrid's intentions are. I've put my foot into it with him and can't go myself, but I specially want to know.'

'H'm!' said Grice. 'He bites.'

Michael grinned. 'He won't bite his benefactor. I'm serious. Will you?'

'I'll try. By the way, there's a book by that French Canadian I've just published. Top-hole! I'll send you a copy – your wife will like it.' 'And,' he added to himself, 'talk about it.' He smoothed back his sleek dark hair and extended his hand. Michael shook it with a little more warmth than he really felt and went away.

'After all,' he thought, 'what is it to Grice except business? Wilfrid's nothing to him! In these days we have to take what the gods send.' And he fell to considering what was really making the public buy a book not concerned with sex, memoirs, or murders. The Empire! The prestige of the English! He did not believe it. No! What was making them buy it was that fundamental interest which attached to the question how far a person might go to save his life without losing what was called his soul. In other words, the book was being sold by that little thing – believed in some quarters to be dead – called Conscience. A problem posed to each reader's conscience, that he could not answer easily; and the fact that it had actually happened to the author brought it home to the reader that some awful alternative might at any moment be presented to himself. And what would he do then, poor thing? And Michael felt one of those sudden bursts of consideration and even respect for the public which often came over him and so affected his more intelligent friends that they alluded to him as 'Poor Michael!'

So meditating, he reached his room at the House of Commons, and had settled down to the consideration of a private bill to preserve certain natural beauties when a card was brought to him:

General Sir Conway Cherrell
Can you see me?

Pencilling: '*Delighted, sir!*' he handed the card back to the attendant and got up. Of all his uncles he knew Dinny's father least, and he waited with some trepidation.

The General came in, saying:

'Regular rabbit-warren this, Michael.'

He had the confirmed neatness of his profession, but his face looked worn and worried.

'Luckily we don't breed here, Uncle Con.'

The General emitted a short laugh.

'No, there's that. I hope I'm not interrupting you. It's about Dinny. She still with you?'

'Yes, sir.'

The General hesitated, and then, crossing his hands on his stick, said firmly:

'You're Desert's best friend, aren't you?'

'Was. What I am now, I really don't know.'

'Is he still in town?'

'Yes; he's been having a bout of malaria, I believe.'

'Dinny still seeing him?'

'No, sir.'

Again the General hesitated, and again seemed to firm himself by gripping his stick.

'Her mother and I, you know, only want what's best for her. We want her happiness; the rest doesn't matter. What do you think?'

'I really don't believe it matters what any of us think.'

The General frowned.

'How do you mean?'

'It's just between those two.'

'I understood that he was going away.'

'He said so to my father, but he hasn't gone. His publisher told me just now that he was still at his rooms this morning.'

'How is Dinny?'

'Very low in her mind. But she keeps her end up.'

'He ought to do something.'

'What, sir?'

'It's not fair to Dinny. He ought either to marry her or go right away.'

'Would you find it easy, in his place, to make up your mind?'

'Perhaps not.'

Michael made a restless tour of his little room.

'I think the whole thing is way below any question of just yes or no. It's a case of wounded pride, and when you've got that, the other emotions don't run straight. You ought to know that, sir. You must have had similar cases, when fellows have been court-martialled.'

The word seemed to strike the General with the force of a revelation. He stared at his nephew and did not answer.

'Wilfrid,' said Michael, 'is being court-martialled, and it isn't a short sharp business like a real court-martial – it's a desperate long-drawn-out affair, with no end to it that I can grasp.'

'I see,' said the General, quietly: 'But he should never have let Dinny in for it.'

Michael smiled. 'Does love ever do what's correct?'

'That's the modern view, anyway.'

'According to report, the ancient one, too.'

The General went to the window and stood looking out.

'I don't like to go and see Dinny,' he said, without turning round; 'it seems like worrying her. Her mother feels the same. And there's nothing we can do.'

His voice, troubled not for himself, touched Michael.

'I believe,' he said, 'that in some way it'll all be over very soon. And whichever way will be better for them and all of us than this.'

The General turned round.

'Let's hope so. I wanted to ask you to keep in touch with us, and not let Dinny do anything without letting us know. It's very hard waiting down there. I won't keep you now; and thank you, it's been a relief. Good-bye, Michael!'

He grasped his nephew's hand, squeezed it firmly, and was gone.

Michael thought: 'Hanging in the wind! There's nothing worse. Poor old boy!'

Chapter Thirty-three

Compson Grice, who had no mean disposition and a certain liking for Michael, went out to lunch mindful of his promise. A believer in the power of meals to solve difficulties, he would normally have issued an invitation and obtained his information over the second or third glass of really old brandy. But he was afraid of Wilfrid. Discussing his simple *sole meunière* and half-bottle of Chablis, he decided on a letter. He wrote it in the Club's little green-panelled writing room, with a cup of coffee by his side and a cigar in his mouth.

The Hotch Potch Club: Friday.

DEAR DESERT,

In view of the remarkable success of *The Leopard* and the probability of further large sales, I feel that I ought to know definitely what you would like me to do with the royalty cheques when they fall due. Perhaps you would be so good as to tell me whether you contemplate going back to the East, and if so when; and at the same time let me have an address to which I can remit with safety. Possibly you would prefer that I should simply pay your royalties into your bank, whatever that is, and take their receipt. Hitherto our financial transactions have been somewhat lean, but *The Leopard* will certainly have – indeed, is already having – an influence on the sales of your two previous books; and it will be advisable that you should keep me in touch with your whereabouts in future. Shall you be in Town much longer? I am always delighted to see you, if you care to look in.

With hearty congratulations and best wishes,

I am, sincerely yours,

Compson Grice

This letter, in his elegant and upright hand, he addressed to Cork Street and sent at once by the club messenger. The remains of his recess he spent sounding in his rather whispering voice the praises of his French Canadian product, and then took a taxi back to Covent Garden. A clerk met him in the lobby.

'Mr Desert is waiting up in your room, sir.'

'Good!' said Compson Grice, subduing a tremor and thinking: 'Quick work!'

Wilfrid was standing at a window which commanded a slanting view of Covent Garden market; and Grice was shocked when he turned round – the face was so dark and wasted and had such a bitter look: the hand, too, had an unpleasant dry heat in the feel of it.

'So you got my letter?' he said.

'Thanks. Here's the address of my bank. Better pay all cheques into it and take their receipt.'

'You don't look too fearfully well. Are you off again?'

'Probably. Well, good-bye, Grice. Thanks for all you've done.'

Compson Grice said, with real feeling: 'I'm terribly sorry it's hit you so hard.'

Wilfrid shrugged and turned to the door.

When he was gone his publisher stood, twisting the bank's address, in his hands. Suddenly he said out loud: 'I don't like his looks; I absolutely don't!' And he went to the telephone . . .

Wilfrid walked north; he had another visit to pay. He reached the museum just as Adrian was having his cup of 'Dover' tea and bun.

'Good!' said Adrian, rising. 'I'm glad to see you. There's a spare cup. Do sit down.'

He had experienced the same shock as Grice at the look on Desert's face and the feel of his hand.

Wilfrid took a sip of tea. 'May I smoke?' He lighted a cigarette, and sat, hunched in his chair. Adrian waited for him to speak.

'Sorry to butt in on you like this,' said Wilfrid, at last, 'but I'm going back into the blue. I wanted to know which would hurt Dinny least – just to clear out or to write.'

Adrian lived through a wretched and bleak minute.

'You mean that if you see her you can't trust yourself.' Desert gave a shivering shrug.

'It's not that exactly. It sounds brutal, but I'm so fed up that I don't feel anything. If I saw her – I might wound her. She's been an angel. I don't suppose you can understand what's happened in me. I can't myself. I only know that I want to get away from everything and everybody.'

Adrian nodded.

'I was told you'd been ill – you don't think that accounts for your present feeling? For God's sake don't make a mistake in your feelings now!'

Wilfrid smiled.

'I'm used to malaria. It's not that. You'll laugh, but I feel like bleeding to death inside. I want to get to where nothing and nobody remind me. And Dinny reminds me more than anyone.'

'I see,' said Adrian gravely. And he was silent, passing his hand over his bearded chin. Then he got up and began to walk about.

'Do you think it's fair to Dinny or yourself not to try what seeing her might do?'

Wilfrid answered, almost with violence: 'I tell you, I should hurt her.'

'You'll hurt her any way; her eggs are all in one basket. And look here, Desert! You published that poem deliberately. I always understood you did so as a form of expiation, even though you had asked Dinny to marry you. I'm not such a fool as to want you to go on with Dinny if your feelings have really changed; but are you sure they have?'

'My feelings haven't changed. I simply have none. Being a pariah dog has killed them.'

'Do you realise what you're saying?'

'Perfectly! I knew I was a pariah from the moment I recanted, and that whether people knew it or not didn't matter. All the same – it *has* mattered.'

'I see,' said Adrian again, and came to a standstill. 'I suppose that's natural.'

'Whether it is to others, I don't know; it is to me. I am out of the herd, and I'll stay there. I don't complain. I side against myself.' He spoke with desperate energy.

Adrian said, very gently: 'Then you just want to know how to hurt Dinny least? I can't tell you: I wish I could. I gave you the wrong advice when you came before. Advice is no good, anyway. We have to wrestle things out for ourselves.'

Wilfrid stood up. 'Ironical, isn't it? I was driven to Dinny by my loneliness. I'm driven away from her by it. Well, good-bye, sir; I don't suppose I shall ever see you again. And thanks for trying to help me.'

'I wish to God I could.'

Wilfrid smiled the sudden smile that gave him his charm.

'I'll try what one more walk will do. I may see some writing on the wall. Anyway, you'll know I didn't want to hurt her more than I could help. Good-bye!'

Adrian's tea was cold and his bun uneaten. He pushed them away. He felt as if he had failed Dinny, and yet for the life of him could not see what he could have done. That young man looked very queer! 'Bleeding to death inside!' Gruesome phrase! And true, judging by his face! Fibre sensitive as his, and a consuming pride! 'Going back into the blue.' To roam about in the East – a sort of Wandering Jew; become one of those mysterious Englishmen found in out-of-the-way places, with no origins that they would speak of, and no future but their present. He filled a pipe and tried his best to feel that, after all, in the long run Dinny would be happier unmarried to him. And he did not succeed. There was only one flowering of real love in a woman's life, and this was hers. He had no doubt on that point. She would make shift – oh! yes; but she would have missed 'the singing and the gold'. And, grabbing his battered hat, he went out. He strode along in the direction of Hyde Park; then, yielding to a whim, diverged towards Mount Street.

When Blore announced him, his sister was putting the last red stitches in the tongue of one of the dogs in her French tapestry. She held it up.

'It ought to drip. He's looking at that bunny. Would blue drips be right?'

'Grey, Em, on that background.'

Lady Mont considered her brother sitting in a small chair with his long legs hunched up.

'You look like a war correspondent – camp stools, and no time to shave. I do want Dinny to be married, Adrian. She's twenty-six. All that about bein' yellow. They could go to Corsica.'

Adrian smiled. Em was so right, and yet so wrong!

'Con was here today,' resumed his sister, 'he'd been seein' Michael. Nobody knows anythin'. And Dinny just goes walks with Kit and Dandy, Fleur says, and nurses Catherine, and sits readin' books without turnin' the page.'

Adrian debated whether to tell her of Desert's visit to him.

'And Con says,' went on Lady Mont, 'that he can't make two ends meet this year – Clare's weddin' and the Budget, and Jean expectin' – he'll have to cut down some trees, and sell the horses. We're hard up, too. It's lucky Fleur's got so much. Money is such a bore. What do you think?'

Adrian gave a start.

'Well, no one expects a good thing nowadays, but one wants enough to live on.'

'It's havin' dependants. Boswell's got a sister that can only walk with one leg; and Johnson's wife's got cancer – poor thing! And everybody's got somebody or somethin'. Dinny says at Condaford her mother does everythin' in the village. So how it's to go on, I don't know. Lawrence doesn't save a penny.'

'We're falling between two stools, Em; and one fine day we shall reach the floor with a bump.'

'I suppose we shall live in almshouses.' And Lady Mont lifted her work up to the light. 'No, I shan't make it drip. Or else go to Kenya; they say there's somethin' that pays there.'

'What I hate,' said Adrian with sudden energy, 'is the thought of Mr Tom Noddy or somebody buying Condaford and using it for weekend cocktail parties.'

'I should go and be a Banshee in the woods. There couldn't be Condaford without Cherrells.'

'There dashed well could, Em. There's a confounded process called evolution; and England is its home.'

Lady Mont sighed, and, getting up, swayed over to her parakeet.

'Polly! You and I will go and live in an almshouse.'

Chapter Thirty-four

When Compson Grice telephoned to Michael, or rather to Fleur, for Michael was not in, he sounded embarrassed.

'Is there any message I can give him, Mr Grice?'

'Your husband asked me to find out Desert's movements. Well, Desert's just been in to see me, and practically said he was off again; but – er – I didn't like his looks, and his hand was like a man's in fever.'

'He's been having malaria.'

'Oh! Ah! By the way, I'm sending you a book I'm sure you'll like; it's by that French Canadian.'

'Thank you, very much. I'll tell Michael when he comes in.'

And Fleur stood thinking. Ought she to pass this on to Dinny? Without consulting Michael she did not like to, and he, tied tightly to the House just now, might not even be in to dinner. How like Wilfrid to keep one on tenterhooks! She always felt that she knew him better than either Dinny or Michael. They were convinced of a vein of pure gold in him. She, for whom he had once had such a pressing passion, could only assess that vein at nine carat. 'That, I suppose,' she thought, rather bitterly, 'is because my nature is lower than theirs.' People assessed others according to their own natures, didn't they? Still, it was difficult to give high value to one whose mistress she had not become, and who had then fled into the blue. There was always extravagance in Michael's likings; in Dinny – well, Dinny she did not really understand.

And so she went back to the letters she was writing. They were important, for she was rallying the best and brightest people to meet some high-caste Indian ladies who were over for the Conference. She had nearly finished when she was called to the telephone by Michael, asking if there were any message from Compson Grice. Having given him what news there was, she went on:

'Are you coming in to dinner? . . . Good! I dread dining alone with Dinny; she's so marvellously cheerful, it gives me the creeps. Not worry other people and all that, of course; but if she showed her feelings more it would worry us less . . . Uncle Con! . . . That's rather funny, the whole family seems to want now the exact opposite of what they wanted at first. I suppose it's the result of watching her suffer . . . Yes, she went in the car to sail Kit's boat on the Round Pond; they sent Dandy and the boat back in the car, and are walking home . . . All right, dear boy. Eight o'clock; don't be late if you can help it . . . Oh! here *are* Kit and Dinny. Good-bye!'

Kit had come into the room. His face was brown, his eyes blue, his sweater the same colour as his eyes, his shorts darker blue; his green stockings were gartered below his bare knees, and his brown shoes had brogues; he wore no cap on his bright head.

'Auntie Dinny has gone to lie down. She had to sit on the grass. She says she'll be all right soon. D'you think she's going to have measles? I've had them, Mummy, so when she's isolated I can still see her. We saw a man who frightened her.'

'What sort of man?'

'He didn't come near; a tall sort of man; he had his hat in his hand, and when he saw us, he almost ran.'

'How do you know he saw you?'

'Oh! he went like that, and scooted.'

'Was that in the Park?'

'Yes.'

'Which?'

'The Green Park.'

'Was he thin, and dark in the face?'

'Yes; do you know him too?'

'Why "too", Kit? Did Auntie Dinny know him?'

'*I* think so; she said: "Oh!" like that, and put her hand here. And then she looked after him; and then she sat down on the grass. I fanned her with her scarf. I love Auntie Dinny. Has she a husband?'

'No.'

When he had gone up, Fleur debated. Dinny must have realised that Kit would describe everything. She decided only to send up a message and some sal volatile.

The answer came back: 'I shall be all right by dinner.'

But at dinner-time a further message came to say she still felt rather faint: might she just go to bed and have a long night?

Thus it was that Michael and Fleur sat down alone.

'It was Wilfrid, of course.'

Michael nodded.

'I wish to God he'd go. It's so wretched – the whole thing! D'you remember that passage in Turgenev, where Litvinov watches the train smoke curling away over the fields?'

'No. Why?'

'All Dinny's tissue going up in smoke.'

'Yes,' said Fleur between tight lips. 'But the fire will burn out.'

'And leave—?'

'Oh! She'll be recognisable.'

Michael looked hard at the partner of his board. She was regarding the morsel of fish on her fork. With a little set smile on her lips she raised it to her mouth and began champing, as if chewing the cud of experience. Recognisable! Yes, *she* was as pretty as ever, though more firmly moulded, as if in tune with the revival of shape. He turned his eyes away, for he still squirmed when he thought of that business four years ago, of which he had known so little, suspected so much, and talked not at all. Smoke! Did all human passion burn away and drift in a blue film over the fields, obscure for a moment the sight of the sun and the shapes of the crops and the trees, then fade into air and leave the clear hard day; and no difference anywhere? Not quite! For smoke was burnt tissue, and where fire had raged there was alteration. Of the Dinny he had known from a small child up, the outline would be changed – hardened, sharpened, refined, withered? And he said:

'I must be back at the House by nine, the Chancellor's speaking. Why one should listen to him, I don't know, but one does.'

'Why you should listen to anyone will always be a mystery. Did you ever know any speaker in the House change anyone's opinions?'

'No,' said Michael with a wry smile, 'but one lives in hopes. We sit day after day talking of some blessed measure, and then take a vote, with the same result as if we'd taken it at the end of the first two speeches. And that's gone on for hundreds of years.'

'So filial!' said Fleur. 'Kit thinks Dinny is going to have measles. He's asking, too, if she has a husband . . . Coaker, bring the coffee, please. Mr Mont has to go.'

When he had kissed her and gone, Fleur went up to the nurseries. Catherine was the soundest of sleepers, and it was pleasant to watch her, a pretty child with hair that would probably be like her own and eyes so hesitating between grey and hazel that they gave promise of becoming ice-green. One small hand was crumpled against her cheek, and she breathed lightly as a flower. Nodding to the nurse, Fleur pushed open the door into the other nursery. To wake Kit was dangerous. He would demand biscuits, and, very likely, milk, want light conversation, and ask her to read to him. But in spite of the door's faint creaking he did not wake. His bright head was thrust determinedly into the pillow from under which the butt of a pistol protruded. It was hot, and he had thrown back the clothes, so that, by the glimmer of the night-light his blue-pyjama'd figure was disclosed to the knees. His skin was brown and healthy, and he had a Forsyte's chin. Fleur moved up and stood quite close. He looked 'such a duck', thus determinedly asleep in face of the opposition put up by his quickening imagination. With feathered finger-tips she gripped the sheet, pulled it up, and gingerly let it down over him; then stood back with her hands on her hips, and one eyebrow raised. He was at the best age in life, and would be for another two years until he went to school. No sex to bother him as yet! Everybody kind to him; everything an adventure out of books. Books! Michael's old books, her own, the few written since fit for children. He was at the wonderful age! She looked swiftly round the twilit room. His gun and sword lay ready on a chair! One supported disarmament, and armed children to the teeth! His other toys, mostly mechanised, would be in the schoolroom. No; there on the window-sill was the boat he had sailed with Dinny, its sails still set; and there on a cushion in the corner was 'the silver dog', aware of her but too lazy to get up. She could see the slim feather of his tail cocked and waving gently at her. And, afraid lest she might disturb this admirable peace, she blew a kiss to both of them and stole back through the door. Nodding again to the nurse, she inspected Catherine's eyelashes and went out. Down the stairs she tip-toed to the floor on which was Dinny's room, above her own. Was it unfeeling not to look in and ask if there were anything she wanted? She moved closer to the door. Only half-past nine! She could not be asleep. Probably she would not sleep at all. It was hateful to think of her lying there silent and unhappy. Perhaps to talk would be a comfort, would take her mind off! She was raising her hand to knock when a sound came forth, smothered, yet unmistakable – the gasping sobs of one crying into her pillow. Fleur stood as if turned to stone. A noise she had not heard since she herself had made it nearly four years ago! It turned her sick with the force of memory – a horrible, but a sacred sound. Not for worlds would she go in! She covered her ears, drew back, and fled downstairs. For further protection from that searing sound she turned on the portable wireless. It gave forth from the second act of *Madame Butterfly*. She turned it off and sat down again at her bureau. She wrote rapidly a kind of formula: 'Such a pleasure if, etc. – meet those very charming Indian ladies who, etc. – Yours, etc., Fleur Mont.' Over and over and over, and the sound of that sobbing in her ears! It was stuffy tonight! She drew the curtains aside and threw the window wider to let in what air there was. A hostile thing, life, full of silent menace and small annoyances. If you went towards and grasped life with both hands, it yielded, perhaps, then drew back to deal some ugly stroke. Half-past ten! What were they jabbering about now in Parliament? Some twopenny-ha'penny tax! She closed the window and drew the curtains again, stamped her letters, and stood looking round the room before turning out and going up. And, suddenly, came a memory – of Wilfrid's face outside close to the glass of the window, on the night he fled from her to the East. If it were there now; if, for a second time in his strange life, he came like a disembodied spirit to that window, seeking now not her but Dinny? She switched off the light and groped her way to the window, cautiously drew the curtains apart a very little, and peered out. Nothing but the last of the artificially delayed daylight! Impatiently she dropped the curtain and went upstairs. Standing before her long mirror, she listened a moment, and then carefully did not. How like life, that! One shut eyes and ears to all that was painful – if one could. And who could blame one? Plenty, to which one could shut neither eyes nor ears, seeped-in even through closed lids and cotton-wool. She was just getting into bed when Michael came. She told him of the sobbing, and he in turn stood listening; but nothing penetrated the room's solid roofing. He went into his dressing room and came back presently in a dressing-gown she had given him, blue, with embroidered cuffs and collar, and began to walk up and down.

'Come to bed,' said Fleur; 'you can't help by doing that.'

They talked a little in bed. It was Michael who fell asleep. Fleur lay wakeful. Big Ben struck twelve. The town murmured on, but the house was very still. A little crack now and then, as though some board were settling down after the day's pressure of feet; the snuffle, not loud, of Michael's breathing – such, and the whispering, as it were, of her own thoughts, were its only noises. From the room above not a sound. She began to think of where they should go in the long vacation. Scotland had been spoken of, and Cornwall; she herself wanted the Riviera for a month at least. To come back brown all over; she had never been properly sun-browned yet! With Mademoiselle and Nanny the children would be safe! What was that? A door closing. Surely the creaking of stairs! She touched Michael.

'Yes?'

'Listen!'

Again that faint creaking.

'It began above,' whispered Fleur; 'I think you ought to see.'

He got out of bed, put on his dressing-gown and slippers, and, opening the door quietly, looked out. Nothing on the landing, but the sound of someone moving in the hall! He slipped down the stairs.

There was a dim figure by the front door, and he said gently:

'Is that you, Dinny?'

'Yes.'

Michael moved forward. Her figure left the door, and he came on her sitting on the coat 'sarcophagus'. He could just see that her hand was raised, holding a scarf over her head and face.

'Is there anything I can get you?'

'No. I wanted some air.'

Michael checked his impulse to turn the light up. He moved forward, and in the darkness stroked her arm.

'I didn't think you'd hear,' she said. 'I'm sorry.'

Dared he speak of her trouble? Would she hate him for it or be grateful?

'My dear,' he said, 'anything that'll do you good.'

'It's silly. I'll go up again.'

Michael put his arm round her; he could feel that she was fully dressed. After a moment she relaxed against him, still holding the scarf so that it veiled her face and head. He rocked her gently – the least little movement side to side. Her body slipped till her head rested against his shoulder. Michael ceased to rock, ceased almost to breathe. As long as she would, let her rest there!

Chapter Thirty-five

When Wilfrid left Adrian's room at the Museum, he had no plan or direction in his mind, and walked along like a man in one of those dreams where the theme is repeated over and over, and the only end is awakening. He went down the Kingsway to the Embankment, came to Westminster Bridge, turned on to it, and stood leaning over the parapet. A jump, and he would be out of it! The tide was running down – English water escaping to the seas, nevermore to come back, glad to go! Escape! Escape from all those who made him think of himself. To be rid of this perpetual self-questioning and self-consciousness! To end this damned mawkish indecision, this puling concern as to whether one would hurt her too much! But of course one would not hurt her too much! She would cry and get over it. Sentiment had betrayed him once! Not again! By God! Not again!

He stood there a long time, leaning on the parapet, watching the bright water and the craft creeping by; and every now and then a passing Cockney would stand beside him, as if convinced that he was looking out at something of sensational interest. And he was! He was seeing his own life finally 'in the blue', unmoored, careering like the Flying Dutchman on far waters to the far ends of the world. But at least without need for bravado, kowtowing, appeal, or pretence, under his own flag, and that not at half-mast.

'I've 'eard,' said a voice, 'that lookin' at the water long enough will make 'em jump sometimes.'

Wilfrid shuddered and walked away. God! How raw and jagged one had got! He walked off the bridge past the end of Whitehall into St James's Park, skirted the long water up to the geraniums and the large stone males, females, and fruits in front of the Palace, passed into the Green Park, and threw himself down on the dry grass. He lay there perhaps an hour on his back with his hand over his eyes, grateful for the sun soaking into him. When he got up he felt dizzy, and had to stand some minutes to get his balance before moving towards Hyde Park Corner. He had gone but a little way when he started and swerved off to the right. Coming towards him, nearer the riding track, were a young woman and a little boy. Dinny! He had seen her gasp, her hand go to her heart. And he had swerved and walked away. It was brutal, horrible, but it was final. So a man, who had thrust a dagger home, would feel. Brutal, horrible, but final! No more indecision! Nothing now but to get away as quick as ever he could! He turned towards his rooms, striding along as if possessed, his lips drawn back in such a smile as a man has in a dentist's chair. He had stricken down the only woman who had ever seemed to him worth marrying, the only woman for whom he had felt what was worthy to be called real love. Well! Better strike her down like that than kill her by living with her! He was as Esau, and as Ishmael, not fit for a daughter of Israel. And a messenger boy turned and stared after him – the pace at which he walked was so foreign to the youth's habitual feelings. He crossed Piccadilly with no concern whatever for its traffic, and plunged into the narrow mouth of Bond Street. It suddenly struck him that he would never see Scott's hats again. The shop had just been shut, but those hats rested in rows, super-conventional hats, tropical hats, ladies' hats, and specimens of the newest Trilby or Homburg, or whatever they called it now. He strode on, rounded the scent of Atkinson's, and came to his own door. There he had to sit down at the foot of the stairs before he could find strength to climb. The spasmodic energy which had followed the shock of seeing her had ebbed out in utter lassitude. He was just beginning to mount when Stack and the dog came down. Foch rushed at his legs and stood against him, reaching his head up. Wilfrid crumpled his ears. To leave him once more without a master!

'I'm off early tomorrow morning, Stack. To Siam. I probably shan't be coming back.'

'Not at all, sir?'

'Not at all.'

'Would you like me to come too, sir?'

Wilfrid put his hand on the henchman's shoulder.

'Jolly good of you, Stack; but you'd be bored to death.'

'Excuse me, sir, but you're hardly fit to travel alone at present.'

'Perhaps not, but I'm going to.'

The henchman bent his eyes on Wilfrid's face. It was a grave intent gaze, as if he were committing that face finally to heart.

'I've been with you a long time, sir.'

'You have, Stack; and nobody could have been nicer to me. I've made provision in case anything happens to me. You'd prefer to go on here, I expect, keeping the rooms for when my father wants them.'

'I should be sorry to leave here, if I can't come with you. Are you sure about that, sir?'

Wilfrid nodded. 'Quite sure, Stack. What about Foch?'

Stack hesitated, then said with a rush: 'I think I ought to tell you, sir, that when Miss Cherrell was here last – the night you went off to Epping – she said that if you was to go away at any time, she would be glad to have the dog. He's fond of her, sir.'

Wilfrid's face became a mask.

'Take him for his run,' he said, and went on up the stairs.

His mind was once again in turmoil. Murder! But it was

done! One did not bring a corpse to life with longing or remorse. The dog, if she wanted him, was hers, of course! Why did women cling to memories, when all they should wish should be to forget? He sat down at his bureau and wrote:

I am going away for good. Foch comes to you with this. He is yours if you care to have him. I am only fit to be alone. Forgive me if you can, and forget me. – WILFRID

He addressed it, and sat on at the bureau slowly turning his head and looking round the room. Under three months since the day he had come back. He felt as if he had lived a lifetime. Dinny over there at the hearth, after her father had been! Dinny on the divan looking up at him! Dinny here, Dinny there!

Her smile, her eyes, her hair! Dinny, and that memory in the Arab tent, pulling at each other, wrestling for him. Why had he not seen the end from the beginning? He might have known himself! He took a sheet of paper and wrote:

MY DEAR FATHER,

England doesn't seem to agree with me, and I am starting to-morrow for Siam. My bank will have my address from time to time. Stack will keep things going here as usual, so that the rooms will be ready whenever you want them. I hope you'll take care of yourself. I'll try and send you a coin for your collection now and then. Good-bye.

Yours affectionately,

WILFRID

His father would read it and say: 'Dear me! Very sudden! Queer fellow!' And that was about all that anyone would think or say – except—!

He took another sheet of paper and wrote to his bank; then lay down, exhausted, on the divan.

Stack must pack, he hadn't the strength. Luckily his passport was in order – that curious document which rendered one independent of one's kind; that password to whatever loneliness one wanted. The room was very still, for at this hour of lull before dinner traffic began there was hardly any noise from the streets. The stuff which he took after attacks of malaria had opium in it, and a dreamy feeling came over him. He drew a long breath and relaxed. To his half-drugged senses scents kept coming – the scent of camels' dung, of coffee roasting, carpets, spices, and humanity in the *Suks*, the sharp unscented air of the desert, and the foetid reek of some river village; and sounds – the whine of beggars, a camel's coughing grunts, the cry of the jackal, Muezzin call, padding of donkeys' feet, tapping of the silversmiths, the creaking and moaning of water being drawn. And before his half-closed eyes visions came floating; a sort of long dream-picture of the East as he had known it. Now it would be another East, further and more strange! . . . He slipped into a real dream . . .

Chapter Thirty-six

Seeing him turn away from her in the Green Park, Dinny had known for certain it was all over. The sight of his ravaged face had moved her to the depths. If only he could be happy again she could put up with it. For since the evening he left her in his rooms she had been steeling herself, never really believing in anything but this. After those moments with Michael in the dark hall she slept a little and had her coffee upstairs. A message was brought her about ten o'clock that a man with a dog was waiting to see her.

She finished dressing quickly, put on her hat, and went down.

It could only be Stack.

The henchman was standing beside the 'sarcophagus', holding Foch on a lead. His face, full of understanding as ever, was lined and pale, as if he had been up all night.

'Mr Desert sent this, miss.' He held out a note.

Dinny opened the door of the drawing room.

'Come in here, please, Stack. Let's sit down.'

He sat down and let go of the lead. The dog went to her and put his nose on her knee. Dinny read the note.

'Mr Desert says that I may have Foch.'

Stack bent his gaze on his boots. 'He's gone, miss. Went by the early service to Paris and Marseilles.'

She could see moisture in the folds of his cheeks. He gave a loud sniff, and angrily brushed his hand over his face.

'I've been with him fourteen years, miss. It was bound to hit me. He talks of not coming back.'

'Where has he gone?'

'Siam.'

'A long way,' said Dinny with a smile. 'The great thing is that he should be happy again.'

'That is so, miss. I don't know if you'd care to hear about the dog's food. He has a dry biscuit about nine, and shin of beef or sheep's head, cooked, with crumbled hound-meal, between six and seven, and nothing else. A good quiet dog, he is, perfect gentleman in the house. He'll sleep in your bedroom if you like.'

'Do you stay where you are, Stack?'

'Yes, miss. The rooms are his lordship's. As I told you, Mr Desert is sudden; but I think he means what he says. He never was happy in England.'

'I'm sure he means what he says. Is there anything I can do for you, Stack?'

The henchman shook his head, his eyes rested on Dinny's face, and she knew he was debating whether he dared offer sympathy. She stood up.

'I think I'll take Foch a walk and get him used to me.'

'Yes, miss. I don't let him off the lead except in the parks. If there's anything you want to know about him any time, you have the number.'

Dinny put out her hand.

'Well, good-bye, Stack, and best wishes.'

'The same to you, miss, I'm sure.' His eyes had what was more than understanding in them, and the grip of his hand had a spasmodic strength. Dinny continued to smile till he was gone and the door closed, then sat down on the sofa with her hands over her eyes. The dog, who had followed

Stack to the door, whined once, and came back to her. She uncovered her eyes, took Wilfrid's note from her lap, and tore it up.

'Well, Foch,' she said, 'what shall we do? Nice walk?'

The tail moved; he again whined slightly.

'Come along, then, boy.'

She felt steady, but as if a spring had broken. With the dog on the lead she walked towards Victoria Station, and stopped before the statue. The leaves had thickened round it, and that was all the change. Man and horse, remote, active, and contained – 'workmanlike'! A long time she stood there, her face raised, dry-eyed, thin and drawn; and the dog sat patiently beside her.

Then, with a shrug, she turned away and led him rapidly towards the Park. When she had walked some time, she went to Mount Street and asked for Sir Lawrence. He was in his study.

'Well, my dear,' he said, 'that looks a nice dog; is he yours?'

'Yes. Uncle Lawrence, will you do something for me?'

'Surely.'

'Wilfrid has gone. He went this morning. He is not coming back. Would you be so very kind as to let my people know, and Michael, and Aunt Em, and Uncle Adrian. I don't want ever to have to speak of it.'

Sir Lawrence inclined his head, took her hand and put it to his lips. 'There was something I wanted to show you, Dinny.' He took from his table a little statuette of Voltaire. 'I picked that up two days ago. Isn't he a delightful old cynic? Why the French should be so much pleasanter as cynics than other people is mysterious, except, of course, that cynicism, to be tolerable, must have grace and wit; apart from those, it's just bad manners. An English cynic is a man with a general grievance. A German cynic is a sort of wild boar. A Scandinavian cynic is a pestilence. An American jumps around too much to make a cynic, and a Russian's state of mind is not constant enough. You might get a perfectly good cynic in Austria, perhaps, or northern China – possibly it's a question of latitude.'

Dinny smiled.

'Give my love to Aunt Em, please. I'm going home this afternoon.'

'God bless you, my dear,' said Sir Lawrence. 'Come here, or to Lippinghall, whenever you want; we love having you.' And he kissed her forehead.

When she had gone, he went to the telephone, and then sought his wife.

'Em, poor Dinny has just been here. She looks like a smiling ghost. It's all over. Desert went off for good this morning. She doesn't want ever to speak of it. Can you remember that?'

Lady Mont, who was arranging some flowers in a Chinese ginger jar, dropped them and turned round.

'Oh! dear!' she said. 'Kiss me, Lawrence!'

They stood for a moment embraced. Poor Em! Her heart was soft as butter! She said into his shoulder: 'Your collar's all covered with hairs. You *will* brush your hair after you've put your coat on. Turn! I'll pick them off.'

Sir Lawrence turned.

'I've telephoned to Condaford and Michael and Adrian. Remember, Em! The thing is as if it never was.'

'Of course I shall remember. Why did she come to you?'

Sir Lawrence shrugged. 'She's got a new dog, a black spaniel.'

'Very faithful, but they get fat. There! Did they say anything on the telephone?'

'Only: "Oh!" and "I see," and "Of course".'

'Lawrence, I want to cry; come back presently and take me somewhere.'

Sir Lawrence patted her shoulders and went out quickly. He, too, felt peculiar. Back in his study, he sat in thought. Desert's flight was the only possible solution! Of all those affected by this incident, he had the clearest and most just insight into Wilfrid. True, probably, that the fellow had a vein of gold in him which his general nature did its best to hide! But to live with? Not on your life! Yellow? Of course he wasn't that! The thing was not plain-sailing, as Jack Muskham and the pukka sahibs supposed, with their superstition that black was not white, and so on. No, no! Young Desert had been snared in a most peculiar way. Given his perverse nature, its revolts, humanitarianism, and want of belief, given his way of hob-nobbing with the Arabs, his case was as different from that of the ordinary Englishman as chalk from cheese. But, whatever his case, he was not a man to live with! Poor Dinny was well out of that! What pranks Fate played! Why should her choice have fallen there? If you came to that, why anything where love was concerned? It knew no laws, not even those of common-sense. Some element in her had flown straight to its kindred element in him, disregarding all that was not kindred, and all outside circumstance. She might never get again the chance of that particular 'nick', as Jack Muskham would call it. But – good Gad! – marriage was a lifelong business; yes, even in these days, no passing joke! For marriage you wanted all the luck and all the give and take that you could get. Not much give and take about Desert – restless, disharmonic, and a poet! And proud – with that inner self-depreciative pride which never let up on a man! A liaison, one of those leaping companionships young people went in for now – possibly; but that didn't fit Dinny; even Desert must have felt so. In her the physical without the spiritual seemed out of place. Ah! Well! Another long heartache in the world – poor Dinny.

'Where,' he thought, 'can I take Em at this time in the morning? The Zoo she doesn't like; I'm sick of the Wallace. Madame Tussaud's! Gaiety will break through. Madame Tussaud's!'

Chapter Thirty-seven

At Condaford Jean went straight from the telephone to find her mother-in-law, and repeated Sir Lawrence's words with her usual decision. The gentle rather timid expression on Lady Cherrell's face changed to a startled concern.

'Oh!'

'Shall I tell the General?'

'Please, dear.'

Alone again with her accounts, Lady Cherrell sat thinking. The only one of the family, except Hubert, who had never seen Wilfrid Desert, she had tried to keep an open mind, and had no definite opposition on her conscience. She felt now only a troubled sympathy. What could one do? And, as is customary in the case of another's bereavement, she could only think of flowers.

She slipped out into the garden and went to the rose beds, which, flanked by tall yew hedges, clustered round the old sundial. She plucked a basket full of the best blossoms, took them up to Dinny's narrow and conventual bedroom, and disposed them in bowls by the bedside and on the window-sill. Then, opening the door and mullioned window wide, she rang for the room to be dusted and the bed made. The Medici prints on the walls she carefully set exactly straight, and said:

'I've dusted the pictures, Annie. Keep the window and door open. I want it all to smell sweet. Can you do the room now?'

'Yes, m'lady.'

'Then I think you'd better, I don't know what time Miss Dinny will be here.'

Back with her accounts, she could not settle to them, and, pushing them into a drawer, went to find her husband. He, too, was seated before bills and papers without sign of animation. She went up to him and pressed his head against her.

'Jean's told you, Con?'

'Yes. It's the only thing, of course; but I hate Dinny to be sad.'

They were silent till Lady Cherrell said:

'I'd tell Dinny about our being so hard up. It would take her mind off.'

The General ruffled his hair. 'I shall be three hundred down on the year. I might get a couple of hundred for the horses, the rest must come out of trees. I don't know which I dislike more. Do you think she could suggest something?'

'No, but she would worry, and that would prevent her troubling so much over the other thing.'

'I see. Well, Jean or you tell her, then. I don't like to. It looks like hinting that I want to reduce her allowance. It's a pittance as it is. Make it plain there's no question of that. Travel would have been the thing for her, but where's the money to come from?'

Lady Cherrell did not know, and the conversation lapsed.

Into that old house, which for so many centuries human hopes, fears, births, deaths, and all the medley of everyday emotions had stamped with a look of wary age, had come an uneasiness which showed in every word and action, even of the maids. What attitude to adopt? How to show sympathy, and yet not show it? How to welcome, and yet make it clear that welcome did not carry rejoicing? Even Jean was infected.

She brushed and combed the dogs, and insisted on taking the car to meet every afternoon train.

Dinny came by the third. Leading Foch, she stepped out of the carriage almost into Jean's arms.

'Hallo, my dear,' said Jean, 'here you are! New dog?'

'Yes; a darling.'

'What have you got?'

'Only these things. It's no use looking for a porter, they're always trundling bicycles.'

'I'll get them out.'

'Indeed you won't! Hold Foch.'

When, carrying her suitcase and dressing-bag, she reached the car, Dinny said:

'Would you mind if I walk up by the fields, Jean? It's good for Foch; and the train was stuffy; I should like a sniff of the hay.'

'Yes, there's some down still. I'll take these along, and have fresh tea ready.'

She left Dinny standing with a smile on her face. And all the way to the Grange she thought of that smile and swore under her breath . . .

Entering the field path, Dinny let Foch off his lead. By the way he rushed to the hedgerow, she realised how he had missed all this. A country dog! For a moment his busy joy took up her attention; then the sore and bitter aching came back again. She called him and walked on. In the first of their own fields the hay was still lying out, and she flung herself down. When she once got home she must watch every word and look, must smile and smile, and show nothing! She wanted desperately these few minutes of abandonment. She didn't cry, but pressed herself against the hay-covered earth, and the sun burned her neck. She turned on her back and gazed up at the blue. She framed no thoughts, dissolved in aching for what was lost and could never be found now. And the hum of summer beat drowsily above her from the wings of insects drunk on heat and honey. She crossed her arms on her chest to compress the pain within her. If she could die, there, now, in full summer with its hum and the singing of the larks; die and ache no more! So she lay motionless, until the dog came and licked her cheek. And, ashamed, she got up and stood brushing the hay-seeds and stalks from her dress and stockings.

Past old Kismet in the next field she came to the thread of stream and crossed it into the disenchanted orchard, smelling of nettles and old trees; then on, to the garden and the flag-stones of the terrace. One magnolia flower was out, but she dared not stop and sniff, lest its lemon-honey scent should upset her again; and, coming to the French window, she looked in.

Her mother was sitting with the look on her face that Dinny called 'waiting for Father'. Her father was standing with the look on his face that she called 'waiting for Mother'. Jean seemed expecting her cub to come round the corner.

'And I'm the cub,' thought Dinny, and stepped over the threshold, saying:

'Well, Mother darling, can I have some tea?' . . .

That evening, after good-night had been said, she came down again and went to her father's study. He was at his bureau, poring, with a pencil, over something he had written. She stole up, and read over his shoulder:

Hunters for sale: Bay gelding, fifteen three, rising ten, sound, good-looking, plenty of bone, fine jumper. Mare: blue roan: fifteen one, rising nine, very clever, carries lady, show jumper, sound wind and limb. Apply Owner, Condaford Grange, Oxon.

'H'm!' he muttered, and crossed out the 'wind and limb'.

Dinny reached down and took the paper.

The General started and looked round.

'No,' she said. And tore the sheet.

'Here! You mustn't do that. It took me—'

'No, Dad, you can't sell the horses, you'd be lost.'

'But I *must* sell the horses, Dinny.'

'I know. Mother told me. But it isn't necessary. I happen to have quite a lot.' She put the notes she had been carrying about so long on his bureau.

The General got up.

'Impossible!' he said. 'Very good of you, Dinny, but quite impossible!'

'You mustn't refuse me, Dad. Let me do something for Condaford. I've no use for it, and it happens to be just the three hundred Mother says you want.'

'No use for it? Nonsense, my dear! Why! With that you could have a good long travel.'

'I don't want a good long travel. I want to stay at home and help you both.'

The General looked hard into her face.

'I should be ashamed to take it,' he said. 'It's my own fault that I've got behind.'

'Dad! You never spend anything on yourself.'

'Well, I don't know how it is – one little thing and another, it piles up.'

'You and I will go into it. There must be things we could do without.'

'The worst is having no capital. Something comes along and I have to meet it out of income; insurance is heavy, and with rates and taxes always going up, income gets smaller all the time.'

'I know; it must be awful. Couldn't one breed something?'

'Costs money to start. Of course we could do perfectly well in London or Cheltenham, or abroad. It's keeping the place up, and the people dependent on it.'

'Leave Condaford! Oh! no! Besides, who would take it? In

spite of all you've done, we're not up to date, Dad.'

'We're certainly not.'

'We could never put "this desirable residence" without blushing. People won't pay for other people's ancestors.'

The General stared before him.

'I do frankly wish, Dinny, the thing wasn't such a trust. I hate bothering about money, screwing here and screwing there, and always having to look forward to see if you can make do. But, as you say, to sell's unthinkable. And who'd rent it? It wouldn't make a boys' school, or a country club, or an asylum. Those seem the only fates before country houses nowadays. Your Uncle Lionel's the only one of us who's got any money – I wonder if he'd like to take it on for his weekends.'

'No, Dad! No! Let's stick to it. I'm sure we can do it, somehow. Let me do the screwing and that. In the meantime you *must* take this. Then we shall start fair.'

'Dinny, I—'

'To please me, dear.'

The General drew her to him.

'That business of yours,' he muttered into her hair. 'My God, I wish—!'

She shook her head.

'I'm going out for a few minutes now, just to wander round. It's so nice and warm.'

And, winding a scarf round her neck, she was gone through the opened window.

The last dregs of the long daylight had drained down beyond the rim, but warmth abode, for no air stirred, and no dew fell – a still, dry, dark night, with swarming stars. From the moment she stepped out Dinny was lost in it. But the old house shrouded in its creepers lived for her eyes, a dim presence with four still-lighted windows. She stood under an elm tree leaning against its trunk, with her arms stretched back and her hands clasping it behind her. Night was a friend

– no eye to see, no ear to listen. She stared into it, unmoving, drawing comfort from the solidity and breadth behind her. Moths flew by, almost touching her face. Insentient nature, warm, incurious, busy even in the darkness. Millions of little creatures burrowed and asleep, hundreds floating or creeping about, billions of blades of grass and flowers straightening up ever so slowly in the comparative coolness of the night. Nature! Pitiless and indifferent even to the only creatures who crowned and petted her with pretty words! Threads broke and hearts broke, or whatever really happened to the silly things – Nature twitched no lip, heaved no sigh! One twitch of Nature's lip would have been more to her than all human sympathy. If, as in the 'Birth of Venus', breezes could puff at her, waves like doves lap to her feet, bees fly round her seeking honey! If for one moment in this darkness she could feel at one with the starshine, the smell of earth, the twitter of that bat, the touch of a moth's wing on her nose!

With her chin tilted up and all her body taut against the tree trunk she stood, breathless from the darkness and the silence and the stars. Ears of a weasel, nose of a fox to hear and scent out what was stirring! In the tree above her head a bird chirped once. The drone of the last train, still far away, began, swelled, resolved itself into the sound of wheels and the sound of steam, stopped, then began again and faded out in a far drumming. All hushed once more! Where she stood the moat had been, filled in so long that this great elm tree had grown. Slow, the lives of trees, and one long fight with the winds; slow and tenacious like the life of her family clinging to this spot.

'I *will* not think of him,' she thought, 'I *will* not think of him!' As a child that refuses to remember what has hurt it, so would she be! And, instantly, his face formed in the darkness – his eyes and his lips. She turned round to the trunk and leaned her forehead on its roughness. But his face came between. Recoiling, she walked away over the grass swiftly and without noise, invisible as a spirit. Up and down she walked, and the wheeling soothed her.

'Well,' she thought, 'I have had my hour. It can't be helped. I must go in.'

She stood for a moment looking up at the stars, so far, so many, bright and cold. And with a faint smile she thought:

'I wonder which is my lucky star!'

Flowering Wilderness: Additional material

A day in the life of John Galsworthy

John Galsworthy was a disciplined and organised man, and as such was a great fan of making lists. Here follows one, written *c.* 1927, quite possibly just for Galsworthy's own amusement, which gives us a small insight into his daily routine:

Sleeping in bed	7 hours
Thinking in bed	1 hour
Trying not to fall asleep in chairs	½ hour
Eating and listening to others talking	2 hours
Playing with dogs	¼ hour
Playing without dogs (on the telephone)	¼ hour
Dressing, undressing, bathing, and Muller exercising	1¼ hours
Exercise in country (riding or walking)	2 hours at least
Exercise in London (walking)	1 hour at most
Imagining vain things, and writing them down on paper:—	
In the country	4 hours
In London	3 hours
Correspondence, and collecting scattered thoughts:—	
In the country	2 hours
In London	4 hours
Skipping newspapers	¾ hour
Reading what I don't want, or otherwise attending to business	1 hour
Reading what I do want to	½ hour
Revision of vain things; and of proofs say	1 hour
Education by life	the rest

Call it an eight to nine hour day.

J.G.

Reading-group questions

- Discuss the character of Dinny. How does she compare to Fleur Forsyte? Who do you like more and why? Are family ties a positive influence in her life, or do they hold her back?

- The Cherrels are an old, titled family from the country in contrast to the city-based, commercially minded Forsytes. How do the opinions and ideals of the two families differ?

- Galsworthy once commented, 'It might be said that I create characters who have feelings which they cannot express'. Consider this in relation to the main characters. How far does this mould and distort their happiness?

- Written at the end of Galsworthy's life, the last three books of *The Forsyte Saga* have been seen to give a rather bleak view of love and marriage. Do you agree? How had attitudes to divorce changed since Soames and Irene's separation at the beginning of *The Forsyte Saga*?

- The thirties were a time of rapidly shifting morals and crumbling traditional values. Discuss specific ways in which Galsworthy captures this clash of the old and new. How do you think he viewed the developments of his day?

THE FORSYTE SAGA

MAID IN WAITING

John Galsworthy

'In this family, the troubles of one were the troubles of all.'

As the 1930s bring dramatic change, so Galsworthy's sweeping family saga turns to the Cherrells, cousins of the Forsytes. Young Dinny Cherrell, seemingly fragile, but strong and determined, is a bright and vivid character who breathes life into all those she encounters. To her, family is everything. So when her brother faces extradition to South America, falsely accused of murder, and her cousin is threatened by her unstable husband, Dinny will do anything she can to shield them from harm.

The heartbreak and scandal continues with another branch of the family – *Maid in Waiting* opens a thrilling new phase in *The Forsyte Saga.*

Since it first appeared in 1906, *The Forsyte Saga* has enthralled generations of readers, and been adapted with huge success for both film and television. These sumptuous new editions of each individual novel include reading-group questions and exciting, exclusive material to introduce them to a whole new audience.

'An immortal achievement . . . it is, at all levels, readability itself' *Financial Times*

978 0 7553 4091 0

THE FORSYTE SAGA

OVER THE RIVER

John Galsworthy

'Every memory she had of him came to life with an intensity that seemed to take all strength from her limbs.'

As *The Forsyte Saga* draws to a close, the future of the Cherrell family, cousins to the Forsytes, seems uncertain. Clare Cherrell has come home, fleeing the clutches of her violent, abusive husband. When he pursues her she vows she will never return and sets about fighting him in vicious divorce proceedings. Dinny supports her sister all the way, but she has her own heartache to conquer, a grief which threatens to embitter her life for ever. Will the sisters make it safely over the river, or is the stream of painful memories destined to engulf their lives?

Over the River is the dramatic, moving and stunning conclusion to John Galsworthy's unforgettable masterpiece, *The Forsyte Saga*.

Since it first appeared in 1906, *The Forsyte Saga* has enthralled generations of readers, and been adapted with huge success for both film and television. These sumptuous new editions of each individual novel include reading-group questions and exciting, exclusive material to introduce them to a whole new audience.

'The satire is sharp, the dialogue, elegant and witty, and the characterisation – dazzling' *Scotsman*

978 0 7553 4093 4